THE PRYCE *OF* PRIDE

KARI BOVÉE

VINCI
BOOKS

By Kari Bovée

The Pryce of Murder

Vinci Books

vinci-books.com

Published by Vinci Books Ltd in 2025

1

Copyright © Kari Bovée 2025

The publisher and the author have made every effort to obtain permissions
for any third party material used in this book and to comply with copyright
law. Any queries in this respect should be brought to the attention of the
publisher and any omissions will be corrected in future editions.
A CIP catalogue record for this book is available from the British Library.
Paperback ISBN: 9781036709273

Chapter One

I stood on the front steps of the Arabella Hotel, taking in the view of the town's main street. La Plata Springs was alive with activity as the Cultural and Historic Festival had begun early that morning. Banners fluttered in the breeze and the street buzzed with a happy cacophony of voices and the clip-clop of horses' hooves as they pulled carriages and wagons carrying supplies and visitors from nearby settlements.

Down in the open field by the river, a group of children, both Tavani and Caucasian, engaged in foot races and a game of Tava-Ha, which consisted of passing around a ball fashioned of stuffed buckskin with broomsticks or long tree branches.

The festival was a time where the diverse cultures of the area came together to celebrate their mutual respect for one another. It was the brainchild of Eleanor Reynolds, a passionate local historian, who had worked tirelessly to bring the event to life. This year, it promised to be more spectacular than ever thanks to the collaboration with

Archibald Archer, the town's founder and acting mayor, and a businessman named Theodore Chase, who was from the neighboring town of Addison. Both men sought to boost tourism and economic growth in the area.

To the south, a large platform was being erected in front of the General, the rival hotel to the Arabella, whose grand reopening conveniently coincided with the festival. Archibald Archer, who owned the hotel, had convinced Miss Reynolds to plan the event at the time of his grand reopening for optimal exposure.

I smiled at the power play. Mr. Archer had made no secret that he wanted to possess all the businesses in the growing community, and owned about ninety percent of them. The jewel in his crown would be the Arabella, built by my late husband and the architect—my supernatural friend—Percival Blank. I had inherited the hotel at my husband's death, and had been directed by a stipulation in his will to run the hotel for one full year in order to gain my full inheritance, which was vast, to say the least. The other request by my husband was to never sell the hotel to Archibald Archer.

One full year. When I received the news of my assignment, I thought I'd never survive it. I had become accustomed to my lavish lifestyle in New York, my renowned theater, and the craft of acting upon the stage which afforded me more than just money. It had been my entire reason for living. To leave it was unimaginable, but leave it I did. Temporarily. And my year-long venture was nearly at an end. I could scarcely believe it. The time had flown.

However, because of the expense of sundry problems with the hotel, my stay had been extended and I would remain here another six months, which now seemed a mere blink of an eye. Having finally felt settled in the little community, the thought of leaving produced feelings in me that were hard to reconcile. I had grown fond of the town and the people who resided in it.

"My goodness, but this is quite impressive," a male voice echoed next to me. I turned to see Percival Blank standing to my left in his transparent, ethereal form. He ran a hand through his thick wavy hair, drawing attention to the hint of gray at his temples. His dark, luminous eyes regarded me with their moody, Byronic charm. Although not among the living, he was a permanent resident of his beloved creation, the Arabella, and he'd become my first friend in La Plata Springs. Clasping his hands behind his back, he rocked back and forth on the balls of his feet, surveying the scene before us. As usual, his pipe was clenched firmly between his teeth, and fragrant wisps of spicy tobacco encircled his head.

"Indeed, it is," I agreed.

He craned his neck to see past me down the street to the south. "It looks like Archibald plans to mesmerize the festival goers with a dazzling speech for the reopening of his flop-house."

I let out a snort. "Come now, Percival," I chided. "He's completely renovated the General. It's much more than just a flop-house now. It's a grand hotel."

Percival scoffed. "Grand, my foot. It will never measure up to the Arabella. I see he is determined at his attempts to steal her shine, since you've refused to allow him to get his grubby hands on her."

I shrugged. "He's making efforts to grow the town, Percival. The mines have attracted a good deal of men whom he's made rich because of those mines, and now he wants to put La Plata Springs on the map with tourism as well. You can't fault him for his ambition. He's a man who makes things happen—although, I will grant you that sometimes his methods can be questionable."

A distinguished man, who looked to be in his early forties, and a lovely woman approached the entrance to the hotel. Percival popped out of sight. The man had a scholarly appearance with short, neatly combed dark hair that was shot through with the occasional strand of gray. His well-fitted suit with bow tie gave him a formal and somewhat pretentious look. His expression was serious and bore a confidence that seemed almost unshakable, radiating a self-assurance that commanded respect.

The woman appeared to be slightly younger than the man. Her auburn hair, the front of which was styled in loose curls framing her intelligent and determined face, shone brilliantly in the sun. Her chocolate brown dress, intricately embroidered in tan, sported lace details and a high neckline, which complemented her coloring and her kind, but slightly strained, demeanor. She wore a beautiful silver brooch at her neck. It depicted a majestic bird in midflight surrounded by delicate foliage.

"Excuse me, please," the woman said. "Is this the Arabella Hotel?"

"Why, yes, it is. I'm the owner, Arabella Pryce."

The woman blinked, as if confused. "Arabella Pryce … You mean THE Arabella Pryce? The actress?"

Pleased at her recognition of my name, I gave her a broad smile. "Yes, guilty as charged."

"My goodness." She laid her hand on her chest. "I've read about your travels to the West and your hotel, but I did not know you'd actually be here. I assumed you'd be in New York, or traveling somewhere abroad." She looked over at the man. "Isn't this amazing?"

The man gave her a polite—but not exactly sincere—

smile, and then he turned his attention to me. "Forgive my wife's exuberance. She has quite forgotten her manners. I'm Warren Baxter, and this is my wife, Bernice."

The woman pressed her lips together in irritation at being chastised by her husband. "Yes, please forgive me."

"It is quite alright," I said to her, wishing to deflect from the awkwardness of the situation. She nodded graciously.

"Mr. Baxter, you are the honored guest of the festival, I understand. I'm looking forward to hearing you speak this evening."

"Thank you. Yes, Archibald Archer reached out to me some weeks ago regarding the festival. He has a great appreciation for my work in native art, artifacts, and antiquities in both South and North America. Recently, I am dedicated to studying the culture of the Tavani. I was happy to comply."

"How lovely. I assume you will stay at the General?"

"Yes," his wife said. "I had hoped to stay here at the Arabella, of course—I've been so curious about your hotel —but since the invitation came from Mr. Archer ... "

"Naturally," I said. "I completely understand. I hear the renovations he's made to the General are quite impressive." As I said the words, a niggle of worry edged its way into my bones. Even though the lien against the Arabella had been recently paid, I still had a lot of financial catching up to do to bring the hotel back to its former glory. It seemed with every step forward I took, I had to take two steps back. I needed to keep the hotel full to occupancy. We were nearly at eighty-five percent now, but I wanted it to be at one hundred percent. Hopefully, visitors for the festival would continue to trickle in.

From behind me, the door to the hotel opened and

Bijou, my little Havanese dog, came scampering over to me. She raised herself up, pawing at my skirts.

"There you are, Arabella," Cordelia, my assistant, companion and best friend, joined me. Her strawberry blond hair was slightly mussed. From this, I knew she'd been reading, or working on my correspondence, as she often had her hands in her hair while concentrating. "Bijou was searching for you."

Chuckling at my pup's smiling face, I picked her up. "Here I am, sweetheart." She happily settled in my arms.

"Cordelia?" Mrs. Baxter stepped forward, looking at her intently. "Cordelia Danson?"

Cordelia's hazel eyes appraised the woman and then grew wide with surprised recognition. "Bernice Madison!"

"Oh, my goodness! I can't believe it," the woman said. "And—it's Baxter now."

Cordelia's gaze bounced back and forth between Mrs. Baxter and her husband. "Yes, yes, of course," she said, apologetically. She clasped her hands together at her waist, and I noted her knuckles instantly paled. Despite her obviously forced smile, her upper lip twitched at the corner.

"You know each other?" The revelation caught me off guard.

"Cordelia and I, we—well, we went to finishing school together in Massachusetts, didn't we, dear?" Mrs. Baxter said.

"Finishing school?" I fixed my gaze on Cordelia, struggling to mask my shock. From what I knew of her background, which I had obviously assumed incorrectly, finishing school was something her family could scarcely afford.

Cordelia's face blanched, causing the light scatter of

freckles across her nose and cheekbones to stand out more vividly.

"Yes," her voice cracked. "Well, I suppose congratulations are in order?" She asked, neatly skirting the subject.

"It's been twelve years," Mrs. Baxter said, looking over at her husband.

He gave Cordelia a brief upturn of his lips and then cleared his throat. "Miss Danson. We had no idea you would be here in La Plata Springs."

"I—I work for Arabella—er, Mrs. Pryce. I've worked for her for ten years." She briefly glanced at me, but would not look me straight in the eye. I gathered this was because she had somehow neglected to mention she knew the famous artifacts historian and his wife, but for what reason? It had me more than curious, and I hate to admit, a little hurt. We'd known he'd be coming to town for a few weeks.

What in the devil's name was she hiding?

Chapter Two

After we said our goodbyes to the couple, Cordelia pivoted sharply and strode back into the hotel, leaving Bijou and me staring after her in complete bewilderment. Without hesitation, I hurried after her through the doors.

"Cordelia?" I called after her. She was rapidly approaching the stairs to go back up to our rooms. Either she didn't hear me, or she was ignoring me. Either way, her behavior was odd. This was not like her at all.

I passed by the reception desk where Mr. Pettyjohn, the clerk, was assisting a couple who were checking in to the hotel. Much to my delight, several others were waiting in line to do the same. The festival, so far, promised to be very beneficial for the hotel, and I hoped we would be at full capacity soon.

As I was about to climb the stairs to go after Cordelia, Sheriff Clayton Marshall and Deputy Dirk Fleming emerged from the Bella with another couple and came into the lobby. My heart lurched at seeing the sheriff—which was completely annoying and unsettling. My feelings for the man often had me confused, and I did not have time for such distractions. I had not seen him for a few weeks, as he had rather abruptly left town—a few days after we had shared a lovely kiss—and his sudden presence sent my emotions reeling. That he had gone away without mentioning it to me was a little inconsiderate. Not that I expected anything from him. The kiss was probably the result of exuberance at our success in solving a recent murder, nothing more. Yet, to my dismay, it felt like something more. I pushed the feeling firmly aside.

Calling upon my acting skill, I put on a pleasant, casual smile and approached the foursome.

"Clayton, Deputy Fleming, how good to see you!" I set Bijou down and she happily raised herself on her hind legs, dancing for the sheriff's attention. He bent down to pet her, and she immediately dropped to the ground and rolled over, exposing her belly. He gave her a few scratches and then rose again.

"Hello, Mrs. Pryce," the young deputy said, his expressive dark gaze meeting mine with a mixture of warmth and boyish charm. A faint blush tinged his cheeks. Tall, broad-shouldered, and with a shock of red hair, Dirk Fleming was a new arrival in town, and I'm afraid he'd become quite smitten with me. He was a darling young man, and while I appreciated his effusive personality and rugged good looks, I did not feel quite the same ardor for him.

"Arabella." Clayton greeted me flatly with a nod. His handsome, weathered face, which featured deep-set, piercing blue eyes, a neatly trimmed mustache and a hint of stubble on his square jaw, was void of a smile. I found it curious, and mildly disconcerting, that he'd addressed me in such an ambivalent manner, quite opposite from the eager deputy.

The gentleman with him, clearly from the local Tavani tribe, looked to be in his late sixties or early seventies. His noble countenance was lined with age and wisdom. Long gray hair swept away from his face and fell loosely over his shoulders. He wore a striped, cotton collared shirt, and a fringed buckskin vest. The woman, much younger—I guessed to be in her late twenties—was strikingly beautiful, with wide expressive eyes, high cheekbones, and glossy dark locks that fell to her waist. Her light tan buckskin dress was fashioned with a frontispiece of elegantly woven beadwork and small shells. Her beaded dangled earrings flashed with color, and a beautiful, almost iridescent deep blue and turquoise feather was threaded into her hair.

"This is Michael Two Trees," Clayton nodded toward the gentleman. "He's an elder and historian of the Tavani tribe, dedicated to educating others about the traditions and history of the native culture here."

"Ah, yes," I said. "You're here for the festival. Welcome."

His warm, kindly eyes settled on me, and he gave me a nod of silent greeting.

Clayton held his hand out toward the woman. "And this is Sarah Redhawk. She's an artist and activist and is passionate about land issues and cultural preservation. She's also on the festival's planning committee." He tilted his head toward me. "This is Arabella Pryce. She owns the hotel."

"It's a pleasure to meet you," Miss Redhawk said. "We are just about to check in to your fine hotel."

"Oh." My brows lifted. "You aren't staying at the General?"

Miss Redhawk and Mr. Two Trees shared a glance.

"No," she said, flatly.

"Ah. Well, we have a few rooms left. I'm sure the General is quite filled up."

Her lips twitched with an attempt at a smile. "I have no idea, but we'd rather be here."

An awkward silence fell among us. I suppose I was waiting for some kind of explanation. Mr. Archer had offered his rooms at a generous discount for the grand opening, probably to entice prospective guests. I had just assumed that anyone involved in the planning committee would stay there.

"I see." I blurted it out, eager to break the silence. "You are most welcome. Please let me know if there is anything I can do to make your stay more pleasant."

"Thank you, gracious lady." The corners of Michael Two Trees' eyes crinkled with gratitude.

The young woman gently took him by the elbow and led him to the back of the line at the reception desk.

"It looks like the festival is off to a good start," Deputy Fleming said. "Are you interested in native historic art and artifacts, Mrs. Pryce? I understand there are some very interesting lectures on the schedule. Will you be attending Mr. Baxter's this evening?"

"I am."

"His theories are quite controversial," he continued. "I'm sure his talk will garner some lively discussion."

"You're familiar with his work?"

"Yes. I dabble in cultural history myself." He straightened his spine and proudly puffed out his chest.

Clayton, not willing to engage in our shared interest, cleared his throat and pulled a watch from his vest pocket. "Deputy, I believe you're on patrol now."

Deputy Fleming's smile faded, replaced with a look of determined seriousness. "Right. Yes, sir." Placing his hat on his head, his fingers lightly touched the brim. "I hope to see you at the lecture, Mrs. Pryce."

"I'll be there," I assured him. His smile returned, and he strode away.

Clayton and I were again left in an uncomfortable and uncustomary silence between us.

"It's nice to see you, Sheriff," I said finally, still confused at his cool demeanor and rather bland introduction of me. Were we not friends? Perhaps more than friends? "You've been away."

He nodded, quietly appraising me with those dazzling blue eyes. "I had some business in Colorado Springs."

"Oh. Law business?" I felt somewhat like I was pulling teeth to get him to talk to me, which was strange. Our conversations in the past had usually come so easily.

He shook his head. "No. Personal."

"Ah. Well. I hope it was a successful trip."

Another awkward silence sucked the air from the room.

"I should get on," he said.

"Yes," I agreed. "Me too. There's a lot going on at the hotel."

He placed his hat back on his head, gave me a polite nod, and walked away. I watched him go with a knot in my belly. Had I done or said something to offend him? Had he regretted the kiss? Did he somehow feel an obligation to me he couldn't abide?

I shook my head, not wanting to face any of these possibilities. After all, what did it matter? I would sell the hotel and leave in six months' time. Leave all of this behind me. Leave him.

I couldn't let these silly emotions derail me from my purpose, which was to get the hotel back on its feet, serve my allotted time here, and get back to my theater in New York. After all, that is where I belonged.

Chapter Three

I returned to the fourth-floor suite I shared with Cordelia, my mind whirling with what had just transpired with her, and with the sheriff. Two people with whom I felt a deep connection, and both who were acting like people I scarcely knew. It felt as though the ground had shifted beneath my feet, settling into an entirely unfamiliar reality.

Stepping into the parlor, I found her sitting at the desk, her head bent over some papers. Bijou scampered over to her and set her paws on the side of the chair, hoping for an indulgent pat on the head. Cordelia obliged, but without her usual enthusiasm toward the impish canine.

"Are you alright, Cordelia?"

She turned and gave me a quizzical look. "Why, yes. I'm perfectly fine. Why do you ask?"

"You seemed unsettled when seeing Bernice Baxter and her husband. I did not know you knew them. Or that you attended finishing school."

"Oh, that." She gave a dismissive wave of her hand.

"Yes. I knew them a long time ago. Bernice and I did go to school together. I met Mr. Baxter a couple of times after we graduated. Bernice worked for him."

"Why didn't you mention any of this to me—particularly finishing school? In Massachusetts no less. Isn't your family from New York? I would think you might have mentioned it when you came to work for me."

She shrugged. "Yes, my family is from New York. I wanted to continue my education, and my mother had a cousin in Massachusetts, so they sent me to stay with her so I could attend finishing school there. When I'd learned of the job in your employ, I made an inquiry. It was Mr. Pryce who interviewed me initially, if you recall, Arabella. You were knee deep in a show at the time—matinees and evening performances. You'd asked him to find a suitable assistant for you. And, when you and I finally did meet, we had an instant rapport. You hired me without asking many questions. I assumed Mr. Pryce told you of my background."

I bit my lip. What she'd said was true. I had asked William to find me an assistant. He was a keen judge of character, and often knew what I needed almost more than I did at the time. I had been working so hard on the show, and with Mr. Blackthorn, my theater manager, to keep the business humming. I had been on the verge of collapse. William had found dear Cordelia, and she was a perfect fit. I would be eternally grateful to him for that.

"But, Cordelia, we're friends. I find it strange that it never came up in conversation."

She gave me an indulgent smile and then chuckled. "It wasn't a secret. It just didn't seem important. The two of us meshed well, and there was ever so much to do when I first came aboard. If you recall, it was quite a baptism of fire. Your life was a complete whirlwind at the time."

I nodded. "Yes. You did walk into quite a mess."

She reached out and touched my arm. "It was a wonderful mess, and I loved every minute. I still love working for you."

Her words warmed my heart. We had become very close, very quickly. Cordelia was a few years younger than me, and our bond felt like that of sisters. Yet, she never took advantage of that. She loved me like family, and respected me as her employer.

"And, Bernice Baxter? Why didn't you mention you knew her when we learned Mr. Baxter would be here for the festival?"

Momentarily, her gaze shifted away from mine. "I didn't realize they'd married. We knew Mr. Baxter would arrive in La Plata Springs with his wife, but I had no idea it would be Bernice—her name was never mentioned."

Her eyes met mine again, and a slight curve of her lips played on her face. Her response was entirely plausible, but I had the sense she was still keeping something from me. Yet, close as we were, I could only pry so much. There were things in my past that I hadn't disclosed to her until recently. Everyone had their secrets.

"He's going to be giving a speech this evening. I plan to attend. Do you care to join me?" I asked.

"Of course. I've read some of his papers on the history and culture of various South and North American tribes. It's fascinating work. He also has an impressive collection of artifacts, including some from this very region."

"The deputy mentioned his work is controversial. What do you suppose he meant by that?" I asked.

She gave a slight nod. "Yes, Warren Baxter seems to find controversy wherever he goes. There has even been some tension between him and the Tavani of this area. Certain members of the tribe feel he has misrepresented the origins of some significant Tavani artifacts and that he has misattributed them to other cultures and history."

"My goodness." I blinked. "It all sounds very interesting."

"One of his most outspoken opponents is a woman named Sarah Redhawk," she continued.

"Really? I've just met her. She and a gentleman named Michael Two Trees are staying here at the Arabella."

"Not at the General?"

"No. I was surprised as well. She said they'd rather stay here."

Cordelia shrugged. "I suppose that is good for the Arabella." She took a small round pocket watch from her dress pocket. "Mr. Baxter's talk is in a couple of hours. Shall we get something to eat in the Bella quickly before we go?"

I nodded. "That sounds like a fine idea. I want to see how things are going in the saloon, anyway."

After we gathered our hats and gloves, and Bijou's leash, we headed down to the Bella.

The place was nearly full to bursting, with every chair at every table occupied and several gentlemen standing at the bar. Cordelia and I made our way toward my booth, which Kitty Carlisle, the manager of the Bella and proprietor of the town's brothel, always kept reserved just for me, Cordelia, or any of our special guests. Bijou ran ahead and hopped onto one of the padded bench seats, while Cordelia and I settled ourselves in beside her.

In moments, Kitty approached us. Always dressed in

black, she was a striking figure with shiny raven hair neatly piled on her head. Her intense, piercing dark gaze could captivate a room and bring even the most hardened men to their knees. Her stern, schoolmarm-like demeanor and meticulous grooming further enhanced her formidable and dignified appearance. But, despite her tough exterior, she cared deeply about the community and was fiercely protective of the Bella's staff and the sporting ladies in her employ, ensuring their safety and well-being with scrupulous attention.

"Ladies." She settled her hands on her broad hips. "What can I bring you?"

"Hello, Kitty," I greeted her. "Champagne and some of Lottie's chicken soup and biscuits will do the trick." I nodded toward all the patrons. "The saloon is certainly humming this afternoon. How are you managing?"

"It's busy, but we are handling it just fine. I've brought in a couple more of my girls to help."

Boisterous laughter caught my attention. I turned to see Archibald Archer and my nemesis, the former theater critic and now journalist Atticus Brooks, sitting at a table with an elegant-looking gentleman. Andrew Archer, Mr. Archer's nephew, was also with them. With his elbow on the table and his chin perched on his palm, his face bore a sullen, bored expression, as if he wanted to be anywhere else. His tanned and sun kissed appearance usually reflected his creative and artistic nature, but at this moment, he looked as if a cloud had settled over his head.

The other gentleman, with his sharp, chiseled features— an angular jawline and pronounced cheekbones— commanded attention. A neatly cropped beard complimented his dark hair, which was touched with gray at the temples. His light gray eyes stood out in striking contrast.

Dressed in an impeccably tailored suit with a double-breasted frock coat, patterned waistcoat, and a neatly tied cravat, he exuded an air of sophistication, authority, and wealth.

"Who is that?" I jutted my chin toward him, unable to hide my interest in such a fine-looking specimen of the male variety. I noted that Atticus Brooks also paid keen attention to his dining companion, while Archibald Archer laughed at something the man said. They, except for Andrew, looked to be having a wonderful time.

"Theodore Chase," Kitty said.

"Ah. He's the businessman from Addison who's helped to sponsor the festival."

"The very one." Kitty smirked. "Known as the most eligible bachelor this side of the Rockies. He's working with Archibald to develop the land between Addison and La Plata Springs. I'm not so sure it's such a good idea. I don't think La Plata Springs is ready for the kind of growth the two of them want. Increased competition from new businesses could threaten the ones already established, including this one and my own."

"Well, I understand his point of view," I said dubiously. "Mr. Archer owns most of the businesses in town, and he's made it no secret that he wants more of them, so of course he wants to expand his reach."

As we were talking, Mr. Chase caught my eye. He leaned over to say something to Mr. Archer, and before I realized it, he was making his way toward the booth. Meanwhile, Mr. Archer and Atticus Brooks also rose, and Andrew, seizing the opportunity for an escape, hurried out of the saloon, looking visibly relieved.

"I'll let Lottie know what you've ordered," Kitty said. "Food should be here in a few minutes."

"Thank you, Kitty."

She turned to leave, but then said over her shoulder. "Don't let Chase's polished and pretty exterior fool you, Arabella. Underneath all that charisma, there's something … rather wily about him."

Chapter Four

Mr. Chase approached the booth with a charming smile.

"Good afternoon, ladies." He gave a gallant bow before turning his attention to me. "What a pleasure it is to meet you in the flesh, Mrs. Pryce. I was fortunate enough to attend one of your performances in 1879 in Chicago. You were marvelous. I'm Theodore Chase."

"Oh, well, thank you, Mr. Chase." His declaration surprised me, but pleased me nonetheless. "The pleasure is all mine. This is my assistant, Cordelia Danson."

The two exchanged pleasantries, and he then refocused his gaze on me.

"How fortuitous for La Plata Springs to have you settle here to manage your namesake hotel. I'm sure with you here, her future is very bright. Although, it is a shame that you will no longer be performing—except at the local theater. What a loss for the world."

A stab of anxiety pierced my chest. Where did he get this erroneous information? My gaze slid over to the most obvious culprit, Atticus Brooks, who regarded me with a smarmy smile. It's true I hadn't told many people that my stay here was temporary. It was important for the staff, guests, and townspeople to know of my dedication to the hotel, but I'd never even breathed the notion that I would stop performing on the national and international stage. For me, it would be akin to death. Mr. Brooks was meddling, that much was clear. He thrived on sowing chaos, and his smirk only confirmed that he enjoyed watching me squirm.

"I assure you, Mr. Chase, I have no intention of leaving the stage—here or elsewhere."

"I'm happy to hear it. But, it must be challenging to run both the hotel and your theater, and continue to perform all at the same time? You must have endless energy."

"I'm only performing here on the rare occasion. And as to managing it all, I have excellent help."

He gave a knowing smile. "That is essential, is it not? A business is only as good as its people, that is what I always say. And your hotel seems to thrive. You are making a fine go of it. But I'm not surprised, given what I've heard about your brilliance." He looked over at Mr. Archer, who'd joined him. "Archibald won't stop going on about you."

Mr. Archer offered me a gracious nod, which I returned with a tentative smile. There was an unmistakable sense that something was brewing, though I couldn't quite put my finger on it. My eyes drifted back to Atticus Brooks, whose smirk seemed permanently etched on his face whenever he looked my way.

"Mrs. Pryce," Mr. Chase continued. "I'd like to speak with you about a business opportunity you might find interesting."

"I see." Slightly intrigued I glanced at Cordelia, who returned my gaze with a skeptically raised brow. "Well, Mr. Chase, perhaps at another time. We are going to have a quick meal and then head over to the Town Hall to hear Mr. Baxter's lecture."

"Of course, of course. At your convenience."

"Are you going to the lecture, Mr. Chase?" Cordelia asked.

A faint smile tugged at his lips. "Yes. I'm curious to hear Baxter's latest historical theories. He never fails to create a commotion."

———

Back in the parlor of our suite, I smoothed my hair into place and then arranged my new Gainsborough hat on my head to elegant perfection. I admired the effect in the mirror which hung above the walnut desk. The hat, crafted by Miss Cynthia Mayes, the town dressmaker, was made from luxurious burgundy velvet with a sleek silk ribbon that wrapped around the base of the crown. Small artificial roses adorned one side, while an ostrich feather arched gracefully over the brim, adding a touch of classic drama—perfectly suited to me.

"Shall we walk to the Town Hall? It seems like a lovely evening." Cordelia took Bijou's leash from the hook on the wall near the door. Bijou leapt from her perch on the Queen Anne loveseat positioned under the large bay window and stood trembling with anticipation as Cordelia clipped the leash to her collar.

"That sounds splendid," I agreed.

Cordelia handed me the leash while she put on her coat. Once we had retrieved our gloves, we made our way downstairs to the lobby. Several guests milled about, and there was a feeling of jubilation in the air. My heart swelled with pride to see so many people in the hotel—none of whom seemed the least bit worried about murder or a curse, despite some of the negative press the hotel had received of late.

Stopping by the reception desk where Mr. Pettyjohn stood sentinel, I leaned over and whispered to him. "Have we many new guests?"

"We are quite full, Mrs. Pryce. Not a room left vacant."

Delighted at this news, I clapped my hands together. "That's excellent, Mr. Pettyjohn!"

Just then, Mr. Johns, the hotel's handyman and some-time bellman, entered the hotel in his role as the latter, carrying the luggage of a couple who came in after him. The couple stopped and took in the elegance, both with delighted expressions on their faces. Their appreciation sent a thrill through me.

After briefly greeting them and a few of the other patrons, Cordelia and I stepped outside and were met with a breathtaking view. As the sun began its descent over La Plata Springs, the sky transformed into a brilliant canvas of colors. Warm golden light bathed the craggy peaks of the surrounding Rocky Mountains. Bijou tugged on her leash as we made our way down Main Street toward the Town Hall, which sat at the south end of La Plata Springs near the train station.

It was a stately, yet modest, building which reflected both the ruggedness of the mountainous setting and the community's, or rather Mr. Archer's, wealth. Constructed from locally produced brick and quarried limestone, it featured large arched windows with wooden shutters. A small bell tower with a mining pickaxe weathervane topped the dark slate roof, and wide stone steps led to elaborately carved wooden doors, which were opened to welcome attendees.

Several of the townspeople mingled in the foyer, while others took their seats in rows of plush-cushioned wooden chairs that faced a raised platform at the front of the room.

Display tables and glass cases showcased Tavani and other native art and artifacts throughout the main hall. The displays contained various items, including basketry, pottery, clothing with intricate beadwork, and ancient weaponry and talismans. Carefully arranged informational placards explained their history and significance.

Mr. Baxter, along with another younger man, stood on the platform near the podium in the company of Atticus Brooks, and Constance Chatterley, the sole reporter and owner of the La Plata Springs Herald—a valiant attempt at a local newspaper. Both muckrakers stood with notebooks poised in hand and, unsurprisingly, appeared to be pelting the pair with questions. Andrew Archer stood on the far side of the group, carefully placing a covered piece of artwork on an easel. I was eager to see what lay underneath.

To the left of them, at the back of the room near one of the curtained windows, Mr. Chase was speaking with Bernice Baxter. I noted with some amusement that they stood quite close to one another. Her face was flushed, and she laughed at something he'd said. He smiled down at her, his charm oozing out into the room.

Bijou, overwhelmed with the crowd, whined, so I picked her up. "Let's find some seats, shall we?" I said to Cordelia.

We headed toward the front of the room, close to the platform. I spotted Michael Two Trees and Sarah Redhawk in the second row, and we took the two chairs next to them.

"Good evening," I said, as Cordelia and I settled into our seats. "I hope you found your accommodations at the Arabella satisfactory?"

"Very," Miss Redhawk said. "I feel quite spoiled. I've never stayed in such a lovely place before."

"Everyone has been very welcoming," Mr. Two Trees added.

I couldn't help but beam at their compliments. "I'm so glad to hear it."

I glanced up at the platform at the foursome near the podium, curious as to the interchange between Mr. Baxter and the two reporters. The gentleman standing next to Mr. Baxter had his arms crossed tightly over his chest, and a thunderous expression on his face. I wondered if Mr. Brooks had asked something offensive, which would have been completely in keeping with his character. With a shake of his head, the man stormed off, took the steps down from the platform, and moved toward the foyer.

"Do you know who that young man is?" I asked Mr. Two Trees, tilting my head toward his retreating back.

He gave a nod of his head. "That is Simon Graves, Baxter's assistant."

"Oh, I see. He didn't look very happy."

"No, he didn't," Cordelia agreed.

Mr. Archer approached the podium, at which time Mr. Brooks and Constance stepped down from the platform. The crowd in the foyer dispersed and people made their way over to the chairs.

"Everyone, please take your seats," Mr. Archer called out. His display of wealth and power was unmistakable. He wore his finest suit, complete with a gleaming gold watch fob on his waistcoat, rings flashing on his fingers, and a diamond ascot pin sparkling like a star in the heavens.

After several words about the festival, and of course, the grand re-opening of the General, he finally introduced the man of the hour, Mr. Warren Baxter, who approached the podium with a vague smile, and the demeanor of someone who merely tolerated the spectacle.

"Ladies and gentlemen, esteemed colleagues," he began. "Today, I am here to share my research on the fascinating Tavani tribe and their most revered artifact, the Tavani Star Amulet. The Tavani, as you know, are indigenous to the Colorado region."

Mr. Two Trees, shaking his head, gave a quiet *hmph*. I wondered at his objection. Was he disputing what Mr. Baxter had said about the amulet, or about the Tavani's origins?

"They have a rich cultural history that is both intricate and captivating," Mr. Baxter went on. "Central to their spiritual practices is the Tavani Star Amulet, an object of immense power and significance."

He pulled from his pocket an eight-sided star, about the size of his palm, which was suspended from a braided leather cord. On cue, Andrew emerged and removed the tarp from the easel, revealing a beautiful, painted rendering of the star amulet. The crowd gasped with delight.

The amulet, carved from obsidian and inlaid with turquoise, had intricate celestial symbols and Tavani patterns captured in fine metalwork. At the center, the eagle's head with amber gemstone eyes seemed almost alive. Vivid strokes of deep crimson framed the amulet, woven into the background design to make the dark object stand out sharply, as if the fiery hue were meant to emphasize its power and mystery.

After a few moments of letting the crowd study the captivating painting, Mr. Baxter continued. "The lovely and talented Sarah Redhawk has painted this beautiful rendering." He extended his hand toward Miss Redhawk, who offered a smile and a nod to the crowd. But when her eyes met Mr. Baxter's again, the smile vanished, replaced by a look far less amiable. Her chin lifted slightly, and a flicker of tension rippled along her jaw.

Mr. Baxter continued. "As legend has it, celestial beings gifted the Tavani Star Amulet to the Tavani. This amulet is said to possess extraordinary powers, including the ability to protect the wearer from harm and to bestow wisdom and prosperity upon the tribe. The amulet's origins are often romanticized as a direct connection to the stars, reflecting the Tavani's deep-seated beliefs in celestial guardianship."

I glanced back at the foyer to see Clayton and Deputy Fleming enter the hall. They made their way over to one of the display tables and stood watching the proceedings from there. I tried to catch Clayton's eye, but to no avail.

I turned my attention back to Mr. Baxter.

"In my research, I have unearthed fascinating details suggesting that the amulet may have also served as a tool for political and social control within the tribe. Leaders who possessed the amulet were often seen as divine intermediaries, thereby consolidating their power and influence. This perspective allows us to understand the amulet not merely as a spiritual artifact but also as a symbol of sociopolitical dynamics within the Tavani community."

Next to me, Michael Two Trees shot to his feet, surprisingly fast for a man his age, and shook his fist in the air. "That is not true. The amulet has never been used to wield political or social power over others. This man is misrepresenting the history of our people. His ignorance in these matters is an insult to our ancestors."

"And furthermore," a woman's voice from the back of the room rang out. I turned to see that Eleanor Reynolds had stepped forward, her mouth rigid with anger. "The man is a thief!"

Chapter Five

An uncomfortable silence fell in the hall. Mr. Baxter, at the podium, grasped the sides of it, his knuckles turning white. His face, now crimson, became all angles and hard lines and a tension, tight as a wire, reverberated between the trio.

Simon Graves had reappeared, standing off to the side of the platform near one of the white columns, his arms crossed. His countenance had lost its severeness and was now quite serene, or perhaps his face bore the look of amusement?

Mr. Baxter cleared his throat, and then proceeded. "My colleague, Michael Two Trees," he gestured toward the man next to me with his outstretched palm, "and I obviously have differing opinions on the history and the culture surrounding the amulet. I have been studying this, and other artifacts, associated with the tribe for more than a decade. But tell me, sir, how have I been in error?"

He did not acknowledge Miss Reynolds, who was standing at the back of the room, her fists balled at her side, as if he hadn't even heard her inflamed and accusatory remark. His jaw had relaxed, and the expression in his eyes resumed their naturally analytical and intelligent demeanor.

Before Michael Two Trees could answer, Miss Reynolds loudly declared again, "He is a thief!" She pointed her finger at him, causing another ripple of shocked murmurs from the crowd.

It was then I noticed the imposing figure standing off to the side, watching her—a man of native descent, tall and regal, with a bearing so still he resembled a statue. His dress was strikingly different from the Tavani men I had encountered, which I found curious. He wore a dark wool coat adorned with narrow, colorful bands of porcupine quillwork on the shoulders and cuffs.

Mr. Archer made his way toward the foyer and stopped beside the sheriff, gesturing subtly toward Miss Reynolds. Clayton responded with a slight tilt of his head toward Deputy Fleming, who then approached her. He leaned in, speaking quietly, but even from a distance, her rigid posture and deliberate turn of her head made it clear she was pointedly ignoring him.

"You people need to know that this man is a fraud!" Her eyes flashed. "He doesn't care about our people, or our history, or our culture. All he cares about is his collection of our belongings!"

"Please come with me," the deputy said, this time more loudly. He took her by the elbow. She didn't resist and let him lead her out of the room, but not before again addressing the crowd.

"He has taken something precious to my people, and he is using it for his own benefit!"

The deputy escorted her out among a fervor of excited voices, but the tall Indian man stayed rooted in place.

Michael Two Trees excused himself and trailed after the deputy and Miss Reynolds as they exited. I glanced at Miss Redhawk. Her eyes, as hard and dark as the obsidian object in question, were fixed on Mr. Baxter, and she was shaking her head in what appeared to be disgust.

Mr. Archer had returned to the front of the room and climbed the stairs leading to the dais. He took the podium, looking aghast, and held his hands out, patting the air, signaling for the audience to settle.

"Did you steal the amulet?" a man seated somewhere behind us shouted. Mr. Baxter again took his place at the podium.

"I'm afraid we've come to a misunderstanding," he addressed the audience with a placating smile. "I assure you, I have stolen nothing. My collection of artifacts from North and South America is a tribute to the peoples from which they came. I am preserving them for posterity and for education. It's my goal to help the white man understand the culture of the native peoples in an effort to create harmony, not disagreement."

"Please, continue with the lecture, Warren," Mr. Archer said, smiling at the crowd. "We'd hate to disappoint these fine folks."

Mr. Baxter gave a nod and continued where he had left off before the disturbance. A handful of spectators quietly left the hall. Perhaps Mr. Two Trees' and Miss Reynolds' comments had struck a chord?

———

After the lecture, the crowd mingled once again in the foyer enjoying refreshments, the outburst forgotten. A small group of people surrounded Mr. Baxter, listening intently to him.

31

Simon Graves was among them, but he stood slightly apart from the group, his hands in his pockets.

He was an attractive young man, with neatly styled, slightly wavy dark hair which added to his refined appearance. His suit was well-tailored, complete with a high-collared shirt and a cravat, giving him a distinguished and sophisticated air. His serious expression conveyed both confidence and depth of character, but he, once again, seemed to brood. I wondered if this was the natural state of his face, or if something had indeed perturbed him.

"Let's get some refreshment," Cordelia said. "I'm parched."

We made our way over to a table laden with baked goods. Betty Gilroy, the wife of Mr. Gilroy, the baker, stood behind the table, serving fruit punch and the sweet delicacies.

"Hello, ladies," she said cheerfully as we approached. "Wasn't that a fascinating lecture?"

"It was indeed," Cordelia said. "I did not know the influence of the Spanish on Tavani art was so profound."

"Shame about Eleanor Reynolds." Betty clicked her tongue. "I've never known her to be so outspoken."

"She has some intense feelings on the matter, no doubt." I took the glass of punch Cordelia had served for me. As the organizer of the festival, I wondered why Miss Reynolds had given Mr. Baxter such a place of prominence in the event, given her feelings about him. Perhaps it had been her agenda to publicly call him out on her claims? Or, more likely, since Mr. Archer had invited him, she hadn't much choice.

I looked over toward the small crowd around Mr. Baxter again. Simon Graves had migrated away and was now speaking with Bernice Baxter and Theodore Chase. Finally, a smile had come to his lips as he and Mrs. Baxter seemed to have landed on a pleasant topic, but I noted she kept glancing at the dashing Mr. Chase.

Catching my eye, Mr. Chase reached out and patted Mr. Graves on the shoulder, interrupting the exchange between him and Mrs. Baxter. Mr. Graves gave a polite nod, but his expression was far from cordial. His eyes lingered on Mrs. Baxter as she and Mr. Chase made their way over to us. I sensed Cordelia stiffen as they approached.

"Ah!" Mr. Chase said. "I couldn't stand another moment without enjoying some of the Gilroy's famous baked goods." He picked up a berry tart. Betty Gilroy smiled with satisfaction, her eyes beaming with pride.

"Oh, Mr. Chase, you are too kind." She handed him a plate overflowing with more small pastries and his eyes lit up as he took it from her and begun sampling each one.

Mrs. Baxter made her way to the punch bowl, where Cordelia was busy pouring a glass for herself and another for me.

"Hello, Cordelia."

"Bernice," Cordelia answered, her tone slightly flat. "Would you like some punch?"

"I'd love some."

I noted Cordelia's hand shaking as she ladled the punch into a glass and then handed it to her. The woman completely unnerved her. But why?

"Did you enjoy the lecture?" Mrs. Baxter asked the two of us.

"It was very interesting," I said, as Cordelia became very busy sipping her punch. "Mr. Baxter certainly seems dedicated to his work."

Of course, I was brimming with curiosity as to Miss

Reynolds' accusations, but it wouldn't be polite to bring it up.

"Warren is nothing if not dedicated," Mrs. Baxter said, her lips thinning. "He works tirelessly." Her gaze moved away from us and landed on her husband, who had moved to a corner of the room. He was speaking intently with Sarah Redhawk, leaning toward her, a look of desperation on his face. *How strange.*

She stood stiffly with her arms crossed tightly over her chest, and her voice, though too low to hear, had a sharp, cutting edge. She shook her head vehemently, clearly unwilling to listen to whatever he was trying to say.

"If you will excuse me." Mrs. Baxter stiffened, her eyes still fixed on the pair. "I'm rather tired from traveling. I'd like to go back to the General."

"Of course. Would you like us to take you? My carriage is just outside," I offered.

"Thank you, no. Mr. Archer has provided his coach and a driver for our use."

"Very well. Get some rest."

"I will. Good night." She turned to Cordelia. "I hope to see you tomorrow. I'd love to catch up."

Cordelia finally lowered her glass from her lips. "Um, well. I'd love to, but, with the festival, things are quite busy at the Arabella—"

"Oh." A look of disappointment clouded Mrs. Baxter's eyes. "I see. Of course."

Cordelia shot me a sheepish glance, and I raised an eyebrow in question. This was unlike her—she must have sensed the awkwardness she'd caused and tried to smooth things over.

"Well, I suppose, if it's all right with Arabella, I could spare an hour or so," she murmured, conceding.

Mrs. Baxter smiled. "That would be lovely."

Cordelia sipped at her glass of punch again, and Mrs. Baxter took her leave, after yet one more glance over at her husband and Miss Redhawk. Things seemed to have cooled a bit between them, but Miss Redhawk still seemed agitated. Perhaps she, too, believed Eleanor Reynolds claims, and had confronted him on the matter?

Cordelia let out an audible sigh.

"Are you all right?" I asked. "You seemed rather tense with Mrs. Baxter."

She blinked, and her face took on a blank expression. "Did I?"

"Yes," I stated matter-of-factly.

"I'm fine. Just tired." She smiled sweetly. "Shall we go back to the hotel? Tomorrow will be a busy day."

"If you'd like." I studied her expression, still puzzled by her odd behavior. I then quickly glanced around the room looking for Mr. Ellis, the Arabella's coach driver. He was standing near the artifacts table speaking with Deputy Fleming, who'd returned after the altercation with Miss Reynolds. "There's Mr. Ellis, over there."

I scanned the room again, looking for Clayton. I hadn't seen him since the lecture, and despite myself, a wave of disappointment washed over me. I tried to ignore the sinking feeling, not wanting to admit how much I had hoped to find him here.

Chapter Six

The following morning, the hotel lobby bustled with activity. The festival committee designated The Arabella as a hospitality station, and Lottie, our cook, along with Kitty and her girls, worked hard to prepare and set out delectable treats, coffee, and tea.

I made my way over to the table with the silver Samovars to enjoy another cup of Earl Grey. As I sipped, pride swelled within me as patrons mingled, enjoying their plates of pastries, while others lounged in the plush Queen Anne settees and armchairs, indulging as well. Strains of gentle piano music filtered in from the Bella Saloon. The atmosphere was warm and inviting, and a feeling of satisfaction washed over me, which was quickly followed by melancholy. It would, indeed, be difficult to leave all of this behind.

I was just about to take another sip of my tea when Constance Chatterley burst through the front doors of the hotel, a look of sheer panic on her face. Afraid she would spoil the mood of the patrons in the lobby, I quickly set down my tea and went to her.

Catching sight of me, she met me halfway. "Oh, Arabella, there you are. It's just terrible. Just terrible!"

"What is it, Constance?"

She swayed, unsteady and breathless, as if her legs might give out.

"Do you need to sit?"

"Oh, I couldn't possibly," she replied, her breath coming in quick, anxious bursts. "Something's happened—something terrible!"

Glancing around the room, I noted several pairs of eyes on us. I gently took her by the arm and ushered her into the hallway, which connected the lobby with the west end of the hotel.

"What's got you so upset?"

She took a shaking breath and then looked up into my face, her eyes bulging. "Mr. Baxter is dead!" She uttered the words in a raspy whisper.

I gasped. "Dead!? When? How?"

"I don't know. All I know was that he was found in his suite at the General. This morning! Oh, this is just awful, I tell you! Doctor Tate is over there right now. What are we going to do about the festival? And—" Her eyes welled with tears and she screwed her face up with anguish. "His poor wife! She was inconsolable."

"Oh, dear. You saw her?"

She nodded, blinking back her emotions. "I was there, at the General, taking coffee with Atticus and Archibald, and she came running down the stairs screaming, 'He's dead! He's dead!' Oh, I tell you, she was in a terrible state, the poor woman."

From the corner of my eye, I saw Cordelia, who seemed

none the wiser about the death of her friend's husband. She was speaking with a group of the guests, her complexion rosy from the recent exercise of Bijou's constitutional. Bijou was enjoying the attentions of a young woman in the group, who had knelt down to rub her belly.

I gently took hold of Constance's arm. "This is indeed sad news, Constance. Are you all right?"

She panted, pressing her hands against the bodice of her dress as if encouraging herself to continue to breathe. "Yes. Yes, I'm fine. It was just such a shock. A man in his prime like that, dead. Such a renowned figure in the world of art and artifacts."

"Well, I think it best that we say nothing yet, until we get more information." Not that it mattered, as Atticus Brooks had been on the scene to learn of the man's death. There was no controlling what he might say or write.

I tilted my head toward the lobby. "Everyone is having such a pleasant time. Let's not ruin their morning until we know more of the facts. All right?"

"Yes, yes, I agree entirely. That's why I was looking for you. I thought you ought to know—being so involved with the festival and all."

"Good. Thank you, Constance."

She gave me an appreciative smile, and then her gaze traveled to the pastries on the table.

"Please, help yourself to the refreshments," I said.

Her previous distress forgotten, she made her way over to the treats while I sought out Cordelia. She had wandered over to the reception desk where Mr. Pettyjohn was busy with some of the hotel's patrons.

When Cordelia caught my eye, I crooked my finger, beckoning her over toward the stairs so we would not be heard.

Bijou scampered over to me, begging to be picked up. I snuggled her against my chest and she rewarded me with many kisses on the chin.

"Is everything all right, Arabella? You look rather pensive," Cordelia said.

I set Bijou down. "I'm afraid I have some bad news."

"Oh, no. Something having to do with the hotel?" she asked. We'd had so many problems, ranging from vermin infestation to structural matters. It seemed the first thing that had popped into her mind.

"No," I shook my head. "It's about your friend Bernice Baxter. Her husband was found dead this morning."

Cordelia's eyes widened, and her mouth fell open. "What? He's dead?"

"Yes. I just heard this from Constance. Mrs. Baxter came down the stairs with the horrible news. She was quite upset, as you might imagine."

"Oh, my goodness, yes." Her gaze drifted away from mine and I could see she was thinking a million thoughts. "I should probably go see her." She lifted her gaze to mine again, her eyes clouded with concern. Or was it trepidation?

"Would you like me to go with you?"

Worrying her lip between her teeth, she nodded.

"Very well." I reached over and gave her arm an assuring squeeze. "I'll get my coat and hat."

We entered the lobby of the General, Bijou in tow, and I was immediately struck with surprise at the new renovations. Mr. Archer had indeed improved the place immensely. In his quest to make his hotel on par or more desirable than mine, he'd certainly made great strides—although, in my humble opinion, it lacked the warmth of the Arabella.

The hotel's interior showcased the new Arts and Crafts style, with simple wooden furniture, a large stone fireplace, muted earthy tones, wood-paneled walls, and wrought iron lighting fixtures. A wooden staircase led to the upper floors, and the lobby was dotted with seating areas with hand-crafted chairs and tables. It was very masculine, which, considering it was lodging for many of the miners working in his mines, was predictable.

Mr. Archer, Dr. Tate, and Clayton stood near one of the paned windows.

"We heard what happened. What a tragedy," I said as we approached them.

Bijou immediately went to Clayton and looked up at him adoringly, waiting for him to acknowledge her. He crouched down and stroked her head, his fingers sinking into her thick hair. Bijou's tail wagged furiously, its long feathers sweeping against the floor like a broom.

Mr. Archer, his lips pale—probably from shock, shook his head. "Terrible business. He seemed in the prime of health."

"Do you know what happened?" I asked, addressing Dr. Tate.

"Not at first glance. The only thing I can determine, based on the condition of the body, is the time of death."

"Which was?" I asked.

"I'd reckon sometime between eleven o'clock at night and one in the morning. We've moved the body to my infirmary for further examination."

"And the cause of death?"

Clayton raised a hand, cutting me off before I could say

more. "Arabella, don't—let's not start down this road. We know nothing yet."

I stiffened, a spark of indignation flaring in my chest at his dismissive tone.

The doctor, seeming to not have noticed the tension between us, continued on. "I am assuming it was heart failure—but don't quote me on that. He was found seated in the desk chair in the parlor of his suite. Mrs. Baxter found him there this morning."

"Where is she?" Cordelia asked.

"She's up in their suite." Mr. Archer tilted his head toward the staircase.

"I've given her a mild sedative," added Dr. Tate.

I glanced again at Clayton, whose focus seemed to have wandered. There was something off in his usually steadfast demeanor—a hint of distraction, or perhaps worry.

"I'll go up to her. What suite?" Cordelia asked Mr. Archer.

"Two thirteen. At the end of the hall."

She nodded and headed for the stairs.

"I'll be right there," I called after her, and then turned again to the men. "What does this mean for the festival?"

"We will proceed as planned," Mr. Archer said. "This is indeed unfortunate, but the festival carries deep cultural significance and serves as a cornerstone for our community and denotes the camaraderie and mutual respect between the native peoples and the town's settlers. This is a time for us to continue to pull together. I'd hate to disrupt that."

The skeptic in me couldn't help but think that the real reason he didn't want to cancel was on account of his grand reopening of the General. Perhaps that wasn't a kind thought. But he had to know that based on last night's alter-cation at the lecture, the sentiment of his remarks fell a little flat. Miss Reynolds, who headed up the festival committee, and Michael Two Trees, and even Sarah Redhawk, demonstrated there was indeed strife between some of the native peoples and the white man, particularly one white man, Mr. Baxter.

"I should go," Dr. Tate said, and then addressed Mr. Archer and the sheriff. "I'll inform you of my findings once I examine Mr. Baxter's body."

"Thank you, doctor," Mr. Archer said. "Well," he turned to Clayton. "I hope we will have smooth sailing for the rest of the festival."

"All seems to be quiet in the town," Clayton reassured him.

"Good, good." Mr. Archer placed his hands behind his back. "Now, if you will excuse me, I need to meet up with Miss Reynolds to see how we are to proceed."

He left Clayton and me standing together in an awkward silence.

"I have seen little of you lately," I finally said, deciding to ignore his previous abruptness.

He shrugged. "I've been busy. We haven't had quite so many people in town before."

"Have there been any problems? Other than this, of course?"

"Not particularly. There was a bit of a scuffle last night —and a few drunkards causing trouble, which I fully expected. But with such a large crowd, the deputy and I have had to stay especially vigilant."

"I'm sure you will be up to the task." I offered a knowing smile.

He pressed his lips together and gave me a slight nod. "All part of the job."

He crossed his arms over his chest and I couldn't shake

the feeling that he was using it as a form of protection, or putting up a wall. But why?

"Is there something wrong, Clayton?"

He gave another shrug of his shoulders. "No, why would you ask that?"

"You seem—it's just that—you know, we've never talked about, well, about what happened between us."

He cleared his throat, clearly uncomfortable with my bringing up our kiss. "Do we need to talk about it?"

I swallowed. Clearly, he didn't feel it was necessary. But what did that mean?

"Look." He softened his tone. "I hope it wasn't inappropriate. I was—I was just caught up in the moment."

"Oh," I flinched. Just caught up in the moment? So, it meant nothing? "Yes, I suppose that is what happened."

I had entertained the very same thought myself, yet knowing he felt the same brought a curious sense of disappointment, quite contrary to what I had expected—or perhaps hoped—he might feel. But really, what could I have expected? It was a simple kiss. And did it truly matter? My life was already tangled in complications far too great for romance. Besides, I was rather enjoying the recent liberty I had found, and a relationship could very well impose restrictions on what I might do with my life.

I further reasoned that I had serious decisions to make about my future, and the distraction of a man was the last thing I needed. It was becoming clear that if I wished to preserve my cherished fame and status in the world, I would have to return to the theater. Yet, to my surprise, the thought of that left me feeling hollow. Fame had always been a reassuring presence, validating my worth and place in the world. And I adored acting, being on the stage, taking on different personas, reaching into the lives of others, whether their stories were fictional or grounded in reality. My theater in New York allowed me to share my art with so many more people than I could ever reach here. Why, it could hold nearly half the population of La Plata Springs within its walls! And in a single day, I could reach twice that number. Could I truly walk away from all of that?

Yet, just as I had embraced the challenge of building the reputation of the theater from the ground up, overcoming countless setbacks to see it thrive, I was now doing the same with the hotel. It would be difficult to leave.

Either way, a committed relationship would only add another layer of complexity to my life, and I could scarcely manage what was already on my plate.

"Well, I'd better get upstairs to check on Mrs. Baxter and Cordelia," I said, overwhelmed with my thoughts and suddenly wanting to get away from Clayton, my feelings for him, and the awkwardness between us.

He held my gaze a little longer than I expected, but then tipped his hat, bidding me a silent farewell.

Chapter Seven

I knocked on the door of the Baxters' suite, and Cordelia answered, ushering me into the parlor. The room was surprisingly spacious, and I couldn't help but wonder if this was the designated 'owner's suite' of the General. Given that Mr. Archer usually stayed at his ranch, it made sense that he'd offer it to Mr. Baxter as the festival's honored guest.

I studied the decor. Rich, earth-toned wallpaper featuring intricate, nature-inspired patterns met dark wooden wainscoting which ran halfway up the walls, show-casing expert craftsmanship.

A stone fireplace, a miniature of the one in the lobby, dominated the room. Above the mantel hung a handcrafted wooden clock, its pendulum ticking gently. Overstuffed armchairs and a settee upholstered in soft, patterned fabrics surrounded the fireplace and a round, wooden table with a polished finish stood in one corner, accompanied by matching chairs—perfect for afternoon tea or a game of cards. Covering the parquet floor was a large woven rug with geometric designs. Everything was in perfect order, except for a small, brilliant red earthen pot on the mantel—which seemed oddly out of place. Also, it had a triangular chip missing, the damage poorly concealed by its awkward positioning. Someone—likely a maid—had broken it and tried to hide her mistake. But the flaw was too obvious, and now it stood out as a silent confession in the otherwise pristine room.

I had to admit, the overall effect of the suite was charming. It made me want to refurbish the fourth floor owner's suite in my hotel, and perhaps the other two suites on the third floor. It pained me to be upstaged. But that would mean more expense, and more money to be borrowed against my estate, which would mean further time before I could receive my inheritance. My pride would have to be put aside for the time being.

"How is she?" I asked Cordelia. I assumed Mrs. Baxter was in one of the other two rooms.

"Shaken, as you would expect." Cordelia bit a nail, which was unusual. I'd never seen her partake of the habit before.

Suddenly, Mrs. Baxter appeared in the doorway. Her eyes were red-rimmed and swollen, and her nose was crimson from crying.

"Mrs. Baxter." I approached her. "Please accept my deepest condolences. This is a terrible, terrible shock. I am so sorry for your loss."

Her lips curved in a polite, fleeting smile. "Thank you, Mrs. Pryce. I still can't believe it." She shook her head. "He—he seemed fine last night."

"Do you mind my asking what happened?"

"Why don't we sit down," Cordelia said. She gestured

for Mrs. Baxter to take the settee. She and I sat in the two armchairs.

Mrs. Baxter pulled a handkerchief from the cuff of her sleeve. Her dress, made from high-quality, lightweight wool in a deep green hue, was simple and refined. The bodice featured a high neckline adorned with a delicate lace collar. Attached to the collar was the beautiful silver brooch—a bird with ruby eyes, its wings spread in flight.

She dabbed her eyes, then composed herself and straightened her expression. "After an early supper, Warren mentioned he had business to attend to with Mr. Archer and Mr. Chase. I had already agreed to assist Simon with a paper he was writing on the textile crafting traditions of the Ayashiri tribe in South America—an area of expertise for the tribe's women, and one in which I had specific knowledge. We were up quite late, well past midnight. When I returned to the room, Warren wasn't in bed. The door to the spare room he had turned into a study was closed, so I assumed he was in there working and didn't want to disturb him. It wasn't uncommon for Warren to work through the night. I went to bed. This morning, I went to check on him and that's when I saw—" Her eyes brimmed with tears, and she quickly pressed the handkerchief to her mouth.

"How awful," Cordelia said, in sympathy.

"Had Mr. Baxter experienced any health problems of late?" I asked.

She shook her head. "No. He is—was—the picture of health."

"Well, I'm sure the doctor will have some answers for you, Bernice," Cordelia said.

Mrs. Baxter reached out and took hold of Cordelia's hand. "It's such a comfort to have you here."

Cordelia gave her a tentative smile.

Mrs. Baxter turned to me. "You are very lucky to have her as your assistant. Cordelia is such a loyal person. And a wonderful researcher. We had many long nights of studying papers on the tribes of South America, didn't we?"

I glanced at Cordelia, who gave me a sheepish smile. She always had her nose in a book, and she often came up with surprising anecdotes about some obscure subject she was interested in, but Mrs. Baxter's comments rang of something more than just a pastime. Another piece in the mysterious puzzle of Cordelia.

"I only dabbled." She shook her head dismissively. "I wanted to study archaeology after finishing school—but things didn't quite work out."

"I see." Again, why hadn't Cordelia mentioned this to me? I thought we knew each other well.

"Is there anything we can do for you, Bernice?" She changed the subject. "Is there family, or anyone, who needs to be informed of Mr. Baxter's death?"

She shook her head. "No, no family. Only colleagues, and Simon will take care of that."

Looking down at her hands, she seemed to retreat inside herself and I suddenly got the distinct impression she wanted to be alone. I understood that sentiment all too well. In the initial days following William's passing, I had no desire to engage in idle conversation with others. I needed time to reflect on what had transpired.

"Mrs. Baxter, if there is anything at all that Cordelia and I could do for you, I hope you will call upon us. Even if it's just to lend a sympathetic ear."

She sniffed and then placed her handkerchief back inside the cuff of her sleeve. "Thank you so much, Mrs. Pryce. I will." Her eyes travelled to Cordelia, but Cordelia would not meet her gaze.

We left Mrs. Baxter with her thoughts and grief, and proceeded down the stairs, Cordelia descending as if there was a fire in the building.

"Cordelia," I called out to her.

She stopped and turned to look up at me. Her mottled complexion and odd expression hinted at unease.

"Are you all right?" I reached out to touch her shoulder.

She shook her head. "No, I'm not. A man has died. The husband of an old friend."

"Yes. A man you said you were only briefly acquainted with," I added.

She looked affronted. "I was only briefly acquainted with him. It's still upsetting," she said, her voice clipped. She turned and continued down the stairs. I followed behind, once again rather confused by her behavior.

We left the General and headed down the main street toward the Arabella. Cordelia walked briskly, nearly losing me in her wake. She had taken the habit of walking everywhere she went, and often into the woods. Her once delicate constitution had grown strong. She'd so transformed since that first day we'd arrived in La Plata Springs. Her chronic headaches had ceased, mostly, and her complexion had taken on a rosy hue from the sun and exercise.

"My goodness," I called out. "What is the rush, my dear?"

Instantly, she slowed, and I caught up with her.

"I'm sorry. I was preoccupied and didn't realize I was walking so fast."

"It's all right." Slightly breathless, I assured her she was

49

forgiven. "Do you want to talk about what has you so preoccupied?"

She stopped and turned to face me. "It's Bernice."

I waited for her to continue, but she only looked up at me in silence.

"You are worried about her?"

"Well—yes. I suppose you could say that."

"She's your friend. She will need your support in the coming days."

"She will," Cordelia agreed, a hesitant look on her face.

"What are you not telling me, Cordelia?"

She sighed, took my hand, and led me to the bench along the boardwalk in front of Archer's Candies and Confections, right under the shop window. The window, framed in weathered wood, was adorned with a lace curtain, slightly yellowed with age. Behind the glass, an array of colorful confections was meticulously arranged to tempt passersby.

We sat down, and Cordelia launched into her explanation.

"You see, Bernice and I had another friend named Anna. I had met Anna after finishing school and introduced her to Bernice. The three of us grew close and did everything together. We were all considering pursuing further studies in archaeology at Radcliffe—especially Anna. She was incredibly driven, and with the money she had inherited from an uncle, she was determined to use it to continue her education. One day, Bernice invited us to join her at an antiquities show where her employer, Warren Baxter, was speaking. Naturally, we thought it sounded delightful, so we went along. Bernice introduced us to Warren, and for Anna, it was love at first sight. It was immediately clear that Mr. Baxter felt the same, and soon, they began courting. I'd never seen Anna so happy. Shortly afterward, she was accepted to Radcliffe and thrilled at the prospect of pursuing her passion for archaeology, especially with someone who shared it. They were completely devoted to each other."

"Sounds like a fairytale romance." I noted the wistfulness in her expression.

"It was. But then—"

Suddenly, her eyes brimmed with tears, and she looked away from me. I took hold of her hand, encouraging her to continue.

"But then Anna died," she said softly.

Sensing Cordelia's emotion, Bijou jumped up and settled herself on the other side of her, resting her paws on her lap. Absently, Cordelia stroked her ears.

"Oh, my." I squeezed her hand. "I'm so sorry."

She sniffed and then wiped away a tear that had escaped down her cheek. "It was devastating. Anna was such a beautiful person. And we were all so young." She flinched slightly, the memory no doubt causing a twinge of lingering sorrow.

"It doesn't seem fair, does it?"

She shook her head. "No." Sniffling, she wiped her cheeks with the back of her hands and straightened herself.

"Bernice and I didn't see much of each other after that. It was... too painful."

"And, it still is?"

She bit her lip and nodded.

"It's funny how grief can either bring people closer together, or drive them apart, isn't it?" I said.

Bijou let out a sigh, nearly asleep in Cordelia's lap.

"Bernice and Warren Baxter started seeing each other after Anna's death. I suppose it was a way of comforting one another, but I thought it was too soon. It bothered me."

"Oh, I see." It probably would have made me raise an eyebrow, too.

She continued. "My father became ill, and I was needed at home, so I left Massachusetts, and my dreams of studying archeology at Radcliff. Shortly after I returned home, I received a letter from Bernice saying that she and Mr. Baxter had broken things off. So, when Mr. Baxter arrived in town, I was surprised to see that they had gotten married after all."

"That's understandable." I squeezed her hand again. "Thank you for telling me. I was a little worried about you."

She gave me an apologetic glance. "I'm sorry for making you worry."

"It's quite all right," I assured her. "And again, I'm sorry about your friend, Anna."

"Thank you." She sniffed and then arranged her face into a forced expression of resolve. "But that was a long time ago. I need to leave it in the past. Besides, I have so much to be grateful for; my employment and friendship with you, this beautiful place we are living—"

Bijou, having awakened from her nap, whined, looking up at Cordelia.

"And Bijou!" she said, her face finally breaking into a genuine smile. Bijou raised herself up and licked Cordelia's chin, making her giggle.

"Oh, Bijou," I said, "you're such an attention-seeking little cherub." The little urchin, panting with satisfaction, simply looked at me, grinning in her canine way.

I glanced up to see the sheriff, Deputy Fleming, Mr. Archer, and Dr. Tate, standing in front of Dr. Tate's infirmary.

"Look over there," I said. "I wonder if the doctor has determined Mr. Baxter's cause of death?"

"Shall we go see?" Cordelia asked.

"Let's."

As we walked down the street, I took a moment to admire the town's transformation for the festival. Banners and flags in bright, festive colors draped across buildings and lampposts, bringing the street to life. Numerous stalls lined the street, offering a variety of traditional and local foods. The aroma of freshly baked bread and sweet treats emanated from Gilroy's Bakery and Mrs. Gilroy, holding a tray of the delicacies, offered them to passersby. Mr. Emerson, the manager of Archer's Dry Goods, stood at a table in front of the store, handing out glasses of lemonade and locally brewed cider.

Booths, occupied by members of the Tavani tribe, displayed handmade crafts from pottery and jewelry to beaded clothing and wooden carvings. Mr. Parkhurst, the town's blacksmith and farrier, was giving demonstrations on various horseshoeing techniques in front of Archer's Livery.

I tightened my grip on Bijou's leash as she eagerly tried to join the children playing games while their families strolled through the festival, enjoying the lively sights and sounds. The thought that Mr. Baxter would no longer be a part of it was sobering indeed.

We approached the men standing in front of the infirmary. Deputy Fleming, surprised at our arrival, quickly swept his hat off his head.

"Mrs. Pryce, what a pleasant surprise," he said, unable to refrain from grinning. He glanced at Cordelia. "Miss Danson, nice to see you."

She gave him a polite nod.

"Have you come to a conclusion about Mr. Baxter, doctor?" I asked.

He shared a glance with Clayton and Mr. Archer. "Yes, I have. The bluish discoloration of the skin, particularly on the lips, face, and extremities, and the pinpoint hemorrhages in the eyes and on the face lead me to believe Mr. Baxter died of suffocation."

"Suffocation? Do you mean—?"

"He was murdered," the sheriff finished for me. "Which is a mystery because there were no signs of a struggle."

The deputy spoke up. "But, there was the—"

The sheriff darted him a warning look. Deputy Fleming's face took on an awkward, tight-lipped expression, glancing away quickly to avoid eye contact.

"What is it?" I looked up into Clayton's face. "What are you not telling me?"

He cleared his throat. "It's nothing. It's not important."

Interesting. Why wasn't he willing to include me?

"I still can't believe it!" Mr. Archer exclaimed, clearly absorbed in his own thoughts. "A man—murdered. In my hotel!"

Unbelievable, indeed, I thought. Maybe now he would cease to feel the need to remind me of the Arabella's precarious reputation because of unfortunate mishaps that had occurred between her walls, and that those tragic incidents were my fault. I knew this was a tactic he used in an effort to get me to abandon her to him. Even so, it had wounded me to the core. I hoped he would be more sensitive to the fact that some things that happened under our roofs were not in our control.

"Was Mr. Baxter incapacitated in any way which would prevent him from fighting back?" I asked the doctor.

"Not that I can tell, so far."

"Perhaps he was poisoned?" Cordelia said.

The doctor shook his head. "I see no evidence of it."

The sheriff turned to Mr. Archer. "You'll have to move Mrs. Baxter to another room at the hotel. We will need to have access to the suite for investigation."

"Of course, of course," he said somberly. "Poor woman."

"If you will excuse me," the doctor said. "I need to get back to the body. I'm missing something, and I won't rest until I find out what it is."

Mr. Archer shook his head slowly, a soft click of his tongue conveying a mix of sadness and bewilderment. "This is an unthinkable tragedy. I hope I can count on you, sheriff, to find out what happened."

Clayton gave him a brief nod. "You know I'll do my best."

Mr. Archer clapped him on the shoulder and then departed.

I looked up into Clayton's face. "If there is anything I can do to help …"

He regarded me for a moment, and then said, "Thanks. But we've got this. Let's go, Deputy."

Deputy Fleming's gaze bounced between Clayton and me. "But, sheriff, Mrs. Pryce is most excellent at—"

"I said, we've got this." Clayton gave him a pointed look.

"It's all right, Deputy," I said, barely able to hide my disappointment. "I'm sure the two of you will have everything in hand in no time."

"Good day, Arabella, Miss Danson." Clayton tipped his hat to us.

I gave him a polite nod, disguising the fact that I did not think it was a good day at all.

Chapter Eight

Later that afternoon, Cordelia and I sat on the settee in our suite, partaking of some tea and toast sandwiches which consisted of freshly churned butter, salt and pepper.

Cordelia, looking pensive, picked at her toast. She hadn't touched her tea, and I imagined it must be quite cold by now.

"Are you thinking about your friend Bernice?" I asked her. "The news of how Mr. Baxter came to his end will be hard to reconcile. I can't imagine how horrifying it would be to discover someone you love was murdered."

A soft, wistful smile played on Cordelia's lips. "I was actually thinking about Anna. She and Warren can now be together. It's all she ever wanted."

I looked at her askance. How odd that she would not be more concerned about Bernice.

Suddenly, the room's temperature dropped, bringing with it the spicy scent of tobacco.

"That is assuredly true." Percival appeared in one of the armchairs. With a pipe gently clasped between his fingers, wisps of curling smoke floated lazily around him, blending into the dim light of the room.

Cordelia's face brightened. "Have you seen them? Are they truly together?"

Only a short time ago, I would have been aghast at Percival's appearing in Cordelia's presence. I had kept my ghostly companions a deeply guarded secret for fear of being discovered as having clairvoyant abilities for reasons stemming back to my youth. Other family members with the same sensitivities had been locked away from society, deemed either insane or evil. Times had changed, as Percival often reminded me, and communication with the beyond was now fashionable. Despite that, the fear was deep-seated and at times overwhelming.

Percival had respected my desire that he not appear to anyone in association with me or the hotel, but after he'd saved Cordelia from the brink of death, she'd become sensitive to his presence. She could not see other spiritual entities that had crossed my path of late, and Percival claimed she probably never would. They shared a specific bond because of her near-death experience.

Constance Chatterley, who had also seen Percival, quite by accident, was another story. She, too, possessed the ability to see ghostly phenomenon, but she was not so keen to fully embrace it. She had come dangerously close to discovering my abilities, but I had successfully evaded her inquiries. I thought Constance was a lovely, if sometimes annoying, person, but given her penchant for gossip, I didn't want the information in her hands.

"I have not seen your Anna and Mr. Baxter, no," Percival answered Cordelia's question. "And, they may not currently inhabit the same ethereal plane, as there are different dimensions in the afterworld, but they will one day most definitely be reunited."

A hint of disappointment crossed her face. "Of course."

Percival gave her a sympathetic smile. "Love crosses all boundaries, my dear. There is no power stronger."

She pressed her lips together in an appreciative smile. "Yes. You're right. But won't Mr. Baxter have trouble reaching Anna as long as his murder is unsolved?"

Percival nodded. "This is also true."

"Then we have to find out who killed him. Arabella, you must put your investigative skills to use once more."

I shook my head. "There is too much to do with the festival, Cordelia. I am stretched to the limit." I also wanted to refrain from stepping on Clayton's toes at the moment. He clearly didn't want me involved.

"I'm sure the sheriff will find the killer. Especially now that he has the capable help of Deputy Fleming," I said with confidence.

"But, you and the sheriff work so well together," Cordelia implored. "He will assuredly want your help."

"Naturally," Percival mumbled under his breath, making clear his annoyance at the notion. I chose to ignore his petulance.

I sighed. "Right now, the man can barely look me in the eye. And you heard him, Cordelia. He doesn't want my help."

"Oh, this is interesting." Percival straightened in the chair, his face all eagerness. I often found his jealousy amusing, but today it didn't seem funny in the least. Clayton's brusque behavior toward me completely confounded me.

Cordelia's brow knit with concern. "Yes. Why is that? Have you two had a falling out?"

I shrugged. "If we have, I certainly don't know over

what. We seemed to be getting along … well… quite famously. But lately, he's been distant. I haven't even had a riding lesson in weeks."

"Pity," Percival said with a mocking pout.

"That's strange," Cordelia said. "I know how much you two enjoyed those lessons together."

"Yes, however, ever since our kiss—"

Cordelia's eyes popped open in surprise. "Your what?! You kissed him?"

I offered a prim smile. "Well, actually, he was the one who kissed me, but—"

"Oh, my goodness. Why didn't you tell me?" she asked, her expression still aghast.

I glanced at Percival to see that his countenance had paled—yes, even a ghost can lose his coloration in times of distress.

"The impudence of the man!" he snarled. "If I were alive, I'd—"

I darted Percival a warning look. "He was a complete gentleman," I said, fondly remembering the heady sensation the kiss had produced.

He scoffed and then popped out of sight in a huff. I shook my head. There is nothing in this world more grievous than a man given to fits of moodiness.

"And, you," I directed my attention toward Cordelia, "don't need to know all of my secrets, dear. Just like I don't need to know yours."

She frowned. "I have kept no secrets from you, Arabella."

"Really?" I laughed. "What about finishing school? Your interest in archaeology? Your knowing the famous Warren Baxter and his wife?"

"Those weren't secrets—exactly."

"Not exactly?" I raised a skeptical brow. "Seeing as your friends were coming to town, I thought you would have at least mentioned it."

"I told you. I hardly knew him, and I most certainly didn't know he and Bernice had married," she said, with a tinge of hurt in her voice. Perhaps I had pressed her too hard on the matter. She was obviously quite distraught over the recent events and those of her past. She didn't need me needling her.

"I apologize, Cordelia. It seems we have gotten off track. I'm sorry if I upset you."

"Thank you, Arabella," she said somberly, her pensive mood returning. "I hope that for Anna's sake, Mr. Baxter's killer will be brought to justice soon."

"And, for Bernice's sake, as well?" I added, curious that she'd left her out of her sympathies.

She blinked and then gave me a tentative smile. "Oh, yes. And, Bernice's sake, of course." She finally picked up her teacup and sipped at her tea with a faraway look in her eyes.

I suspected that I still didn't know the entire story of Cordelia's past with Bernice Baxter and her now deceased husband.

Chapter Nine

The following morning, I rose and dressed before dawn. Despite my resolve to let the professionals investigate the murder of Mr. Baxter in order to give Clayton the space he obviously needed from our friendship—if there was one — I couldn't help but be curious about his death. Thoughts of scenarios of how he could have succumbed to suffocation clouded my sleep, making for a restless night.

After slipping down to the kitchen to make a pot of tea, I went back to my rooms, built a fire, and sat at the desk, working on some correspondence. I realized I had not received a letter from Mr. Thomas Blackthorn, the manager of my theater in New York, for a few weeks, which was a little unusual. He, at my request, was fairly diligent about keeping me abreast of what was happening with the most current show and the players involved, not to mention the running of the business.

Perhaps Cordelia had come across a letter and had placed it on the desk of my office in the annex? I would have to check later.

From her little bed under the window, Bijou whined. I glanced over to see the sky pink with the break of dawn. Bijou most likely needed to go outside to do her business. Besides, a walk might be nice to clear my head.

I straightened the papers on the desk and then rose to put on my coat and hat. Bijou jumped about, delighted when I took the leash from the hook beside the door.

"All right, my little *chou chou*. Let's get some of that early mountain air, shall we?" I clipped the leash to her collar.

She smiled and wagged her tail in agreement.

The lobby of the hotel was blissfully quiet. Mr. Pettyjohn stood at the reception desk, a steaming cup of coffee in his right hand, reviewing the guest register and ledger, and making notes with the other.

"Good morning," I whispered, not wanting to disturb the silence.

"Good morning, Mrs. Pryce," he replied quietly.

"All well at the hotel?"

He glanced up from behind his wire-rimmed spectacles. "Yes, aside from some initial unease over Mr. Baxter's murder. A few of the General's guests have inquired about rooms—they're uneasy staying there after what happened."

"I imagine so. Have you been able to accommodate them?"

He shook his head. "We are full to the brim, madam."

"Right. I thought so. Well, I am off for a walk."

"Enjoy the morning, madam."

Bijou pulled at the leash, conveying the urgency of her bladder, so I smiled at Mr. Pettyjohn, and bid him goodbye.

Outside, the air was crisp, but not quite cold yet—the September mornings still clung to a hint of warmth, refusing to give in to the bite of frost. Off in the distance, I could hear the familiar chug-chug of the early morning train. I turned and started south, making my way toward the station to watch that magnificent engine pull into town, all iron and steam, cutting through the quiet of morning.

As I walked down the street, the businesses on each side were slowly awakening. Shopkeepers were milling about their stores, preparing for the day ahead, but none seemed to take notice of me, until I passed by the Post Office and Telegraph Exchange. The postmaster, Mr. Crawford, stepped outside, making the bells on the door jingle merrily.

"Ah, Mrs. Pryce. How fortuitous." His round, ruddy face broke into a grin. "I have just sorted some mail for you. Would you like to take it now?"

I returned his smile, but then said apologetically, "I'm just taking Bijou for a walk. I'm not sure I can carry all of it."

"It's just two envelopes, but if you'd like, you can come back for it later."

I supposed I could carry two envelopes. I hoped one of them would be from Mr. Blackthorn. Besides, it would save Cordelia a trip. "Very well. If it's just two, I'll take them now."

He held up a finger. "I'll be back in a moment."

Bijou found a nearby bush, so while we waited, she conducted her business.

"Here you are." Mr. Crawford returned, sending the bells jingling again. He handed me both missives. One was a bill, and the other appeared to be a letter, but from the handwriting on the front of the envelope, I knew it was not from Mr. Blackthorn.

"Bad luck about that traveling Art Dealer," Mr. Crawford shook his head. "I heard he died at the General the other night."

I offered a sympathetic smile. "I'm afraid so."

63

"Do you know what happened?"

"Dr. Tate is trying to ascertain just that," I said, not wanting to divulge that the man had been murdered.

Mr. Crawford *tsked*. "Well, it just goes to show—you can't take anything for granted. You never know when you might just give up the ghost."

"I couldn't agree more," I said, eager to be on my way. "Thank you for the mail, Mr. Crawford."

After Bijou and I had walked a few yards, I stopped to look down at the letter. My name was written in a hasty scrawl, with The Arabella Hotel noted below. Curious about the sender, I turned it over, but the back was blank. I opened the envelope, took out the letter, and read.

Dear Mrs. Pryce,

I am writing to you regarding my visit to La Plata Springs for the cultural and historic festival. While my visit is partly professional, I also have a very personal reason for coming—to seek your help.
I fear for my life.

I have read about your exceptional crime-solving abilities and am certain you can assist me. I only hope this letter reaches you in time.
I am forced to communicate by letter because we cannot risk meeting in person. I am being watched, and I fear for both your safety and that of your loved ones.

I understand if you are hesitant to take on the challenge of uncovering who is behind this threat. However, I believe you are my only hope.
If you find it in your heart to help me confront the perpetrator of my fears, please write back to me immediately. Address the envelope to my alias, Vincent Morley, and place the letter beneath the painted yellow stone under the footbridge leading to the woods. Take care to ensure you are not followed.
I also have one other request. If I should, God forbid, come to my

demise before you receive this letter, please protect my wife, for her close association with me and my work puts her in grave danger.
Sincerely yours,
Warren Baxter

Chapter Ten

In a daze, after reading Mr. Baxter's letter, I went back to the hotel. There were several guests and townsfolk enjoying the pastries, tea, and coffee that had been laid out. Kitty and Lottie bustled in and out of the kitchen, bringing new trays of finger foods out to the tables.

I stopped Kitty as she went for one of the Samovars. "Everything going all right here?"

She nodded and removed the large beverage container from its stand. "Busy, but all going well. Just going to refresh the tea."

"Very good. I'm headed upstairs for a while. Just have Clarence come fetch me if you need me."

"Will do," she said with a wink.

I ascended the steps slowly, contemplating what to do about the letter. Should I inform Cordelia? Given that Mrs. Baxter was her friend, she deserved to know. And if Mrs. Baxter was truly in danger, could that also place Cordelia at risk by association? If they were often together, then surely it would. Yet, then again, Cordelia had not been too eager to reunite with her old friend, for reasons that were still a mystery.

But the larger question remained: should I comply with the request? Mr. Baxter's fears had come to pass, and he had implored me to help. Yet, I now faced the added complication of my fragile relationship with Clayton.

What a quandary. I needed some time to think this through. I wondered if Cordelia was in our suite, or if she was out? I was hoping to have a few moments to myself to consider how to proceed.

When I opened the door to the parlor, the pungent scent of pipe tobacco enveloped me. Percival, in his transparent form, was prone, lounging on the settee. He had blown a series of smoke rings into the air and poked at them with his finger, creating a variety of odd shaped designs.

"What are you doing?" I asked, my voice a little sharper than I intended.

"Resting," he said. "Is that all right with you?"

"I'm sorry. I've just received a rather distressing letter."

He raised himself to sitting, planting his feet on the floor. He leaned forward and rested his elbows on his knees, his pipe firmly between his teeth.

"Do tell," he said with some interest.

"Is Cordelia here?" I whispered.

He shook his head.

I sat down on the chair next to the settee and pulled the letter from my handbag and relayed its message.

"Distressing indeed," Percival said. "What do you intend to do?"

I shrugged. "I'm not sure. The man needed my help—and now he is dead. I feel somewhat obliged to find his killer. Especially given that his wife could be in danger. And,

I suppose as she and Cordelia are friends, I must warn Cordelia."

"Warn me about what?" She had appeared in the doorway that led to the bedrooms.

I glared at Percival, who merely shrugged his shoulders. He could have at least told me she was in the other room.

"Come sit, dear." I pointed to the chair opposite mine. I then handed her the letter.

Reading it, she gasped, laying a hand on her chest. "He knew he might be killed?"

I nodded. "It seems so."

Cordelia lowered the letter to her lap. "There you have it. We must find his killer."

I let out a sigh and shot her a skeptical glance.

"I've been thinking about it, Arabella. Mr. Baxter will not rest until his murder is solved. And if he cannot be at peace, then he cannot find Anna. And from what he wrote in the letter, Bernice is in danger, too. We have to get involved."

"I got a faint glimpse of Warren Baxter during the night, but he was unreachable," Percival offered.

"Is that because he is caught between the spiritual realms?" I asked. Percival had once explained the complex web of realms a spirit must pass through to reach the Afterworld.

He shook his head. "No. He is not between realms. I believe he exists in the most enigmatic and most tightly guarded plane of all. The Veiled Realm."

"You have not mentioned this realm before," Cordelia said.

He shrugged. "I understand very little about it. Only that those in its grasp are tied to arcane beliefs or practices."

"Does this have something to do with his work?" I asked.

"He was a historian and dealer in ancient artifacts, was he not?" Percival said. "It only follows that he would have been aware of such beliefs and practices associated with those items. Perhaps he even partook of them?"

"If he's in this realm, does that mean he can't be reunited with Anna?" Cordelia asked.

Percival let out a sigh. "I am afraid so. The esoteric nature of the Veiled Realm makes communication with those in the other realms highly difficult. Its mysteries run deep."

Cordelia stood up abruptly and began pacing the room, wringing her hands. She bit her lip, a look of dire concern, or perhaps even fear, passing over her features.

"My goodness, Cordelia. Why do you look so distressed?" I asked, surprised at her sudden agitation.

Still pacing, she raised a hand to her forehead and pinched it between her thumb and fingers. "We have to solve Mr. Baxter's murder," she repeated. "We have to ensure he gets out of the Veiled Realm. He and Anna simply must be together. I owe it to her."

I blinked. "You owe it to her? Whatever do you mean?"

Cordelia stopped pacing, placed her head in her hands, and let out an exasperated breath. I had never seen her so flustered. I glanced at Percival, who seemed as confounded as I was.

Finally, Cordelia lowered her hands. "I have to make it right."

I shook my head in confusion. "My dear, what on earth are you talking about?"

She winced, as if a wave of pain assaulted her body. When she opened her eyes again, they glistened with tears.

She took a deep breath and then let it out slowly. Her demeanor had calmed somewhat from the exercise.

"I must ensure Anna's happiness in the afterlife."

"Yes, so you keep saying, but why?"

She let go a defeated sigh. "Because I'm the one who put her on that path."

I stared at her, dumbfounded. "Put her on that path? Surely you can't mean—"

Cordelia threw herself down in the chair. "I'm partially to blame for her death."

"You can't be serious," I said in disbelief. Surely, she was exaggerating.

Cordelia leaned forward in the chair to explain. "Anna's parents did not approve of her courtship with Mr. Baxter— or her pursuit of archaeology at Radcliffe. They had planned for her to marry one of her father's business acquaintances—a very wealthy man—and become a rich socialite and housewife. But Anna confided in me about her feelings for Mr. Baxter, and I encouraged her. I told her she should follow her heart and not let her parents control her life."

"That seems reasonable advice," I said.

"Perhaps." Cordelia shook her head. "But it set everything in motion. They became closer, more defiant of her parents, and their passion—well, it led to a pregnancy."

"Oh, I see," I said, a little thrown off guard.

"Anna came to me, desperate. She didn't know what to do. Her parents had already arranged for her to marry the man of their choice, and she felt trapped. I didn't know how to help her, so in my desperation, I broke Anna's confidence and confided in Bernice. Bernice said she'd heard of a woman, a licensed apothecary, who could 'take care' of the matter. Well, unfortunately, Anna died because of this woman's ministrations. I trusted her, Arabella. I trusted Bernice. I later discovered that the woman had no license and a questionable reputation at best. Anna died because of my encouragement and my blind faith in Bernice's solution."

"How tragic," Percival said.

Cordelia pressed her hand to her mouth, her voice trembling. "I was the one who put her on that path, and it ended in tragedy. I've carried this guilt with me for years. If I can help reunite her and Mr. Baxter, if I can believe they are at peace together with their child, then maybe—just maybe—I can forgive myself."

Pressing my lips together, I considered her plea, and it seemed I had little choice. After all, I would do anything for Cordelia—as she would for me. Whether I was in the good graces of the sheriff or not, I would help my dear friend find the peace and closure she needed.

"Of course, dear," I said. "We'll get started right away."

Chapter Eleven

Early the following day, after I'd checked that all was in order at the hotel, I summoned Mr. Ellis, the driver of the hotel's coach, to take Bijou and me to the Aurora Mystique, the new theater on the outskirts of town.

Andrew Archer, Archibald's multi-talented nephew, had written a play titled, "Bridging Worlds: The Settlers and the Tavani Tribe" to be performed at the theater on the last day of the festival. The piece aimed to educate and engage the audience through a balanced portrayal of historical events, emphasizing the importance of mutual respect, understanding, and cooperation. It highlighted both the challenges and successes in the relationship between the settlers and the Tavani tribe, and he hoped it would foster a deeper appreciation for the diverse history of La Plata Springs.

The bright young man had not only written the play, but also took on the lead role of his uncle, the founder of La Plata Springs. It impressed me he had not written the role in complete deference to his uncle, but portrayed him quite honestly, flaws and all, and I wondered if it had caused friction between the two. Humility was not one of Archibald Archer's stronger traits.

The play detailed the history of the town's founding, starting with the arrival of the railroad, followed by the discovery of ore in the area. It covered the introduction of the mines and the building of the General hotel, the first permanent structure in the town, and portrayed the often challenging relations between the Tavani and the new settlers, but ultimately showing how they came to coexist peacefully. There was also a scene highlighting the building of the Arabella hotel, which delighted me, as it gave homage to both my late husband and Percival.

As the young man considered himself my protégé of sorts, he'd asked me to come watch the final rehearsal, for which I was happy to oblige, despite the early hour. He'd scheduled this rehearsal at the break of dawn because several of the cast members had businesses to return to before the events of the day began.

Bijou, nestled on my lap, snored contentedly as we bumped along the deeply rutted road. I enjoyed taking in the view. This was my second September in Colorado, and I noted the month came with a teasing of fall as the shadows elongated and there was a crispness to the early morning air that quickly gave way to higher temperatures, culminating in a balmy afternoon.

Soon the Aurora Mystique came into view. Although just a few months old and built from an abandoned warehouse, it already blended into the landscape, as if it had always belonged there.

We alit from the coach, and I instructed Mr. Ellis to return for me in two hours' time. I didn't want to be away from the hotel for too long, as today would be one of the busier days of the festival.

As I entered the theater, I found a flurry of activity inside. Several townsfolk—including Miss Mayes, Bob Parkhurst the blacksmith, Sally Dean, a barmaid at the Bella, and Mr. Emerson, both the manager of Archer's Mercantile and Sally's sweetheart—were busy with various tasks or deep in conversation.

Miss Mayes was making some final adjustments on Mr. Parkhurst's costume while Sally Dean, Mr. Emerson, and two young people from the Tavani tribe stood together rehearsing their lines. Andrew was busy with some of the backstage crew working on the fly system, testing the lowering and raising of the two backdrops that were stunningly painted—no doubt at Andrew's direction. Despite his other gifts, Andrew was, first and foremost, a wonderful painter.

Michael Two Trees, Sarah Redhawk and Eleanor Reynolds stood by having a quiet conversation while they watched the activity on the stage. Bijou scampered over to them, eager to receive a warm welcome.

"Good morning." I approached the trio. "What brings you here?"

"Good morning to you, Mrs. Pryce." Michael Two Trees dipped his head in greeting. As always, his expression remained stoic, but there was a warmth in his eyes that belied his reserved demeanor.

"Andrew asked for our collaboration to make sure the play represented an accurate depiction of the history of the area from the Tavani perspective and that of the settlers. He wanted to give us a special preview before the actual performance," he said.

Sarah Redhawk bent down and swept Bijou into her arms, delighting the little canine.

Eleanor Reynolds regarded me with a restrained smile.

Dressed in her unique style, she wore a high-necked Victorian dress of the era, complimented with Indian beadwork on the bodice and sleeves, along with a shawl featuring tribal patterns. She carried with her, as she had for the last few weeks, a clipboard containing a stack of papers. She was highly organized and had been doing a wonderful job of keeping the festival running smoothly.

"We were just talking about Warren Baxter," Sarah Redhawk said, pushing a lock of glossy dark hair away from her face, revealing a pair of stunning bright blue and green feathered earrings that were so long, they dusted the top of her shoulders. "He seemed to be so robust. We had no idea he was ill."

Ill? They obviously did not know Mr. Baxter's true cause of death.

"Yes," I demurred. "It was quite shocking."

Eleanor raised her chin, a guarded defiance in her features. "Do you know what happened exactly?"

I shook my head. "No. Not exactly."

I did not feel it appropriate to comment on what I knew, that he was indeed murdered, until the sheriff started his inquiries. The last thing I wanted to do at this point was to cause further isolation between Clayton and me, as he was already giving me the cold shoulder.

"Really?" Sarah Redhawk's brows lowered in concern.

"Yes," I said. "It's quite a mystery."

She looked away, and I detected a wistfulness in her expression.

"Did you know him well?" I was curious at the sense of melancholy I detected in her demeanor.

"We met two years ago at a Native American artifacts exposition in St. Louis. His knowledge impressed me and he seemed genuinely interested in preserving the cultural heritage of some of the South American tribes. We exchanged many ideas on how to incorporate cultural preservation into community development on confiscated lands. Warren and I had a deep professional connection rooted in our mutual passion for cultural preservation." She then crossed her arms over her chest, and her expression darkened. "Unfortunately, our differing visions and personal boundaries eventually led to a significant misunderstanding, which strained our collaboration."

"Warren Baxter was a complex figure, deeply invested in the culture of the Tavani tribe, as well as others," Michael Two Trees added. "Though his theories and methods of research and artifact collection were controversial, and I often felt he misappropriated many things about our culture, he was a worthy adversary, challenging my perspectives and pushing me to defend the integrity of our heritage. We may have disagreed, but his passion for the Tavani culture was undeniable."

Eleanor Reynolds softly scoffed. "Don't fool yourself, Michael. He might have shown a keen interest in Tavani cultural preservation, but it was only to satisfy his greed. He has stolen precious historical and cultural artifacts from indigenous peoples, and he needs to be made accountable."

"Miss Reynolds, I'm curious. If you believe Mr. Baxter was such a problem for your people, why would you agree to have him speak at the festival?" I asked.

She sighed heavily. "I really had little choice in the matter. Mr. Archer was insistent he come, and the festival was important to me, so I thought it would be a good time to confront Mr. Baxter about the artifacts. I tried to talk with him when he arrived in town, but he wouldn't speak with me."

"And that made you angry?"

"Naturally. He rebuffed me. I only wanted to speak with him to make him see how important it is the items he's found remain with their people."

"So you called him out publicly," I said.

She gave an unapologetic shrug. "It was the only way he would hear me. It's one thing to misappropriate historical culture and some of its artifacts, as Michael said, but to hold a claim on objects of reverence that have significant spiritual meaning to our native peoples is another. I was hoping to make him see sense, and return the items. But he shut me down. So, yes, I was angry at him and I wanted people to know and understand what he has done."

Bijou, who was still in the arms of Sarah Redhawk, whined. Glancing over at them, I understood why. The woman's whole body went rigid, her jaw clenching as a dark shadow flickered across her face. Her eyes sharpened, and a tightness pulled at the corners of her mouth.

"Are you not doing the same, Eleanor?" she said.

Eleanor shot her a look and was about to comment when, from the stage, Andrew clapped his hands together to get everyone's attention.

"We are ready to start the rehearsal. Please take your seats," he gestured toward us.

Sarah Redhawk set Bijou down, and we all slipped into one of the front rows. I casually observed my companions as we settled into our seats, wondering about the obvious tension between Miss Reynolds and Miss Redhawk—and also if their conflicted feelings about Warren Baxter might have turned to a motivation for murder.

Chapter Twelve

The rehearsal went splendidly, and it was apparent that Andrew had expertly cast the characters of his play. Each actor brought a natural realism to their part and helped to portray the story in a most convincing light.

Andrew, although unseasoned as a director, showed a good understanding of character and story, and exhibited strong communication and collaboration abilities. His passion for theater, combined with a knack for problem-solving and the ability to inspire and motivate the cast, would do him in good stead if he continued as a director. It was thrilling to see his fresh perspective and enthusiasm, and my heart swelled with pride at his achievement.

"That was wonderful." I turned to Mr. Two Trees and Miss Redhawk.

Mr. Two Trees gave a nod of approval. "He's represented all parties well."

Miss Redhawk didn't give an opinion, and addressed her companion. "We need to get back to town."

"Of course," he said. "Good day, Mrs. Pryce."

I bid them both farewell, and they left the theater.

"The play's debut will be a great success," I said to Andrew when he came over to get my opinion. "It really came together for you."

"Thank you, Mrs. Pryce. You've taught me a great deal over the last few weeks."

I waved a dismissive hand in the air. "You're quite a natural. But, I'm glad I could help."

From behind the wings, Miss Mayes appeared and made her way over to us. A woman of mature years, she carried herself with the grace of a swan. Meticulously styled auburn hair, streaked with gray, framed her angular yet attractive face. Her deep-set, dark eyes held an intense, knowing gaze that seemed to penetrate the very soul of anyone she looked at.

"Miss Mayes," I greeted her warmly. The woman and I had a rocky start soon after my arrival in La Plata Springs as I inquired, quite directly, if she had murdered one of the town's inhabitants. I'll admit my approach was less than tactful, and after the true killer was found, I gave her my deepest apologies. It had taken her some time to feel at ease around me, but I believed the entire matter had been forgotten.

"You have done a marvelous job," I said. "Not only with the costumes, but the final touches on the stage curtain are sublime. You truly are a master of your art."

She offered a polite smile, and her eyes betrayed a flicker of satisfaction. "Well, thank you. That is high praise coming from you, Mrs. Pryce."

"Well, I think you are incredibly talented."

"Such a shame about Mr. Baxter," she said, changing the subject.

"Quite," I agreed, wondering if she had heard the cause

of death. Given her close friendship with Miss Chatterley—and Miss Chatterley's notoriously nosy nature—she might have, especially with their regular evening chats by the fireside at Miss Mayes's shop.

"I just don't understand how someone could do such a thing."

So, she had found out it was murder.

"It's quite unbelievable," I agreed.

"While most respected the man, he was not terribly liked I'm afraid. Stepped on too many toes, he did." She gave a defiant nod.

"Oh?" I played coy, eager to hear her point of view. "Upon whose toes did he tread?"

"Well, as you saw the other night at his lecture, certain members of the Tavani tribe were not too fond of him. And, he definitely rubbed Mr. Chase the wrong way."

"Mr. Chase?"

"They have been squabbling about a parcel of land the railroad wants to lay track on at the behest of Mr. Chase. Mr. Chase would like to stand up a depot in Addison. Apparently, the two-hour coach ride from La Plata Springs is too much of an inconvenience." She raised her nose with a sniff.

"It is surprising that given Addison's superior size, there is not already a depot there. Yet there is one here in La Plata Springs."

Cynthia gave a knowing smile. "That's on account of my cousin Archibald's influence—you know he was with the railroad for quite some time before he opened the mines and founded the town."

"Yes, so I've heard."

"Now that Mr. Chase is eager to grow the area between La Plata Springs and Addison, he felt it only made sense for a line to be built between the two towns, but Mr. Baxter insisted that the land needs to be protected as he believed it to contain ancient and important artifacts. He's been negotiating with the government to excavate the area, which the Tavani aren't too keen about. He also had plans to build a museum on the site, to showcase his collection of art and artifacts. As it stands now, Archibald has the rights to that land, but Mr. Baxter was making things uncomfortable for him."

"So, Mr. Baxter stood in the way of Mr. Chase and Mr. Archer's plans?"

She shrugged. "I think they were trying to come to some kind of an agreement."

"And what about Mr. Archer? How does he feel about all of this?"

She gave a slight chuckle. "You know Archibald. He's always eager for progress. He agrees with Mr. Chase about developing the area between the two towns, but he also feels that Mr. Baxter's contributions would benefit La Plata Springs. I believe he was trying to facilitate a compromise between all the parties involved."

Or, could both gentlemen have been eager to get Mr. Baxter out of the way?

Miss Mayes said something, but I was too lost in thought to catch her words.

"Pardon me?" I said.

"Are you going to be helping the sheriff with the investigation?"

I wasn't sure how to answer, given Clayton's recent mood. Saying I'd be helping him felt dishonest, as he clearly didn't want me involved. But had he ever really wanted me involved? He'd always tried to dissuade me from investigating—though in the end, he'd tolerated it. Barely.

Now, however, it felt different. He was shutting me out in a way he never had before.

Would he tolerate my 'help' this time? Considering his recent behavior, I wasn't sure. But I had given my word to Cordelia, and I supposed I'd just have to face the consequences if Clayton disapproved.

Miss Mayes, undaunted by my silence, went on. "With your knack for detective work, I'm sure justice will be served and quickly. It would be a shame to have the terrible incident of Mr. Baxter's murder taint this and future historic and cultural festivals in La Plata Springs. I would think that knowing we have such a clever sleuth in our midst will help to deter such crimes in the future."

I smiled at her appreciation of me. "You flatter me, Miss Mayes. I am sure the truth will come out, one way or another."

Chapter Thirteen

I stood in front of the sheriff's office and jail, gathering the courage to enter. Investigating Mr. Baxter's murder without his knowledge didn't sit well with me. Besides, he needed to know about the letter I'd received from the deceased, as it provided a place to begin. In truth, I wanted us to collaborate, as we had in the past. I needed to confront him about his recent distant behavior toward me.

Bijou tugged on the leash, wanting to go in. She loved her visits here, and was often welcomed with her favorite thing—lots of affection.

"All right, girl. I suppose it's now or never." I tried to ignore the flutter in my chest.

Clayton and Deputy Fleming sat at their desks, opposite one another.

"Mrs. Pryce, what a pleasant surprise." The deputy stood up. Bijou scampered over to him and danced on her hind legs, begging for attention. He bent down and scooped her up into his arms. "Hello, girl. How's Miss Bijou?"

She eagerly licked him on the chin, making him chuckle.

"Arabella," Clayton said, his demeanor stoic. "What brings you here?"

I had wanted to speak with him about our personal matter first, but found myself flustered at what to say—and I didn't want to say it, whatever it was, in front of the deputy.

I cleared my throat. "I received this." I pulled the letter out of my reticule and set it on his desk.

He opened the envelope and read it.

"When did you get this? Why didn't you tell me about it before Mr. Baxter's murder?" His tone was accusatory, which sent a twitch of annoyance through me.

"I only just received it today," I said pointedly. "I thought you should know about it, so I am here."

Deputy Fleming strode over and reached for the letter. Clayton handed it to him.

"Well, thank you for letting me know." The sheriff's tone now carried a forced politeness, laced with a hint of dismissal—which only vexed me further.

I straightened my spine. "I'd like to help with the case."

"I thought I'd made myself clear. That won't be necessary."

"Mr. Baxter wanted me to help find his killer," I reminded him.

Clayton's sea swept blue eyes took on a darker, stormier hue. "Mr. Baxter is no longer here. I'm sure you're busy with the festival. The deputy and I can handle this case."

His cold, curt delivery made me grit my teeth. This treatment was unacceptable.

"May I speak with you in private, sheriff?" I asked, mirroring his steely tone.

He exhaled audibly and, glancing at the deputy, tilted his head toward the door. Deputy Fleming, looking somewhat wounded, rolled his eyes, set the letter on his desk, and left the room, taking Bijou with him.

The sheriff regarded me with raised brows and an expectant look on his face.

"I don't understand your behavior, Clayton. Our personal issues aside, you know we work well together. I can help with this case. I am closer to the situation than you may think."

"How so?"

"Cordelia has a past with Mr. and Mrs. Baxter. Her knowledge of them could help provide some insights into the case. She and Mrs. Baxter were quite close at one time, and Mrs. Baxter is comfortable with her. Besides, Mr. Baxter asked that I protect his wife."

"Which will only put you—and Miss Danson—in danger." He shook his head. "I don't think it's a good idea."

"So, she should just be on her own at the General?"

"I'll have Archibald put one of his men in charge of her safety."

I balled my fists at my sides. "Clayton, why are you shutting me out?"

Suddenly, he slapped his hand on the desk, making me flinch. The angular planes of his face had hardened and there was a look of turmoil in his eyes. "Look, Arabella, I said we can handle this."

Shocked at his mini outburst, my mouth dropped open and I took in a sharp breath. "I beg your pardon, sir. So—that is your last word?"

"It is," he confirmed quietly.

Shaking with rage, I swiped the letter off the desk,

crammed it into my handbag, spun on my heel, and marched to the door.

As I reached for the handle, he called out, "Arabella." His tone had softened. I froze, but did not turn around. Suddenly, I sensed his presence behind me—so close I could feel his breath on my neck.

With a reluctant sigh, I pulled the letter from my handbag and held it out to him, simmering with resentment despite my compliance. Our gazes locked.

"I care about you, Arabella, but you need to leave this to me."

I searched his eyes, hoping for more of an explanation, but none was forthcoming.

I flung open the door, walked out and slammed it behind me, more determined than ever to find the killer.

Down the street, near the booth set up in front of Archer's Confections, the local candy shop, I noticed Deputy Fleming chatting with a young woman tending the booth. Bijou remained contentedly cradled in his arms.

He did not see me, so I slipped into the narrow alleyway between the sheriff's office and Dr. Tate's infirmary, to hide away for a moment to recompose myself.

Tears stung the back of my nose and pricked behind my eyes. With a trembling hand, I reached into my reticule for a handkerchief and then dabbed at my lashes, all the while blinking to stop any seepage from flowing. I would not cry! How stupid I had been to let myself enter-tain any romantic thoughts of the sheriff whatsoever! It was utterly ridiculous! Any melancholy thoughts I had about leaving La Plata Springs suddenly vanished, and my remaining six months seemed a lifetime. The sooner I left, the better.

I took in a deep breath, and squaring my shoulders, let it out in a cleansing *whoosh*. I wished I could leave tomorrow, but remain for the duration of the final six months, I must. For the wealth I was about to obtain would mean one very important thing: freedom. I would be beholden to nothing and no one ever again. I could leave this town and its infuriating sheriff behind, and return to my true happy place.

But steady on, girl. Why should I let my errant and misguided feelings for Clayton Marshall chase me away from my hotel and the life I was building here? Away from William's legacy? Why couldn't I have both my life in New York and a life here? I had invested much of my time and energy in both places. There was so much more at stake here than my silly feelings for a man I had absolutely nothing in common with.

Oh, I had been so foolish!

I dabbed at my eyes again and then shoved the handkerchief back into my handbag. I sniffed, smoothed my hair and then my dress. Straightening my shoulders, I emerged from the alleyway into the sunlight and headed for Deputy Fleming to collect my dog.

He and the woman were still talking, and she was laughing at something he said. She was beautiful, with long dark hair, bright blue eyes, and a sprinkling of freckles across her nose and well-defined cheekbones. Her slender neck and long arms made me think of a graceful gazelle.

I approached the booth, but neither one of them took notice of me. Bijou casually swiveled her head in my direction and smiled at me in her little canine way, but made no effort to detach herself from Deputy Fleming, who was grinning at the young woman like a Cheshire cat.

I cleared my throat to get the deputy's attention, which was successful—after the second attempt.

"Oh, Mrs. Pryce. Hello."

A little annoyed at being previously ignored, I nodded at him and pointed to Bijou.

"Ah, right." He handed her to me. "She was a good girl. Oh, have you met Mary Frakes?" He looked over at the young woman again—with an expression of admiration on his face that was usually reserved for me.

"No." I frowned, but then turned a polite gaze on her. "Pleasure to meet you."

"The pleasure is mine," she said sweetly. "I've seen you around town, but I was too afraid to introduce myself."

I scoffed. "Whatever for, my dear?"

"Oh, well, I didn't want to disturb you. You're such an important person, and all."

"Fiddlesticks," I said. "Come to the Bella and have tea with me sometime."

Her eyes popped open. "Really? You mean it?"

I waved a hand in the air. "Of course. You are always welcome."

She beamed at the Deputy, and he beamed right back at her.

"Very well," I said. "Thank you, Deputy Fleming, for watching Bijou."

He didn't seem to hear me and continued to gaze at his lovely companion. Since he'd arrived in town, he'd fallen at my feet at every turn. Now, it seemed his affection for me had been replaced.

I shook my head in confusion. *Men! Would I ever understand them?*

Chapter Fourteen

Back at the Arabella's lobby, I wove through the crowd gathered around Maggie, our head maid. Earlier in the week, she had come to me with an idea: to offer a hotel tour during the festival, showcasing its history and significance to the town.

She believed it would be fascinating to highlight some of the ghostly happenings that often took place at the Arabella —strange noises from the attic, the occasional disappearance of a guest's belongings, or the mysterious scent of pipe smoke that lingered in the air despite no one being nearby to light one.

I had at first been apprehensive, worried about people knowing my secret, But, then I remembered what Percival had told me, that people—even the likes of Mary Todd Lincoln, Mark Twain, Sir Arthur Conan Doyle and Queen Victoria herself—took an interest in spiritual phenomena. It occurred to me this could, in fact, bring in more business.

I was still uncomfortable with the idea of publicizing the

hotel as haunted as my fear of a tarnished reputation had controlled me for most of my life, but I had stepped out of my comfort zone and allowed her this one tour. It seemed a small step for me in facing my fears. I hoped it didn't come back to haunt me—no pun intended.

The crowd gathered around her *oohed* and *aahed* as she spoke. Swallowing down my anxiety, I approached Mr. Pettyjohn at the reception desk who was assisting an elderly man by giving him directions to Kitty's place in the annex. I stifled a smirk. Would someone of his age have the endurance for what Kitty's girls offered? Perhaps he just wanted to be in the company of pretty female companions?

I suddenly realized the irony of my fears. I had been so worried about my reputation should word get out about my clairvoyant propensities, yet there was a bordello operating under my very roof! When I'd first arrived, I had intended to do away with the henhouse, but over time I had grown quite fond of Kitty's girls, and the madam herself had become a great confident and ally. It had become glaringly clear to me I could never displace her and her flock of pretty birds.

The elderly man nodded his thanks to the clerk and made his way toward the hallway leading to the annex.

"Mr. Pettyjohn, have you seen Cordelia?"

His eyes peered over the rims of his round spectacles, and he raised his caterpillar brows.

"I believe she is in the Bella, madam." He delivered the words with absolute seriousness. Though polite, diligent, and devoted to the hotel, he rarely smiled, treating everything as if it were of grave consequence. Still, guests and staff alike—myself included—liked him and relied on him.

"Thank you, Mr. Pettyjohn."

I made my way to the opposite end of the lobby and pulled open the polished wood and beveled glass door leading into the Bella. The saloon was full to the brim with those seeking a tipple or two and a bite to eat. Several of Kitty's girls, wearing their vibrant costumes in eye-catching colors of red, gold, and purple, with low-cut bodices, ruffles, lace, and tightly corseted waists, were busy waiting on customers.

I scanned the room for Cordelia and found her in the back booth. I set Bijou down and she quickly scampered over to her, jumped up on the bench and into her lap.

"How did it go with the sheriff?" she asked, as I slid in opposite her.

I shook my head. "He isn't interested in my help."

"But he's always protested at first, then the two of you end up working together, anyway."

I shrugged. "It's different this time. He seems to have a bee in his bonnet over something, but it is of no consequence. We will proceed with our own investigation."

Cordelia's shoulders relaxed, and she gave me a faint smile. "Thank you, Arabella. It means a lot to me."

"I know, dear. You are welcome."

"Where shall we start?"

"We start with the letter Mr. Baxter sent me. Although it is no longer in my possession. The sheriff confiscated it," I said between clenched teeth. "But that is of no consequence —the words are burned in my memory. Mr. Baxter wrote he believed he and his wife were in danger from someone close to him, a friend or colleague. Who do we know who fits that profile?"

"Well, there's his assistant, Simon Graves. He probably works the closest with him."

"Yes," I agreed.

"Sarah Redhawk was closely associated with him at one time, and she has also been outspoken in her disagreements with him."

"If they were once close, it now seems she's become an adversary," I said. "As well as Michael Two Trees—who was opposed to the spread of Mr. Baxter's theories regarding the Tavani's history and culture."

"And don't forget Eleanor Reynolds outrightly accused him of theft," Cordelia reminded me.

I nodded. "Indeed, she did. We also may need to consider Theodore Chase and Archibald Archer."

"Oh, why is that?" Cordelia slathered some honey over a piece of brown bread.

"Well, as you know, Mr. Chase and Mr. Archer want to develop the land between La Plata Springs and Addison. In addition, Mr. Chase wants to expand the railroad to Addison, but Mr. Baxter opposed it, arguing that the land to do so contains ancient artifacts that need protection. Mr. Baxter had been negotiating with the government for excavation rights and planned to build a museum on the site, which also put him at odds with Mr. Archer, who currently owns the land, and also has some clout with the government."

"Mr. Archer? But he invited Mr. Baxter to attend the festival as the guest of honor." Cordelia set down the bread. "He insisted he stay at his hotel—" Suddenly, her eyes widened as if some new revelation dawned on her—"where Mr. Baxter was killed."

We stared at each other, both of our minds racing with the notion that perhaps Mr. Archer had lured Mr. Baxter to his hotel to do away with him.

"But would Mr. Archer risk everything he has here in La

Plata Springs by killing someone, and potentially being found out?" I whispered, worried about being overheard. "Yes, he wants the railroad to expand into Addison, and to develop the land between the two, but would he resort to murder instead of using his influence with the railroad and the government to get what he wants?"

Cordelia nodded, thoughtfully. "I see your point. It seems Mr. Chase has more to lose—Addison simply cannot grow without better access to resources and markets, which would require the expansion of the town and the railroad."

"Right," I had to agree. "Mr. Archer has been clever enough to build his wealth and influence right here, and it makes little sense for him to jeopardize all that for a controversial venture. Besides, several of the Tavani work in his mines. Would he want to jeopardize his relationship with them? They oppose laying track on the land. Building a museum near it is different. Sacred sites can be avoided."

"That's true," she said. "But I don't think we can completely count him out. Mr. Archer's ambitions have a tendency to get in the way of his ethics."

I recalled his dubious means of obtaining the land in La Linda, a nearby town that he'd founded before La Plata Springs. Although ambitious to the point of greed, would Mr. Archer actually kill to get his way? Would Mr. Chase? So far, I wasn't convinced.

"But Mr. Baxter mentioned he was in danger from someone close to him," I said. "That indicates some kind of intimacy. How close were he and Mr. Archer? Or he and Mr. Chase?"

"Hard to say." Cordelia shrugged.

"Well, it looks like we have a lot of work ahead of us. Let's begin with Bernice Baxter and ask about some of these connections, starting with Mr. Baxter's assistant,

Simon Graves. Aside from her, he was likely the closest to the deceased. I'd also like to look at Mr. and Mrs. Baxter's suite at the General."

Cordelia's face brightened. "All right, then. Sounds like we have a plan!"

Chapter Fifteen

We entered the lobby of the General to find Archibald Archer speaking to a small group of people gathered near the gigantic stone fireplace which crackled with a robust blaze. I thought it odd that he should have a fire in the fireplace as the September temperatures were still warm, particularly in the afternoons. Perhaps he was trying to imbue the cozy atmosphere of the place. Thumbs tucked into the pockets of his waistcoat, and his chest sticking out proudly, he looked like a king holding court in his self-made palace.

Bijou tugged on the leash, eager to dash over to the group of potential attention-givers, but I kept a firm hold. It wouldn't do to distract Mr. Archer's audience from his little speech.

Cordelia and I silently joined the group, and Bijou sat quietly at my feet. Mr. Archer spoke about his work with the railroad, his founding of the town, and now his plans for its glorious future. After expounding on these subjects for about fifteen minutes, Tilly Weston, a young woman who worked at his mercantile under the management of Mr. Emerson, approached the group. Mr. Archer introduced her and then told the group she would conduct a brief tour of the hotel.

After the small crowd followed Miss Weston toward the back of the room, Mr. Archer took notice of us.

"Mrs. Pryce! How nice to see you! And, you, too, Miss Danson."

"How do you do, Mr. Archer?" I greeted him. Bijou waddled over to him and he bent down to give her a brief pat on the head, and then he straightened again, placing his thumbs back into the pockets of his waistcoat.

He rolled back and forth on the balls of his feet. "As well as to be expected after such a tragedy as we've experienced recently."

"You're offering tours of the hotel." I wondered if he'd heard about our tour at the Arabella. I wouldn't put it past him to capitalize on our idea. I also thought it was strange considering a murder had just been committed here.

He scratched at his neatly groomed silver beard. "We mustn't let this unfortunate event cast a cloud over the festival. It is too important to La Plata Springs. We will carry on as normal. Will you be attending the La Plata Games tonight? I expect there will be a grand turnout."

"Possibly, though I'll have to see how things are faring at the hotel." It was plain enough that Mr. Archer wouldn't allow anything to stand in the way of his ambitions.

"How unfortunate, though, that Mr. Baxter's murder took place at your hotel—and during the grand reopening." I couldn't resist the remark; after all the grief he'd given me about my hotel's reputation, I thought it only fair to plant a tiny burr under his saddle. Perhaps trite of me, but undeniably satisfying.

"Yes," he grumbled, a deep crease forming between his eyebrows. "I'm sure you quite understand with the many transgressions that have been committed at the Arabella."

Touché. I sighed.

But my reasons for coming to the General went beyond a bit of playful sparring with the esteemed Mr. Archer. I then graced him with my most coquettish smile.

"Yes. Please accept my sympathies, Mr. Archer. But, like me, you will rise above this terrible situation and turn straw into gold—or in your case, ore into gold, as you always do."

As I knew he would be, he seemed pleased with my observation. A brief smile tugged at the corner of his lips. "What brings you two to the General, Mrs. Pryce? Would you like a private tour? I'd be happy to oblige."

"Actually, we would like a tour—of a sort. I wonder if you'd allow me to look around in Mr. Baxter's suite?"

His smile broadened. "Ah, intent on investigating, after all, are we?"

I blinked at him, confused as to his meaning. "Well, if you must know, yes."

"The sheriff said you might come by."

"He did?" I shared a glance with Cordelia.

"Yes, and I am to tell you we have Baxter's room locked and cordoned off as a crime scene, as instructed by the sheriff. He explained you would not be working with him on the investigation because you were otherwise engaged with the festival and the activities at the Arabella."

Stunned that Clayton had gone so far as to tell Mr. Archer to prohibit me from going into Mr. Baxter's room, I gritted my teeth, not sure how to respond.

"Of course," Cordelia cut in. "And we are indeed quite busy with the festival, but we have another reason for wanting to get into the room—as a favor to Mrs. Baxter.

You see, she and I are old friends, and she told me she'd forgotten to get something—" she batted her eyelashes and her cheeks flushed prettily—"of a personal nature, when you so graciously moved her to another room. It's far too painful for her to go back there, so she asked that I retrieve the item."

Mr. Archer pressed his lips together and then shook his head. "I'm sorry, Miss Danson. It is completely off limits. The sheriff wants nothing moved, nor anything taken from the room. Please give Mrs. Baxter my apologies."

"We will," I said a little too brusquely, but I was still stinging from the sheriff's barring me from the case. "At this very moment. What room does she now occupy?"

"One-twelve," he said.

"Thank you. Shall we, Cordelia?"

"Yes," she agreed. "Good day, Mr. Archer."

Once we reached the staircase and were out of earshot, Cordelia gently grabbed my elbow and whispered, "What are we going to do, Arabella?"

"I'm not sure yet. I need some time to think it over. For now, the only thing we can do is speak with Mrs. Baxter and see if she can shed any light on the threat Mr. Baxter believed he was facing."

We started up the stairs, and I turned to her. "Nice performance, by the way. That flirtatious blush was brilliant. I am quite impressed."

She smiled with pride. "I only wished it had worked."

When we found room one-twelve, Cordelia gently knocked on the door. I was flummoxed to see Theodore Chase open it.

Mute, I blinked at him and then found my voice. "Mr. Chase, what are you doing here?"

A casual smile crossed his handsome face. "I've just

stopped by to give Mrs. Baxter my condolences. I was just leaving."

"Oh, of course." I was still a little mystified at his presence here, given the disagreements he'd had with Mr. Baxter. But then I remembered that he and Mrs. Baxter had been speaking cozily at the lecture the other night. *How interesting.*

She appeared behind his shoulder and then peeked around him. "Mrs. Pryce, Cordelia. To what do I owe the pleasure?"

"We've come to see how you are faring, Bernice," Cordelia said. "May we come in?"

"Certainly," she said.

We bid our goodbyes to Mr. Chase and entered the room. This suite was smaller than the one she'd previously occupied, but contained a quaint little parlor. A closed door to the right indicated the location of the bedroom. The parlor's furnishings were sparse, with only two armchairs and two footstools, and a small table between them, but still the room seemed comfortable.

"Please sit down." She held her hand out toward the chairs in front of the wood-burning stove.

"I'll sit on the footstool," Cordelia offered. "Please, Bernice, take the chair."

"Very well." She seated herself next to me.

"How are you holding up, Mrs. Baxter?" I asked, eager to get to the point but mindful of easing into the conversation. Despite her grief, she looked well—though a bit tired —and, as always, impeccably attired. Her dress, though simple, was a striking creation of deep sapphire fabric that caught the light with her every movement.

She sighed, shaking her head.

Cordelia reached out and grasped the distraught

woman's hands to comfort her. Bijou, who had been sitting at my feet, went to Mrs. Baxter and raised herself on her hind legs, setting her paws on the chair next to her.

"I'm managing," she said. "There is ever so much to do. I'll have to make arrangements for Warren's burial. I'm not sure if we will lay him to rest here or elsewhere, and I also need to consider what's to be done about his business. It's quite a bit to undertake."

"There are so many decisions to make when a spouse dies," I said. "I went through it myself in the not-so-distant-past."

She looked up at me with sympathy in her eyes. "I'm very sorry for your loss."

"Thank you. Mrs. Baxter. I'd like to speak with you about something that has occurred since your husband's death, which I find very curious. I received a letter just this morning. From your husband. In it he claimed that his life was in danger."

Her brow furrowed in confusion. "This morning? But—"

"It was obviously sent before his death. Which means your husband knew someone was out to kill him."

She bit her lip and raised her gaze to meet mine, tears welling in her eyes. "Oh, my poor Warren. Can I see the letter?"

"The sheriff has taken it as evidence," I explained.

"Did you have any idea that he feared for his life?" Cordelia asked.

She shook her head. "No. Warren—well, we—" she paused, pressing her fingers to her lips. "We hadn't been speaking much. Warren was very absorbed in his work. He'd stay up very late at night, and then would often go to bed around the time I was waking up—or he'd be out.

Lately, it felt like we were strangers occupying the same space." Her voice wavered, and she pulled a handkerchief from her pocket. "He'd been so distant. I did not know he thought he was in danger."

"Oh, dear. I'm so sorry," Cordelia said, shooting me a glance.

Mrs. Baxter continued. "We did occasionally talk about things pertaining to his work. I was helping him with some further research on the Noya'Keen tribe in South America."

"Do you know of anyone who might want to kill your husband?" I asked.

She sighed sharply through her nose. "As you might have gathered, Warren had a tendency to ruffle some feathers. People did not understand that he was trying to bring greater awareness of tribal cultures to the settlers in the west. He was using the artifacts he found to educate people."

"But what about the claims that he obtained them rather dubiously, as Miss Reynold's stated during his lecture?"

She shook her head. "Miss Reynolds was referring to the Sun Stone. An artifact Simon and Warren found on a dig in Brazil. It had been buried for centuries. He added it to his collection, but it disappeared shortly after."

"You mean it was stolen?" Cordelia's brows pinched together.

"Yes. It's been gone for two years. Warren tried to explain this to Miss Reynolds, but she is convinced he still has it."

"But Miss Reynolds is Tavani. I'd have thought she'd be more focused on the Star Amulet. Why is she so passionate about the Sun Stone?" I asked, then quickly realized her powerful feelings might extend to artifacts from all native cultures.

Mrs. Baxter let out a soft, weary sigh. "She is also half Noya'Keen."

"Oh, I see." So, Eleanor Reynold's anger was deeply personal—and palpable the night of Warren's lecture. Could she have killed him for revenge? It bore looking into.

"Mrs. Baxter—"

"Bernice," she said. "Please. Any friend of Cordelia's is a friend of mine."

I nodded. "Very well. Bernice. Is there anyone else you can think of who might want to harm your husband? Anyone else who had a grievance toward him?"

Her jaw tightened, and a look of disdain crossed her features. "Well, I know that Warren and Miss Redhawk had a falling out." She clutched at the handkerchief tighter.

I recalled the tension between the two after the lecture and how Miss Redhawk had mentioned their association had ended. "Do you know what it was about? Did it pertain to their prior collaboration?"

She scoffed, her eyes as hard as flint. "Collaboration? Is that what you'd call it?"

Cordelia and I shared a confused glance.

"Yes, Miss Redhawk said they had once worked together," I said. "What do you mean?"

A bitter smile twisted her lips. "What I mean is that their falling out was more personal."

"How so?" Cordelia asked.

Bernice huffed. "You'd have to ask her. She was one of Warren's conquests."

Chapter Sixteen

The lobby of the Arabella was a flurry of activity that afternoon as I had volunteered the Arabella as a hospitality station for the festival. Funds were tight, but several of the businesses had pitched in to share the expenses, as it would benefit everyone. Lottie, and some temporary kitchen help, were to set out a continental breakfast, coffee, and tea in the mornings, and provide some pastries—with the help of Mrs. Gilroy—and more coffee and tea, for an afternoon repast.

I made my way over to one of the tables for a quick inspection and was delighted to find it tastefully arranged with delectable goodies, our finest plates and silverware, and cloth napkins monogrammed with the hotel's insignia—one of Cordelia's projects. There was even a centerpiece of early fall blooms, provided by Cynthia Mayes, who not only created fashionable garments but also had a marvelously green thumb and enviable flower garden.

I admired the colorful bouquet comprising zinnias in shades of pink, red, and orange, marigolds, their golden-yellow and deep orange blossoms adding a cheerful glow, and nestled between them, geraniums in crimson and soft pastel hues which provided a striking contrast. The combination exuded a rustic charm and fragrant delight, perfect for brightening any space.

The other table held an array of hot and cold beverages, along with our China teacups and coffee cups. A miniature bouquet of the same flowers graced the opposite corner of the table.

I was so absorbed in the lovely bouquet before me I didn't immediately notice the altercation on the other side of the room. Glancing up, I spotted Miss Reynolds and Mr. Simon Graves near the stairs. She was pointing a finger close to his face, her voice an urgent, loud whisper. He glared down at her, his eyes blazing and cheeks flushed with anger. Concerned they might disturb the other guests, I was about to intervene and suggest they continue their argument elsewhere. But just then, the stoic gentleman I'd seen with Eleanor at Simon Baxter's lecture suddenly joined her. He reached out to take her elbow, and she turned on her heel and marched down the hallway toward the hotel's back entrance. The man followed her. Simon Graves, noticing the glances of several onlookers—including my own—looked momentarily abashed before disappearing into the hallway that led to the annex.

"Ah, Mrs. Pryce." A deep male voice interrupted my musings over their argument. It was Theodore Chase. Dressed once more in an impeccably tailored suit of the latest fashion, he truly cut a dashing figure. He offered a winning smile, the corners of his gray eyes crinkling with charm.

"Good afternoon, Mr. Chase," I greeted him.

"Lovely spread, here." He nodded at the tables. "You provide every luxury at the Arabella, don't you?"

Pleased with the compliment, I smiled at him. "We try, Mr. Chase. Have you had one of the lemon scones? They're delicious."

He chuckled and patted his stomach. "Oh, yes. Far too many, I'm afraid."

"I'm glad to hear it," I said, delighted that he'd enjoyed them so much.

"Mrs. Pryce, about that business opportunity I mentioned."

"Oh, yes?"

"Do you have a moment to hear about it?"

I glanced around the lobby, the foyer, and the reception desk. All seemed to be calm and in order. "I have a few minutes. Shall we go to my office?"

"That sounds perfect," he said.

I led him down the hallway toward the annex. Once we settled ourselves in my office in front of the wood-burning stove, Mr. Chase fixed his captivating gaze on me.

"I'll just come right out and say it, Mrs. Pryce. I've read things about the Arabella that have been, well, less than desirable since you've taken management of it."

I nearly choked on his bluntness. "I see."

He was, of course, remarking on the recent articles in the *La Plata Herald* and the *Addison News*.

"It seems Mr. Brooks has taken a keen interest in you," he added.

I scoffed. *You don't know the half of it.* "Mr. Brooks is keen on sensationalist journalism." *If you can call it journalism.*

I stopped there lest I say something I may regret.

He indulged my comment with a chuckle, and then continued. "I've heard from other sources as well that there has been some trouble at the Arabella in the matter of some nefarious goings on."

I swallowed, not sure what to say to that, for it was true. "You are referring to the rumors of the hotel being cursed, I suppose?"

The Arabella had seen its fair share of tragedies, and these—along with earlier rumors of a murderous ghost (of which Percival was certainly not one)—had spun into a foolish tale of the hotel being cursed. Of course, that rumor had long been dispelled; otherwise, why would so many people want to stay here? The recent guests might be intrigued with ghostly phenomena, but would they have clamored to stay here if the hotel was truly cursed? I think not.

Mr. Chase gave me a sympathetic smile. "Yes. That is what I am referring to."

I laughed to disguise my discomfort at the subject at hand. "We've had a few challenges, but we've overcome them, thank goodness."

"I understand Archibald believes the hotel should be torn down on account of her dubious reputation. He feels it will affect the well-being of the town."

I gritted my teeth. Dubious reputation, indeed. "He's told you that, has he?"

"Yes." His eyes danced with amusement, which further discomfited me. I found nothing at all funny about the situation.

I cleared my throat. "Well, despite Mr. Archer's feelings about the Arabella and her 'dubious' reputation, I'll have you know that we have been nearly full for the last several weeks, and I've just been told that we are sadly now having to turn people away. You saw the lobby. We are brimming with festival goers, travelers, and longtime guests. Despite what Mr. Archer thinks or says, or what Mr. Brooks writes, people still want to stay here. But, I understand that the General still has availability," I said to further my point.

He gave me a pleasant smile. "I am certainly glad to hear that the Arabella's popularity has not been affected, but I am not surprised."

I blinked at him, confused at his change of tack. "Not surprised? But, I thought you——"

His eyes took on a thoughtful glow. "You see, I don't agree with Archibald. I am not surprised that the Arabella is more popular than ever. People are curious beings. Visiting places with dark or perhaps even supernatural reputations provides an escape from everyday life. It offers an opportunity to step into a different world, one filled with mystery and excitement, away from the mundane."

I raised my eyebrows, astonished at his point of view.

"But that is not the only reason people want to stay at the Arabella," he continued.

"Oh?" I said, still taking in what he'd just said.

"You are the primary draw, Mrs. Pryce. Not only are you a glamorous and famous actress, you've made a name for yourself in solving the crimes that have befallen the Arabella, and La Plata Springs at large. People see value in that. And, with the new theater in town, my goodness, people will continue to clamor to the area to see you perform. Archibald tells me he'd like for you to take over management of the Aurora Mystique?"

"He's mentioned that, yes." I bristled at the memory. The last thing I would ever undertake is to work for the man who coveted my hotel—and had told me it needed to be destroyed and rebuilt—under his ownership.

"But, I have too much to do here at the Arabella." I did

my best to infuse warmth in my words. "There are still some renovations I'd like to take care of before—"

I hesitated, unsure if I could trust Mr. Chase—or anyone—with my plans to leave. If I told him, he might go straight to Mr. Archer, giving him yet another reason to press me to sell.

"Before?" He urged me to continue.

"Before the winter snows arrive," I said.

"Ah, yes. We do have rather harsh winters here, don't we?" he mused. "But back to the business prospect. As I mentioned, I happen to be in violent disagreement with Archibald about the Arabella. I believe she should be completely restored and preserved, as you do. She is the heart of the town and she will be instrumental in bringing visitors to the area, as will you, my dear Mrs. Pryce."

I gave him a demure smile. "I'm glad to hear it. I owe it to my late husband and to the architect, the late Percival Blank—both of whom breathed life into the hotel—to carry on their legacy."

"Precisely. That is why I am proposing a partnership."

My hackles rose. "A partnership? What exactly do you mean?"

"I'd like to have ownership in the hotel. You'd have the controlling interest, of course, but—"

"Mr. Chase, as I've told Mr. Archer, I'm not at the moment prepared to sell—"

"And I'd like to build a sister hotel to the Arabella in Addison, giving you partial ownership. I would keep the controlling interest there."

Stunned, I stared at him, open-mouthed. What a novel idea: sister hotels. Not only would I have the opportunity to preserve William's and Percival's legacy, but I could also expand and grow it.

"I see." I tried to mask my excitement at the prospect.

"Please, do not decide now, Mrs. Pryce. You have much to manage with the festival. We shall continue this discussion later. Would that be agreeable to you?"

I blinked, still dumbfounded at the notion. "Yes, yes, of course. That sounds perfectly acceptable."

He rose from the chair, gave a graceful bow, and left me to contemplate a future beyond my wildest dreams.

My gaze shifted to the desk, reminding me to check for any correspondence from Mr. Blackthorn. Sure enough, a letter from him lay there, penned on Pryce Theater stationery.

I ripped it open. After a few pleasantries, Mr. Blackthorn launched into a report on the current financials—which were, to my chagrin, not what I had hoped. I read further.

Arabella, the theater needs your return. While the public is fascinated with your life on the frontier—and the running of your charming hotel—they are aching for your return to the stage, and I am afraid it is reflected in the financial ledger. You ARE the theater, Mrs. Pryce, and with your continued absence, its prosperity is in jeopardy.

Two of the seven who sit on our board have been entertaining positions elsewhere. Those who remain steadfast are doing their best to find a compelling show for which to entice a new talent named Maude Adams to take the lead. She is an admirer of yours and wishes to perform at the theater, but her manager insists it be a play of the highest quality. I will keep you informed on our progress.

Faithfully yours,

Thomas Blackthorn

My heart sank at the sobering news. I had explained to Mr. Blackthorn the conditions of my stay—the stipulation that I remain in La Plata Springs for a year, now extended to a year and six months because of funds I had borrowed against the estate. It was all terribly complicated, and it had pained me to tell him the truth, but as my business partner, he'd needed to know. However, his—and my public's—patience was wearing thin.

My stomach in knots, I went back to the hotel lobby, my mind buzzing with the contents of Mr. Blackthorn's letter, and with Mr. Chase's proposal. Sister hotels. And I would have ownership of the hotel in Addison.

When I first arrived in La Plata Springs, I'd hardly wanted ownership of a single hotel, but now the thought of owning two stirred an excitement in me I couldn't quite reconcile. Perhaps it was the idea that, in six months' time, I could leave La Plata Springs without selling the Arabella as I had planned—and with Mr. Chase's help, we could combine our resources to find a capable manager to run things for me. William would be pleased to see me keep hold of his treasured creation, as would Percival, no doubt.

Going into business with Theodore Chase might solve all of my problems. But, in doing so, would I be entering into a partnership with a murderer?

Chapter Seventeen

That evening, after one of Lottie's scrumptious meals, Cordelia and I relaxed on the settee in the parlor of our suite, enjoying a sherry digestif and discussing Lottie's growing talents in the kitchen. She had definitely improved her palate, and with it, her culinary skills. Of late, she had been working on perfecting Beef Wellington, which we had enjoyed at dinner. I'd had Cordelia write to Maximillian, my chef in New York, for some of his specialty recipes, including that for the fillet of beef wrapped in delicate puff pastry.

Luckily for me, Maximillian had opted to remain under my employment to cook for my staff. William had written in his will that the staff remain employed until my return, for which I was grateful. To go back and have to start all over acquiring the personnel to run my household would have been a daunting task. Maximillian was well known in my social set and could have opted to seek an opportunity to cook for other wealthy patrons, but he remained loyal to me, which I appreciated.

"Were you surprised to learn that Warren Baxter and Miss Redhawk had had an affair?" I asked Cordelia. "Had you known him to be the wandering sort?"

Cordelia sighed. "I honestly did not know him well at all, so I cannot say. From what Anna had told me of their relationship, it seemed he was entirely devoted to her. But I really cannot comment on his relationship with Bernice, as we had grown apart after Anna's death."

The room's temperature plunged without warning, and a familiar chill crept up my spine. Cordelia felt it too, her body giving a slight shudder in response.

"What are we discussing?" Percival appeared in the chair facing us, looking as if he'd been there for quite some time. He casually crossed his legs at the knees, rested his elbows on the chair's arms, and neatly tented his fingers under his chin.

"Hello, Percival," Cordelia greeted him with a smile.

"We're talking about Warren Baxter," I said. "And Miss Redhawk. According to Bernice, the two had an illicit affair."

"Oh my. Do you consider her a suspect for his murder?" he asked.

I nodded. "Mr. Baxter mentioned that someone close to him wanted to harm both him and Bernice. I'd say that puts Miss Redhawk on the list of suspects."

"And, Miss Reynolds, too," Cordelia added. "She was angry with him for the disappearance of the Noya'Keen Sun Stone."

"Do you know anything about the item?" I asked her, as she had been studying native cultures since we'd learned about the plans for the festival.

She shook her head. "No, but I imagine we could find

out about it through Simon Graves, his assistant. Didn't Bernice say they discovered it together?"

"She did," I affirmed.

"Mr. Baxter wrote extensively about his finds," she added. "He might have brought his journals with him."

"Which, if he did, are most likely in his suite at the General. We have to get in there."

"But the sheriff has barred you from entering it," Cordelia reminded me.

"Still trouble in paradise?" Percival said, attempting to sound doleful, but I knew he was being sarcastic.

I ignored his comment. "Then we'll have to find another way. Mr. Baxter's suite is on the second floor—" An idea suddenly sparked. "Percival, you could help. You could get into the room and let us in," I suggested.

"Perhaps. But only if there's a mirror facing the door."

"Right." My excitement dimmed as I remembered I hadn't recalled seeing if there were any mirrors present in the suite. Without a mirror, Percival couldn't physically engage with inanimate objects. "But you could go over there and peruse the room for us. See if anything stands out?"

He shrugged. "I suppose it's worth a try."

"Excellent!" I clapped my hands together. "We'll wait right here. Now, off you pop!"

He regarded me with knitted brows. "You're assuming quite an authoritative tone."

I gave him a sympathetic look. "Very well, I apologize. Percival, would you please go to Mr. Baxter's suite at the General and survey his rooms for us?"

His lips curved up in a satisfied smile. "I'd be delighted." He then disappeared.

"He's quite temperamental," Cordelia stated.

I raised an eyebrow at her. "You're just now realizing this?"

We both burst out into laughter.

Several minutes later, Percival returned.

"Well?" I inquired.

He shook his head. "I saw nothing out in the open that would be any sort of clue, but I noticed something very peculiar. It was something carved on the back of the door."

"On the back of the door? What was it?"

"A symbol of some sort, carved on the back of the door to a room off the parlor. It looked like he was using the room as his office, or study."

"That's strange," Cordelia said. "The sheriff, Mr. Archer, or Bernice made no mention of a symbol carved in the back of the door."

I sniffed. "Either they did not see it, or the sheriff didn't want me to know about it. Considering that Clayton doesn't want me investigating—and going so far as to bar entrance of the suite to me—it makes perfect sense."

"Or, the carving was done later—after the body was removed," Cordelia suggested.

"That's possible. And if that is the case, does Clayton know about it?" I mused.

A silence filled the room, each one of us caught up in our own thoughts.

"Percival, what did this symbol look like?" I asked.

"It was round, with—well, the best way to describe it is like the iris of the human eye. It had jagged lines radiating from the edge toward the dark center. The rim of this stylized eye was surrounded by a circle of geometric patterns and motifs that looked almost tribal. And at the dark epicenter, the image of a flame."

"Fascinating," I murmured. "I wonder what it means?

Obviously, the killer was conveying a message. I'd like to see this symbol for myself."

"But we can't get into the room," said Cordelia. "It's locked tight."

"Perhaps there is a way." Percival raised his eyebrows.

"Which is?" I asked.

"The room faces the street to the south. There is a window, and it is opened. Large enough for a slim body to fit through."

"That's brilliant!" I said. "All I have to do is climb through that window."

"Arabella!" Cordelia gasped. "It's on the second floor. How will you get up there? And with no one seeing you?"

"It's almost dark now. And everyone will be at the La Plata Games. The timing is perfect!" I said. "But how to get up there poses a problem. The General, and the Arabella, for that matter, don't have fire escapes like some buildings in New York," I mused out loud. I'd have to see about rectifying that—for the Arabella at least. "Perhaps I could have Mr. Johns fetch me a ladder from Archer's Mercantile."

"Don't you think he would ask you why you needed the ladder?" Cordelia said. "And, seeing as he is the Arabella's handyman, he would expect it was for a job you wanted him to do."

I tapped a finger against my lips. "You're right."

"There is a tree next to the window. A Poplar, I believe," said Percival. "Been here since before the town was built, as are several trees among the buildings. Despite some of his failings, Archer is a friend to the flora and fauna of the area and left as many trees as possible while building the town, which is commendable."

"Indeed, it is," I said. "I'll have to change out of this dress. I believe my riding skirt would fit the bill." Miss

Mayes had fashioned for me a beautiful, yet practical skirt that was split down the middle. Beneath it, I wore slim fitting trousers and boots. The effect was quite flattering, if I say so myself. But my appearance was the last thing on my mind at the moment.

Cordelia's eyes clouded with concern. "You're not thinking of climbing the tree, are you, Arabella? You could fall and break your neck, and then what would we do?"

"Oh, don't be such a pessimist, darling," I scolded. "Where's your sense of adventure?"

She sighed, rolling her eyes at me. "I suppose you are determined, then?"

I reached out and gently cupped her chin. "My dear, have you ever known me to be anything else?"

Chapter Eighteen

Cordelia and I stood at the base of the Poplar tree, looking up toward the second floor of the General Hotel.

"Those branches are pretty high off the ground," she said, her skepticism making its case.

"Then you'll have to give me a boost." I offered her a cheerful smile, which she met with a disapproving frown.

A group of people strolled along Main Street, which ran perpendicular to the hotel's south wall. Fortunately, they were too absorbed in their conversation and merriment to notice us.

I glanced at the streetlamp on the corner. "I'd feel better if that gas flame didn't shine so brightly down this way."

Percival, who hovered nearby, glided over to the lamp, snapped his fingers, and the light went out. He floated back over to us with a satisfied smile on his face. "At your service, m'lady," he said with a grand bow.

"All right, Cordelia. Do you think you could support me for a few seconds while I reach for that branch?"

She crossed her arms. "No, Arabella, I don't think I can.

You're taller and bigger-boned than me. You're just too heavy. And besides, I don't think this is a good idea."

I tried not to be offended by her comment. I had never been called heavy before, though I was taller than your average woman, and more solidly built. Still, I suspected her reluctance to help had more to do with the plan itself than with my weight.

I scanned the area and then started walking east toward the river.

"Where are you going?" she called after me.

Ignoring her, I made my way around the building. Behind the hotel, I spotted several waste receptacles and—yes! A few pallets and, even better, a couple of discarded supply crates. Feeling quite smug, I picked up two of the crates and headed back, nearly colliding with Cordelia, who'd come after me.

"Here." I handed her a crate. "You can hold them steady while I stand on them to reach the tree branch."

I made my way back to the poplar with Cordelia, carrying the other crate, on my heels.

"Are you sure about this, Arabella? Maybe you could talk to the sheriff again. Try to convince him to let you help with his investigation. Or get the deputy to help you. He's awfully sweet on you. I'm sure he'd get you into the room— without having to sustain any injuries."

"It would be a waste of time, Cordelia. The sheriff has made it clear he doesn't want my help. And I don't want to get the deputy into any trouble. This will be fine. Stop worrying." I set my crate down and then took hers and set it squarely on top of the other.

I glanced at Percival, who casually leaned against the trunk of the tree with an amused grin on his face.

"What?" I questioned, suddenly feeling self-conscious.

"You are simply adorable, my dear. I do love your spunk." Still grinning, he placed his pipe between his teeth and his luminescent eyes glowed with mirth.

I gave him a wry smile. "I don't know if it's spunk, or stupidity, but I thank you for your confidence in me."

I tested the stability of the crates. "All right. This looks pretty solid. Cordelia, place your hands firmly on the top crate."

With a dramatic and audible sigh, she finally relented. Once I steadied myself on the crates, the lowest branch stood at chest height. Gripping it with both hands, I pushed off from the crate and hauled myself up, swinging one leg over to straddle the branch. From there, I used the branches above to pull myself upright. Steadying myself, I found strong handholds and footholds and began climbing further up the tree.

"I say, you are quite good at this, my dear." Percival had settled himself on a branch.

"Yes, I suppose I am," I agreed. "A talent I did not know I possessed. Tree climbing was something my mother would never allow—even if I'd had time for it. It's something I've always wanted to do."

I set my foot on another branch, and immediately it snapped, throwing me off balance. I went to grasp a limb above my head, but missed and was suddenly in mid-air. I was plummeting to the ground. Below me, Cordelia let out a squeal, and then by some miracle, I found myself cradled between two of the larger boughs, my ribs shouting their discontent.

"Are you all right?" Cordelia said in a hissing whisper.

"I'm fine," I said, my heart pounding at the speed of a runaway locomotive.

"That was a close call." Percival hovered above me. "Do you think you can right yourself?"

"Yes," I groused, my fear now turning to embarrassment at my predicament. It took some doing, but I got myself to my feet again on one of the sturdier branches. I began to climb, but this time with more concentration, and soon, I was at the open window.

"Are you there, yet?" Cordelia said from below.

"Yes. I just need to figure out how to get in the window." I studied the opened sash. The space was indeed tall enough for me to fit through. The problem was, if I scooted out on the small branch closest, it would no doubt break, sending me to my death. I looked above me. If I climbed a little higher, I could get my feet onto the sill and could reach down, take hold of the sash and go in feet first.

"Do be careful," Cordelia hissed, her voice filled with concern.

I made my way further up the tree. Grasping a limb above me, I stepped out onto the sill and then took hold of one below me. Carefully, I pulled myself forward, got my bottom on the sill and then slipped into the room.

"Bravo!" Percival clapped his hands. Relief swept through me, and I gave him a broad smile.

"You made it?" Cordelia called up.

"Yes!" I whispered down, quite proud of myself. Glancing at my mode of transportation into the room, I realized that getting back out onto the tree might be problematic, but I would think about that later.

Peering into the dimness, it was clear I had entered the bedroom. I scanned the area and spotted a gas lamp on the bureau beside the door. Fortunately, a box of matches lay nearby, and soon I had light. I glanced around, searching for anything of interest, but found nothing. Where I needed to be was the adjoining room—the one Mr. Baxter had used as an office.

I stepped from the bedroom into the parlor and saw the opened door leading to the spare room. Unlike the bedroom, which had been stripped clean of any evidence of habitation, this room remained untouched, as if Mr. Baxter would return at any moment. There were papers littering the desk, a man's scarf tossed across the back of the desk chair, and several items lay on top of the low bookshelf.

"The carving is here." Percival pointed to the back of the door. I went to it and swung it shut. Sure enough, there was the symbol, carved in a crude and hurried fashion. A chill slipped down my spine.

"How eerie." It was just as Percival had described.

"There is something else on the desk." Percival had drifted over to it and was pointing at something. A piece of paper. The same symbol was drawn on it. Below it a message, written in bold block letters, read: "Take heed. The Eye of the Ancestors is watching you."

"The eye of the ancestors. I wonder what this means?" I mused.

"The symbols could be Tavani," Percival said.

"Do you know anything about this eye?"

"Regrettably, I don't. I would have liked to learn more about the Tavani, their culture, and their practices during my lifetime, but alas, my time here was cut short."

"Perhaps there is something more about it among these other papers." I scanned the desk and my gaze stopped at an object lying next to the inkwell. It was a smoking pipe carved from what appeared to be bone, with an integrated bowl that seamlessly connected to the slightly curved stem. Intricate tribal motifs were carved into it, with inlays of turquoise and possibly malachite. A small, bright blue and red feather was fastened to the stem with thin leather strips.

I picked it up and showed it to Percival. "This is beautiful."

"Ah. A pipe. Looks ceremonial to me," he said.

I examined it closer and noticed something around the rim of the bowl. A powdery residue of some kind. Deep red in color.

"This is strange. Does pipe tobacco have this red hue?"

"Yes. Some of the Red Virginia's are often orangish-brown."

The sound of footsteps in the hotel corridor startled me and I absently slipped the pipe into my dress pocket. Someone was walking past the suite. I held my breath, listening, hoping I would not hear the click of a doorknob. The sound grew fainter and sharing a glance with Percival I breathed a sigh of relief.

"I'd better hurry," I said. "I'd hate to be caught here." The thought of the sheriff deciding to do a search at this very moment in the evening's quiet—an optimal time for such doings—sent my heart racing.

I rushed through the other papers, but there was nothing more about the eye of the ancestors or the symbol. I took a clean sheet of paper, and copied the symbol the best I could and then tucked my hasty drawing into my skirt pocket.

I noticed two leather-bound books on the corner of the desk. I picked one up and quickly perused it. It was a diary with scheduled appointments. Nothing of interest jumped out at me. I picked up the other. A journal. I flipped through the pages and stopped when my gaze landed on a drawing of the Tavani Star Amulet. I read the passage below, out loud.

The Star Amulet is truly a marvel, unlike any artifact I've ever encoun-
tered. I am convinced now that it is more than just an ancient relic—it
is a vessel of life itself. Since acquiring it, I have felt a surge of vitality
that I haven't known in the last two years. The silent invader within
me, that dark shadow gnawing at my very core, seems to have lost its
grip, as if the amulet is driving it back into the abyss. The Tavani
must have known of its power, using it to extend their lives and main-
tain their strength. I cannot help but feel that I have uncovered a secret
long buried, a gift that will allow me to defy the natural course of time.
This amulet is my key to longevity, perhaps even immortality, and I
will guard it with my life. For as long as it remains in my possession, I
am untouchable.

"Well," Percival said with a snort. "He couldn't have been more wrong."

Chapter Nineteen

The following day, Bijou and I went to the town hall to view the exhibition of artifacts, hoping I could glean more information about the Eye of the Ancestors and the Tavani Star Amulet.

Cordelia had volunteered to manage affairs at the hotel for me. She also planned to keep an eye out for Sarah Redhawk to strike up a conversation with her to find out more about her relationship with Warren Baxter. We planned to meet in the Bella for lunch later.

I stood in front of one of the glass cases, admiring the lovely beadwork on a buckskin warrior's shirt and matching moccasins. I marveled at the intricacy of the design and how much time it would have taken to sew the thousands of beads onto the garments. From the corner of my eye, I saw Mr. Graves standing at another case, speaking with a group of people. Slowly, I made my way in that direction.

As I neared, I overheard the conversation. A woman was asking him about an item in the case behind him. He went to the case and, pulling a key from his pocket, opened it and took the item out to show it to her. It was a small clay pot, decorated with beautiful symbols. I couldn't make out what he said about it, but after a few moments, the group moved on and Mr. Graves placed the item back into the case.

Bijou scampered over to him and sat down quietly at his feet as he locked the case. He paid her no mind, and not at all pleased with him, Bijou let out a sharp yip. While I normally would have been a little embarrassed at her demands, I was actually grateful, for it gave me the perfect opportunity to approach him.

"I'm so sorry about my dog," I said, picking her up. "She doesn't mean any harm. The little thing is shameless in her demand for attention."

"It's no bother." Mr. Graves placed the key back into his pocket and then reached out to pat Bijou's head. A ghost of a smile broke through his serious expression, softening the tension in his strong jawline. His clean-shaven face emphasized his youthful yet mature demeanor.

"Those are lovely." I pointed to some pottery in the case, deep red earthen jugs. They reminded me of the pot I saw on the mantel in the Baxter's suite when we had gone to see Bernice, right after he'd died, and before she'd moved to room one-twelve.

He nodded. "Yes, they are."

I marveled at the color. "Are they painted?"

"No, it's their natural hue."

"More of Mr. Baxter's excellent finds," I mused.

"Yes, they came from a dig in South America."

"And these?" I gestured toward a cluster of rustic pots in a more muted, brownish-red color.

The tension in his jaw returned. "We found them buried

in an ancient ruin near an old hunting ground up north, near the South Platte river."

"Were they made by the Tavani?"

He shook his head. "No. We aren't sure who made them, but it could have been ancestral Puebloans."

"Oh, I see." I admired them once again, and without looking up at him, asked. "And, where did Mr. Baxter find the Star Amulet?"

He scoffed softly. "It was discovered southeast of here, near what is now the Mexican border, where the Tavani ancients once lived. They migrated north centuries ago. While some intermarried with the Puebloans, among other tribes, most of their lineage remained purely Tavani."

I looked up at him, puzzled by his caustic tone when speaking of the discovery of the amulet.

"Is that surprising? I mean, that Mr. Baxter found the amulet there, near the border of Mexico?"

He cleared his throat. "No. It wasn't surprising at all. It's just that — well—just between us, Mrs. Pryce, Warren wasn't the one who actually discovered the amulet."

"Really?" I blinked, waiting for him to continue.

"I'd known about an ancient burial ground in the New Mexico Territory long before I started working for Warren. I'd been researching the area but didn't have the money to fund an excavation. When Warren hired me, I told him about the site, and he agreed to partner with me on the dig. We uncovered several valuable artifacts, also proving the theory of the intermingling with the two tribes—but it was I who found the Tavani Star amulet, the most valuable arti-fact of all." His gaze hardened, sending a chill down my spine.

"And he took credit for it," I said. "That must have made you angry."

126

He let out a loud sigh, clearly annoyed.

"I needed the job to continue my work and research. Not all of us have the luxury of a rich wife."

"Of course," I said, suddenly feeling very awkward. I recalled the journal and how Warren had written about 'the silent invader within me.' "I've heard the amulet is said to have powers. Powers of longevity."

"That is the myth," he said. "Warren certainly believed it."

"Does the amulet cure illness?"

"I suppose if you believe in something strongly enough, it might seem to work miracles." His tone was now gentle, but tinged with doubt. "But I believe the amulet's value lies in what it can teach us about culture, not in a wishful belief that it has supernatural powers."

"Right," I chuckled. "What will become of the amulet now that Mr. Baxter is gone?"

He shrugged. "I imagine it will stay with the collection."

"And you? What will you do?"

"We haven't spoken about it in depth, but Bernice— Mrs. Baxter—has encouraged me to continue with Warren's work. She's always believed in me, and her support means a great deal. She's been more than generous, really … quite remarkable." Simon's voice softened as he spoke her name, a flicker of admiration in his eyes.

"That must be pleasing to you. To continue with Mr. Baxter's work."

"It is an honor," he said with a nod.

"Did you see Mr. Baxter after the lecture?" I ventured. I was curious to hear what he would say, given Bernice had told me they had worked together that night.

"I had a meal with him—and Bernice, but he said he

had a meeting. Bernice was kind enough to help me with a paper I'm writing."

"Yes," I said, "She mentioned it. You burned the midnight oil?"

He laughed softly, as if remembering the evening fondly. "We could talk for hours. I'm not sure what time it was when we finished."

Since he seemed in the mood for conversation, and no one was presently requiring his attention, I thought it a good time to make some more inquiries.

"Mr. Graves, have you ever heard of 'The Eye of the Ancestors?'"

His lips pursed in a thoughtful frown. "It sounds familiar —could you be more specific?"

"I really know little about it, but there is a symbol associated with it." I pulled my crude drawing out of my pocket and showed him the crumpled paper. A look of surprise briefly crossed his features.

"Where did you get this?" he asked with an edge to his voice that I found a little intimidating.

"I—erm—I found it. At the General. I noticed it in a trash bin and thought it was interesting. I knew you'd know what it was." I batted my eyelashes to charm him, and it seemed to work as a faint smile tugged at the corners of his lips.

"Ah. Yes. This is South American. Noya'Keen, I believe. A traditional warning sign. It signifies that those who encounter it are being watched and judged by the spirits of the ancestors. The symbol is deeply embedded in their cultural and spiritual practices. It is believed to serve as a mark of spiritual protection and a warning to those who might desecrate sacred grounds or steal sacred objects. The symbol's appearance signals that the tribe's ancestral spirits are aware of the transgression and will take action to protect their heritage."

My heart skipped a beat. Miss Reynolds was half Noya'-Keen. And she had accused Mr. Baxter of stealing from the native American tribes.

"I suspect it could very well have been drawn by the hand of Eleanor Reynolds," he said, confirming my suspicions. He tilted his head toward the far end of the room where she was standing with a group of people, clipboard in hand. "She had been hounding Warren from the moment we got into town. She wasn't pleased about Mr. Archer giving Warren a platform."

"Right," I said, remembering their tiff. "Had you and Mr. Baxter met her before coming to La Plata Springs?"

"Oh, yes. We met her at a symposium in Denver after we discovered the amulet. She was quite aggressive in her opposition to Warren keeping it for his collection—and she hasn't let up since."

"Was that what you were upset about? In the hotel's lobby?"

His eyes widened with surprise and his cheeks flushed. "Oh, you saw that?"

I nodded.

"Yes. She was—she was disparaging Warren, again. I didn't want to hear it."

"Was this regarding her claims that he stole the amulet?"

"Yes." He shook his head. "Among other things. Things more personal to her. Sometimes I can't say that I blame her. Warren and I had differing opinions on proper handling of artifacts."

"I noticed a very handsome gentleman with her. At the lecture, and at the hotel. Do you know who he is?"

He shook his head. "Only that he's Noya'Keen, and I only know that because I recognize their style of dress."

I was about to inquire further about the 'things more personal' to Miss Reynolds—which I assumed was the Sun Stone—when two elderly women approached us at the display. Mr. Graves greeted them and they asked him a question about the origin of the items in the case.

He turned to me with a polite smile. "If you will excuse me, Mrs. Pryce."

"Yes, of course," I replied.

I glanced over at Eleanor Reynolds, who was now speaking with Michael Two Trees. She was gesturing sharply toward the podium; her face etched with intensity. She looked quite displeased. I couldn't tell if her frustration was directed at him or if she was fervently explaining something else entirely.

She was undeniably a woman of deep conviction. Particularly when it came to educating the public about Native American cultures in the West, and equally dedicated to preserving cultural artifacts—so much so that she had accused Mr. Baxter of theft.

I gave Mr. Graves a nod of farewell and then stooped down to pick up Bijou.

"Come on, girl," I whispered as I hefted her into my arms.

I mulled over his words. Miss Reynolds had certainly shown combativeness during Mr. Baxter's lecture, and now she was aiming her aggression at Michael Two Trees. Could that pugnacity have driven her to deface the door of Mr. Baxter's suite? Or perhaps even commit murder?

Chapter Twenty

With Bijou in my arms, I made my way over to Miss Reynolds and Michael Two Trees to glean what the apparent disagreement was about, but my efforts were thwarted when Atticus Brooks appeared out of nowhere.

"Ah, Mrs. Pryce. You look like you're on a mission."

I let out an irritated sigh. Atticus Brooks was the last person I wanted to speak with at the present moment—or any moment. We had a long history fraught with unpleasantness. Besides writing slanderous things about the Arabella, the man had been intent on ruining my public reputation—ever since William had the man banned from his private club for cheating at cards. Brooks retaliated by writing scathing reviews of my performances, for which William then used his powerful connections to have the writer fired from his position as theater critic at one of New York's preeminent papers.

While William had only my best interest at heart, the feud had had the opposite effect and now I bore the brunt of Mr. Brook's pettiness.

"I'm really rather in a hurry, Mr. Brooks," I said dismissively, setting Bijou down. She sniffed at the hem of his trousers, then sat down, staring up at him. She emitted a low growl.

"Sticking your nose into Warren Baxter's murder, no doubt?" he said, ignoring her.

I raked my eyes over the length of him. He was ever the flamboyant dresser—and his ensembles were almost as garish as Constance Chatterley's. I wondered if this was an eccentricity particular to sensationalist journalists.

"Shouldn't you be writing a scintillating article for Miss Chatterley's paper, exploiting his death?" I asked back, not withholding my sarcasm.

His smug grin faded. "Archibald has asked that we hold off for the time being."

"Ah, of course he has." Anger prickled under my skin. When it came to a murder at his hotel, he wanted the news kept quiet.

"But, still, I'm curious. What have you discovered thus far?"

I let out a derisive snort. "Believe me, Mr. Brooks, if I were investigating his murder, you'd be the last person with whom I would share my findings." I didn't want to outright admit that indeed I was intent on finding Mr. Baxter's killer, as I knew it would surely get back to Clayton.

"My, my." He twisted the end of his ridiculous mustache. "Then you probably wouldn't want to know what I've discovered."

I blinked at him, wondering if this was some kind of trap. "If you know something that might be pertinent to Mr. Baxter's murder, why would you tell me and not the sheriff?"

"Who says I'm not giving Mr. Marshall the same information?" He looked at me blankly.

"Mr. Brooks," I said, unable to hide the irritation in my voice. "I'm not interested in playing games. Now, if you don't mind—" I gestured with a tilt of my head in a request that he let me pass.

He stood rooted to the spot. "I overheard an argument between Sarah Redhawk and our deceased Mr. Baxter. It got quite heated."

I narrowed my eyes at him, skeptical and confused at his need to relay information of Mr. Baxter's murder to me. What was in it for him? Would he try to get me off track so he could write about my meddling and consequential failure?

"Bully for you," I said. "I suggest you take the information to Mr. Marshall."

"She threatened him. Said he ruined her life, and he would suffer the consequences."

His words gave me pause, but I would not indulge him. "That's very unfortunate. Now, if you will excuse me—"

"Mrs. Pryce—Arabella—" he looked at me with doleful eyes. "Don't you think it's time we buried the hatchet? Let bygones be bygones?"

My mouth dropped open. Now this was quite stunning, to say the least. I couldn't help but laugh. "I don't know what you are up to, Mr. Brooks, but like I said, I have not the time, nor the inclination to play games—"

He held up his hands in surrender. "It's no game. Since we are residing in such a small community together, there's really no room for animosity, is there? I'm willing to make peace."

I took in a deep breath and let it out slowly, not sure how to respond.

"I may have misjudged you," he continued. "And I realize my disagreements were not with you, but with your late husband. May he rest in peace. I shouldn't have directed my anger toward you when it was meant for him. It was petty and—"

"Damaging?" I finished, crossing my arms over my chest.

His jaw tightened and his Adam's apple bobbed as he swallowed. Was he swallowing down regret, or was it his pride?

"Whatever I have written about you in the past has been quite overshadowed with all the positive press you've received both then and now. I can't deny that you are a genius at your craft, and that your immense talent extends beyond the stage."

Now he was flattering me and laying it on quite thick. Although I was skeptical of it, I must admit, it had a most welcomed effect. However, my instincts were telling me not to let my pride get swept up in this little *mea culpa.*

I cleared my throat. "I will think about what you've said, Mr. Brooks, about our... relationship."

He placed his hands behind his back and gave a shrug of his shoulders. "Fair enough."

I pushed my lips to the side, perplexed by this entire exchange. What did he want?

"Did you overhear anything else between Miss Redhawk and Mr. Baxter?" I asked. It was possible he was trying to lead me astray. Even so, I was curious.

"No, but I saw her leaving the second floor of the General at around eleven thirty that night. My room is also on the second floor. I could not sleep, so did some reading in front of the fireplace in the lobby."

Interesting. "Well, Mr. Brooks, this is information the

sheriff would indeed need to hear about," I said, still not sure why he would be so forthcoming with information to help me.

"Of course," he said.

I did not want to prolong this conversation further, so gave him a polite nod. "Good day, Mr. Brooks."

He gave a slight bow and moved aside to finally let me pass. My loyal little canine had remained as unmoving as Michealangelo's David, her eyes locked onto his face.

"Come along, Bijou." I tried to shake off a shiver as we walked away. Between Mr. Brooks and the Sheriff, I couldn't decide who was acting more peculiar.

Chapter Twenty-One

By the time I had finished with Mr. Brooks, Eleanor Reynolds had disappeared. Michael Two Trees was still standing next to the podium, going over some papers.

Bijou scampered up the stairs onto the stage and then danced at his feet, eager to greet him. Watching her little performance, a gentle smile broke out on his face. I joined them.

"Hello, Mr. Two Trees."

"Your little dog has a cheerful spirit." His eyes, though softened by age, remained sharp, reflecting a wisdom borne of time and life experience.

I chuckled at his observation. "She does. If we all had her cheerfulness, the world would be a better place."

"Indeed it would," he agreed.

"I was looking for Miss Reynolds," I said. "Do you know where she has gone?"

"I believe she was going to check on the booths and demonstrations along Main Street. She is very thorough and organized. I've been impressed with how she has managed the festival."

"It's a big undertaking," I added. "And the death of Mr. Baxter has put a strain on everything, I imagine. He was, after all, the principal attraction."

Mr. Two Trees made no comment, but simply regarded me with his gentle gaze.

"But Miss Reynolds has been steadfast in her commitment to making the festival a success. I must say, it's quite admirable," I remarked.

"She is deeply passionate about preserving Native American culture in this country. She wants to educate others about our heritage, hoping to sustain our way of life. Since the government began relocating so many of our people, she's become an outspoken advocate. Especially about our spiritual life, and the sacred totems we hold so dear."

"Much like you," I added with a nod of respect.

He gave a slight tilt of his head. "Sometimes we must walk paths others wouldn't dare to tread. We are guided by our ancestors to see that these items are returned."

"I see." I pondered the strength of his convictions.

"You might check in at Archer's Livery," he said, changing the subject. "Eleanor mentioned something about going there first."

I got the impression he wanted to be left alone with his papers.

"Thank you, Mr. Two Trees. I won't keep you."

He held them up. "I struggle with public speaking. I need to go over these notes for my lecture tonight."

"I understand. Come on, Bijou."

We bid him goodbye. Curious at the cryptic tone of his

words, I wondered if the guidance of his ancestors advocated getting the spiritual artifacts back at any cost? Even murder?

I spent the next hour searching for Miss Reynolds, to no avail. Mr. Parkhurst at the Livery said she'd never come by.

Later that night, when Cordelia and I had finally retired to our suite, exhausted from the day's and evening's activities, we requested a pot of chamomile tea and two slices of Lottie's latest delicacy, Pound Cake glazed with sugar syrup, to be brought up to our rooms.

As I gazed into the fire, I sank deep into my chair, completely absorbed in the delightful blend of the tea's delicate floral notes and the rich decadence of the vanilla and almond sauce drizzled over the dense, buttery cake.

Cordelia let out an audible, satisfied sigh, indicating that she, too, appreciated Lottie's handiwork.

Having finished pressing the last of the delectable crumbs of cake onto my fork, I savored the remains and then set the plate aside. Holding the teacup between both hands, I let the aroma swirl around my head.

Suddenly, another more pungent aroma filled the room and Percival appeared on the loveseat to the left of us.

"How wonderfully cozy," he remarked.

"Hello, Percival," Cordelia greeted him.

I gave him a warm smile.

"Oh, I forgot to tell you," I said to Cordelia. "I had an interesting discussion with Atticus Brooks."

Her brows knit together in confusion. "I beg your pardon. You had a discussion with him?"

I shrugged. "For some reason, he's trying to get in my good books. Obviously, I don't trust him, but he mentioned something about an argument between Sarah Redhawk and Mr. Baxter."

"Well, I saw that too, at the lecture. You did as well," she said.

"I know. But he also said something about seeing her leave the second floor of the General at about eleven thirty the night of his murder."

"Huh." Cordelia frowned. "Didn't the doctor say he guessed the time of death to be between eleven o'clock and one o'clock?"

"He did."

"That seems suspicious," Percival said.

"But Bernice said Warren was out," she commented.

"She was as well, remember?" I added. "She said she came back and went to bed. She didn't check to see if he was in the spare room."

Exhausted from the day, and from thinking about the murder, I slumped further into the chair, stretching my legs out in front of me. Something clunked against the chair seat. Something in my pocket. I reached in and pulled it out. It was the ceremonial pipe I'd found in Mr. Baxter's suite. "Oh, dear."

"What is it?" Cordelia asked.

"I found this in Mr. Baxter's rooms. I picked it up, but when I thought I heard someone in the hallway approaching the suite, I slipped it into my pocket. I completely forgot about it until now."

Cordelia's eyes grew wide. "You removed evidence from the scene of the crime?"

"It's only a pipe," Percival stated. "It's not like you stole the implement with which the intruder carved the symbol into the door."

I shook my head. "I doubt Clayton would see it that way. Oh, gosh. If he finds out I have this..."

"Perhaps you can put it back?" Percival suggested.

"Absolutely not!" Cordelia said. "I'm not going through that worry again."

I turned the pipe over in my hands for further inspection. "It is indeed a beautifully carved piece."

"May I see it?" Cordelia asked.

I handed it to her, and she scrutinized it closely. "You know, I came across an illustration of an object in a book I've been reading on the South American tribes Mr. Baxter has been studying, and it bore a striking resemblance to this design."

"Really?" I said. "Was it a smoking pipe?"

"No. It was a bowl. Probably used for food. Very ancient and hard to come by. That's probably a valuable piece, Arabella. You will have to find a way to return it—and NOT by going through the window."

"Yes," I agreed, wondering how in the world I would do that without looking as if I had stolen the piece.

"I thought you should know something," Percival said. "It's about Eleanor Reynolds."

I pulled my focus away from Cordelia and the pipe and looked over at Percival.

"I saw her going out into the forest."

"When was this?" I asked. "I was looking for her earlier."

"Just a few minutes ago."

"Perhaps she was going for a walk?" Cordelia, who had grown fond of such activities, suggested.

"Perhaps, but it's rather a dark night, and she had no means with which to light her way," he said.

"I suppose that is rather strange. I wonder what she was doing out there?"

"And I believe someone was following her," he added.

"Who?" Cordelia asked.

"I don't know. The figure was wearing a cloak."

"That sounds ominous." I wondered if it was the man I'd seen her with twice before. "Could you tell where she might be going?"

"No idea."

"Did you follow her?"

"I lost sight of her. I looked for some time, but having no luck, returned here."

"How strange indeed," Cordelia said. "I hope she's not in danger. Do you suppose we should alert the sheriff?"

"And what would we tell him?" I asked. "That our friend, the ghost of Percival Blank, saw her being followed into the woods, and then lost sight of her? And if we told him we saw her going into the woods, he might suspect that I was working on the case."

"I beg your pardon!" Percival said. "You know I abhor the word 'ghost.'"

I rolled my eyes. "Very well, *spirit*, then. Maybe she had plans to meet this cloaked figure. An assignation, perhaps?"

A knock on the door interrupted our conversation.

"Who could that be?" Cordelia said as Percival disappeared into the ether.

I rose and opened the door. Clarence, our young bellman, stood there with a note in his hand.

"Hello, Mrs. Pryce. Sorry to intrude at such a late hour, but I have this note for you. Mr. Andrew Archer brought it to the front desk. Said he didn't want to bother you, ma'am."

I took the note. "Ah, yes. Well, thank you, Clarence." I was about to shut the door when something dawned on me. "Shouldn't you be at home? Why are you still working?" Still a teenager, the young man needed his sleep. It wouldn't do for my bellman to be dead on his feet during his working hours.

"Mr. Pettyjohn said I could stay in the room that is being refurbished on the first floor. With the hotel so full, he's needed some extra hands. That's all right, isn't it, ma'am?"

"Of course it's all right. You are always welcome, Clarence. But, perhaps you should go to bed soon? Mr. Pettyjohn will need you fighting fit in the morning."

"Yes, ma'am. Right away, ma'am. Good night."

"Good night, Clarence." I shut the door and then opened the note.

"What is it?" Cordelia asked.

"It's from Andrew. He's asked if I can go to the theater first thing in the morning. The play is in two days and I'm sure he's anxious about his debut as director. Our coaching sessions have gone well, but he must have some lingering jitters."

"I imagine so," Cordelia said with a yawn. "Well, I think I'd better turn in. I can barely hold my eyes open."

"Good night, dear. I'll do the same in a few minutes."

She rose from her chair and went into her room. I returned to the fireplace to finish the last of my tea. As my gaze fell upon the pipe Cordelia had left on the table, I picked it up, turning it over in my hands. Its intricately carved surface was worn smooth in places where countless hands had held it over the years. The once-sharp details of the images had softened with time, eroded by the gentle touch of lips and fingers—a testament to both its age and the reverence with which it had been used.

The reddish residue clinging to the bowl drew my attention. I whisked it with my fingertip, feeling the powdery texture, like fine dust. Lifting my finger to my nose, I detected no scent, which was unusual for tobacco, which commonly had a very strong odor.

I didn't know what to do with the pipe, but I knew I certainly could not keep it. Suddenly feeling exhausted, I set the pipe back down on the table, finished the last of my tea, and made my way to the comfort of my bed.

Chapter Twenty-Two

"I'm glad you decided to join me," I said to Cordelia as the coach bumped along the rutted road. Bijou, resting her head in my lap, emitted a long, contented sigh.

"Everything is running smoothly with the hospitality service at the hotel," she said with a smile. "Kitty is amazing. She seems to have her finger on the pulse of everything at the hotel. She has everything and everyone under control and never seems to tire. So, I thought it would be nice to get out and see how Andrew is progressing with the play. I haven't been to the theater since your mother was in town."

"Haven't you? You don't pass by this way on your daily walks?"

She shook her head. "I usually go in the other direction. Out toward the meadows. I love the expansiveness of them. The forests are a little too dark and close for me."

"Yes, they are quite dense," I agreed, noting the thick copse of trees as they passed by outside the window. I wrapped my shawl more snugly around my shoulders, bracing against the damp chill of the early morning air.

Finally, the coach driver, Mr. Ellis, steered the two muscled gray horses up to the theater entrance. After helping us out of the coach, he tipped his hat, said he had a quick delivery to make, and would be back for us within the hour.

The entrance to the theater—once a giant warehouse—had been made inviting, with three barrel kegs cut in half, each half serving as a flower pot. Planted with early fall blooms—Black-eyed Susans, Shasta daisies, and vibrant zinnias—the pots warmly welcomed us to the closed front doors.

I tried the latch, but it was locked. I then knocked.

We waited for several minutes, but no one came to the door.

"Why isn't anyone here?" Cordelia asked.

"Andrew asked that I meet him here at eight o'clock. The others aren't supposed to arrive until eight-thirty." I pulled my watch necklace out from under my coat and looked at the time. "It's ten minutes after eight."

"We might try the back door," Cordelia suggested. "If he's near the stage or backstage, he might not hear us."

"Good idea," I agreed.

We made our way around the east side of the building. Several piles of scrap, still left over from the recent renovations, were heaped up against the wall, so we had to swing wide around them. Bijou scampered away from us, going after a bird that was pecking at the ground.

"Bijou, come back," I called after her. The bird had taken wing, but Bijou remained transfixed on something at the edge of the forest.

"Come, Bijou!" Cordelia said in a sing-song voice, but still, the little urchin did not budge. Her ears were pressed forward and her whole body was rigid as a board. She emitted a high-pitched whine.

"What in the world?" I said, slightly irritated. "Bijou! Come here!"

She only whined louder.

"For heaven's sake." I lifted the hem of my skirt above my ankles and hurried through the tall grass toward her. But as I neared, I saw what had captured her attention. In the distance, beneath the shadow of a large pine tree, lay what appeared to be a person sprawled on the ground. My breath caught. "Oh, no!"

"What is it?" Cordelia came up beside me, her voice tight with concern. I pointed silently at the figure. She gasped.

We moved closer, cautious and tense, until the body's identity became unmistakable. It was Eleanor Reynolds. Her eyes were wide and staring, and there was an odd discoloration around her mouth. I bent down to get a closer look and noted that the discoloration was a smattering of a red substance—a powdery substance. Bijou sniffed at the dead woman's gloved hand.

"Look at this, Cordelia." I pointed to Miss Reynold's mouth.

She knelt next to me. "What is that?"

"I don't know, but it looks like the same substance that rimmed the bowl of the pipe I accidentally took from Mr. Baxter's suite."

"How odd," she said. "Why do you suppose it's on her face like that?"

I shook my head. "I can't imagine."

"Do you suppose she was killed?"

"It's hard to say. There is no blood. No sign of a struggle." In fact, her clothing was only slightly mussed. I scanned the area around her and noticed a large rock about fourteen inches away from her feet.

"It was a dark night," I said. "She could have tripped on that rock."

"But wouldn't she be face down, then?"

"Perhaps. But Percival said he saw her in the forest last night, and that someone was following her. Maybe whoever followed her startled her—she turned around, lost her footing, tripped over the rock, and when her head hit the ground, it killed her."

"Poor woman," Cordelia said.

"I feel terrible," I said under my breath. "We should have come looking for her."

"But Percival said he'd lost her," Cordelia reminded me. "If he couldn't find her with his ability to float above and cover ground far faster than we can, how could we possibly have found her?"

"You're right," I agreed, but still felt guilty about the whole thing. "We might have been able to prevent this somehow, though."

"We can't think about that now, Arabella. There was really nothing we could have done."

I sighed. She had a point. "We'll have to get Dr. Tate out here."

"And the sheriff," she added.

I bit my lip, not at all looking forward to another frosty encounter with him.

"I'll stay here with Miss Reynolds. You go see if Andrew or any of his other crew has arrived yet. Someone will have to go back to town to get Clayton and the doctor."

"Will do." She left Bijou and me with the body. My eyes

skimmed her clothing, looking for any sort of further clue as to what might have happened to her, but I saw nothing of note. I went to the rock and again examined it. There was no scuff mark, or anything to show that her boot might have hit it. Looking around the dense carpet of pine needles, nothing odd or unusual stood out. I decided to go a little further afield and walked a twenty-foot perimeter around the body.

Finding nothing of interest, I sat on a nearby boulder to wait. A few minutes later, Andrew appeared around the corner of the building. The moment he saw me, he rushed over, stopping just short of Miss Reynolds. He ran a hand through his sandy blond hair, his eyes filled with anguish as he looked at me.

"Oh my God, what happened?" The shock of seeing the body turned his usually ruddy complexion white.

"I don't know. I've been trying to find something that might indicate how she came to her death, but there is nothing transparently evident."

"How long have you been here?"

"Just a few minutes. Where is Cordelia?" I was surprised she had not come with him.

"I came with Mr. Crawford in his wagon. He and Cordelia are headed back to town to get the doc and the sheriff."

"Good," I said.

Andrew joined me at the rock and I scooted over to make room for him. Bijou raised herself up and set her front paws on his knee, both offering comfort and requesting attention. He absently stroked her head.

"How long has she been out here, I wonder," he said. "She usually comes by in the afternoon to see if there is anything I need, or to check on our progress with the play.

You don't think she's been out here since yesterday afternoon, do you?"

I shook my head. "Probably not. I think this happened more recently than that." Not only did I know this for a fact, but if she had, her body might have fallen victim to some of the forest's animals or insects, and there was no evidence of such happenings.

"I can't believe it." Andrew leaned his elbows on his knees and held the sides of his head between his palms. "First Mr. Baxter, and now this."

I shook my head. "I know. It's quite unfortunate."

"Does the doc know how Mr. Baxter died?"

"As far as I know, he believes Mr. Baxter died of suffocation, but cannot determine the cause."

"Suffocation. So that means he was murdered?"

I nodded.

"Do you think Eleanor was murdered as well?"

"I don't know," I said, honestly.

He let go a robust sigh. "It's just so strange that two people have dropped dead within the space of a few days. Eleanor was so proud of this festival. She worked so hard. This is such a terrible tragedy."

I reached out and laid a hand on his back. He was a sensitive man and had obviously worked closely with Miss Reynolds.

"I—I should probably go back to the theater. I'm expecting the rest of the cast and crew to arrive at any moment," he said, downcast.

"Best that you not mention this to them until we know more about her death," I said. "Maybe you can keep everyone busy inside the theater until the doctor removes the body?"

He nodded. "That shouldn't be too difficult. We've got a

dress rehearsal, and the crew's still busy with the backdrop and building the set." He gave me a soft, affectionate smile before standing up and leaving me alone with the stillness—and the deceased Eleanor Reynolds.

Chapter Twenty-Three

A calmness settled over the forest, the only sounds the occasional birdsong and the faint whisper of wind threading through the pines. Bijou had wandered off to explore the bushes near the forest's edge—wild roses, if I wasn't mistaken—likely in pursuit of a squirrel or some other small creature. I kept a watchful eye on her, letting her roam.

I let my gaze drift back to Miss Reynold's face, her vacant eyes fixed on the canopy of trees above. I narrowed in on the fine red powder that circled her mouth. What could it be? Had she eaten something seasoned with paprika, or perhaps the chili powder used in some Tavani dishes? Lottie often used beet powder when curing meats or adding an earthy flavor and vibrant color to her baked goods. But none of those seemed likely here. Certainly, it wouldn't explain the substance on the ceremonial pipe—if what clung to it was the same as what rimmed Miss Reynold's lips. However, Percival had explained that some pipe tobaccos were red.

The sudden sound of a twig snapping diverted my attention away from the body. Where is Bijou?

I spotted her, tail wagging, nose deep in a bush, completely unaware. Then another sharp snap cut through the air. My breath caught in my throat as I turned toward the sound. There, barely twenty feet away, a mountain lion crouched low, its eyes locked on her. Time seemed to stop. The predator, muscles tensed, was ready to pounce.

A sharp, instinctive panic seized me, and my heart hammered against my ribs, as if my body already knew the danger before my mind fully caught up. Every nerve screamed at me to move, or to shout a warning to Bijou, but I was paralyzed, unable to tear my eyes from the deadly focus in the mountain lion's gaze.

"Keep still," a man's voice, low and calm, echoed from behind. "Don't turn away from the lion and don't make a sound."

I sucked in a breath and waited, frozen to the spot.

The cold, metallic click of the gun being cocked rang out, and then a sudden explosion of sound tore through the silence, so close it left my ears ringing and my heart racing.

The Mountain Lion startled and then turned and dashed away, deeper into the forest. I let out the breath I had been holding and turned to see Theodore Chase standing behind me, his gun aimed at the heavens.

I shot to my feet, but the adrenaline still rushing through my body made my head spin and my knees turn to water. I faltered and in seconds he had his arms around me, supporting my weight.

"Are you all right?" he asked, his voice low and gentle. I looked up into his cool gray gaze and my breath caught in my throat. I blinked my eyes rapidly, trying to get my bearings again.

"Yes, yes, I think so. Just a little light-headed."

Bijou, who'd emerged from the bush, barked at something in the distance, breaking the moment, and we both turned our heads to see Dr. Tate and Sheriff Marshall striding toward us. The doctor, older and shorter, was struggling to keep pace with the long-legged sheriff, but they reached us quickly enough. Dr. Tate immediately crouched down, beginning a swift examination of the body.

I wanted to step back from Mr. Chase, but my feet felt rooted to the ground. Slowly, he let me go. Clayton's eyes met mine, and in them, I saw shock—and something else. Disappointment.

"There was a mountain lion," I said, as if that could somehow explain why Mr. Chase and I were caught in such a tight embrace, which it was, but why did I feel guilty about it? "It was getting ready to go after Bijou. Mr. Chase scared it away."

"Haven't seen one of them in a while," Mr. Chase said. "And certainly not this far down the mountain. I imagine it came to the river in search of water."

Clayton's gaze, still locked onto mine, showed a mix of concern, relief, and disbelief that was impossible to ignore.

"Excuse us," he said to Mr. Chase. He took hold of my elbow, his grip firm but gentle. "I'd like a word with Mrs. Pryce."

My nerves tingled as he guided me a few steps away from Mr. Chase and the doctor. Mr. Chase asked Dr. Tate something about the body, but I couldn't hear the words.

Clayton released my arm, crossing his own as he stared down at me. His expression was tight—frustration clearly written in the set of his jaw and the hardness of those stormy blue eyes—but beneath it, something else flickered, something he clearly didn't want me to see. Could it be jealousy? For a moment, his gaze softened, almost as if he was about to say something different, something personal. But just as quickly, the walls went back up, and the stern mask slipped into place.

Finally, his voice broke through the tension between us. "What are you doing here, Arabella?"

"Andrew asked me to come early this morning to help with the final touches on the play. He wanted me to watch the dress rehearsal."

"And Mr. Chase?" he asked, his tone sharper.

I shrugged, feeling defensive. "I—I don't know why he's here. I didn't get the chance to ask him before that mountain lion showed up—"

His eyes narrowed slightly. "What brought you out here?" He gestured at the surrounding area. "This isn't part of the play."

"Well, no." I was beginning to feel like I was being interrogated.

"Did you come out here with Chase?"

I squinted at him. "No. What exactly are you implying?"

"Was Chase with you when you found the body?"

I exhaled sharply, frustration bubbling up. "If you're asking whether I came out here with Mr. Chase for some kind of romantic tryst, the answer is no," I said, my voice hardening. I couldn't help but feel insulted that he'd even suggest such a thing. Besides, he'd made it clear he wanted nothing to do with me—so why should he care?

Mimicking him, I crossed my arms over my chest. "Like I said, I have no idea why Mr. Chase is here, but I am certainly glad he is. Who knows what would have become of Bijou if he hadn't shown up?"

"Sheriff?" Dr. Tate called out, interrupting us. For

which I was grateful. He gestured for Clayton to join him, and I trailed behind. Mr. Chase stepped up to my side, settling in next to me.

"Everything all right?" he asked, his voice almost a whisper.

I nodded, not wanting to go into the details of Clayton's strange interrogation with him.

Clayton's gaze momentarily slid our way, but then he addressed the doctor. "What do you have, doc?"

The doctor, leaning over the body, glanced up and said, "I can't be certain yet, but upon initial inspection, I'd say the cause of death was asphyxiation."

"Just like Baxter," Clayton said. "Are there any ligature marks?"

The doctor shook his head. "No. Also, just like Mr. Baxter."

"But you think she was murdered?" I asked the doctor.

"Like I said, I'm not absolutely certain, but I think it's likely."

"What is that around her mouth?" Clayton asked.

Using his index finger, the doctor touched the area below her lower lip and then lifted his finger to his face for closer inspection. He rolled the substance between his forefinger and thumb. "Feels slightly gritty, like powdered clay, or perhaps powdered paint."

I pressed my lips together to avoid mentioning the pipe I'd found with a similar substance around the bowl. How would I tell Clayton without him knowing I'd somehow gotten into Mr. Baxter's suite?

"Do you think that's what killed her?" Mr. Chase asked.

"Possibly. I'll have to find out what it is before I make that determination," Dr. Tate said. "I'll pull the wagon

155

around so I can take her back to town." He struggled to his feet and then left us.

"This is incredible," Mr. Chase said. "Two people dead. And both involved with the festival. What have you discovered about Mr. Baxter's murder?" he asked Clayton.

The sheriff's expression flickered with irritation. "I'm not going to go into the details with you. But I do have some questions for you."

"For me?" Mr. Chase chuckled, looking mildly affronted. "Why me?"

"You were seen at Kitty's with Mr. Baxter the night he was killed," Clayton said.

Mr. Chase shot me a quick, furtive glance, and I responded with a questioning raise of my eyebrows. He cleared his throat and then put on a gracious smile. "Yes. Warren thought it would be a good place to discuss business. You know, away from all the crowds in town."

"Right," the sheriff said, crossing his arms over his chest again. "Why don't we go back to my office and discuss this further? I'm sure Mrs. Pryce needs to get to the dress rehearsal."

"Oh, well, of course, sheriff. But could we do it another time? I'd like to speak with Mrs. Pryce."

"No. We really can't," Clayton said, his voice edged with impatience.

"Very well," Mr. Chase said with a sigh, then looked over at me with a heart-warming smile. "Then I'll just have to ask Mrs. Pryce if she'll join me for dinner tomorrow night? If you're up to it. This has all been rather upsetting."

"I'm fine, Mr. Chase."

"I'm glad to hear it. There's a great little restaurant in Addison that I quite enjoy. And I'd like to show you the site for the new hotel."

The muscles in Clayton's jaw rippled under the surface, but he refused to look at me, icing me out once again. I set my mouth in a hard line. This was beyond the pale.

Then I gave Mr. Chase the brightest smile I could muster. "I'd love to join you for dinner."

Mr. Chase, looking more confident than ever, gave me a gracious nod. "Excellent. I will pick you up at eight o'clock."

Chapter Twenty-Four

The dress rehearsal for the play went off without a hitch. Considering how shaken up he'd been only two hours earlier, Andrew had done a remarkable job directing, all while playing a role himself. I couldn't help but admire how effortlessly he balanced both demanding tasks—especially given that he'd just discovered a dead body. His focus, despite whatever turmoil might be simmering beneath the surface, was the mark of a true thespian.

Watching Andrew play his uncle made me wonder how much time he was spending with him, preparing to one day take the reins of Mr. Archer's business ventures. The poor young man had no desire for such a future, but with no direct heirs, Mr. Archer was determined to make Andrew his protégé in running the mining company. As far as I knew, Andrew hadn't yet begun the formal training to oversee the town—that responsibility, for now, Mr. Archer seemed content to keep for himself.

I made my way to the stage, offering congratulations to Andrew, Miss Mayes, and a few other cast members.

Cordelia, deep in conversation with Everett Emerson—the Dry Goods manager who was playing the role of himself—stood with Sally Dean, who played Kitty, and Constance Chatterley, likely on the lookout for a story or the latest gossip. Cordelia waved me over, and with a courteous nod, I excused myself from the others. Before long, Andrew and Miss Mayes had fallen into step behind me.

"It's so terrible what happened to Eleanor Reynolds," Sally said.

Concern flickered across Miss Mayes's face, and Constance gasped. "What happened to Eleanor?"

I threw an annoyed glance at Andrew. He shrugged and said, "She was supposed to be here to watch the rehearsal. Sally and Mr. Emerson asked why she hadn't shown up. I was so stunned by what I saw, I couldn't keep quiet. I'm sorry."

I could hardly blame him. The young man was nothing if not honest. "It's all right, Andrew. Word will get out eventually." I then addressed the others. "We found Miss Reynolds outside, at the edge of the forest—deceased."

Miss Mayes drew in a sharp breath, clutching at her throat. Constance immediately pulled a small notepad and pencil from her handbag. She licked the tip of the pencil and then directed her gaze at me. "She's dead? What happened?"

I reached out and gently removed her pencil from her hand. "We aren't sure. The doctor and the sheriff arrived a little while ago to remove the body, but please—" I implored her and the rest of the group. "Let's keep this quiet for the time being."

"But I must have the scoop," she said. The others in the group looked at her, aghast. "When it's appropriate, of course," she added, sheepishly.

"Did the doc know what killed her?" Mr. Emerson asked. He was a hulking figure, gruff in manner but with a heart of gold.

"There's nothing conclusive yet, I'm afraid," I said.

"It's awfully disconcerting that two people who were involved with the festival have died within one week," Miss Mayes said. "It hardly sounds like a coincidence. We very well may have a murderer on the loose. Do you think the rest of us are at risk?"

"I think we should all be on alert," I said. "But until we know exactly what happened, we shouldn't jump to conclusions."

I wanted to give them comfort that whoever killed Mr. Baxter was most likely someone who was close to him, as he'd mentioned in the letter, and the act was personal, but I didn't want to divulge anything further. Yet, I must say, Miss Reynolds's death added a layer of complexity to Mr. Baxter's murder.

"What about Mr. Baxter?" Sally asked. "Have you and the sheriff gotten any closer to finding his killer?"

Cordelia and I shared a glance.

"I'm sure we will get to the truth of the matter," Cordelia answered for me. "With the sheriff's determination and Arabella's sleuthing skills, I'm sure Mr. Baxter's killer will be found in no time."

I was impressed with how quick she had been on her feet to answer the awkward question about the sheriff and me working together—or not.

"Have any of you noticed anything odd or unusual regarding Miss Reynolds?" I asked. "Did she seem to be unwell?"

They all shook their heads.

Constance raised her hand like a schoolgirl in class, her

eyes glimmering with excitement. "Oh, well, I saw her last night at the Bella," she began, her voice dripping with intrigue. "She looked positively distressed, and—would you believe it?—she was arguing with Simon Graves. He marched right up to the table where she was sitting with Miss Redhawk—they seemed to be having quite the tête-à-tête, very intense—and from the shock on her face, I'd wager Mr. Graves said something rather scandalous. A few more sharp words, and then Miss Reynolds stormed off!"

"What did Mr. Graves do then?" I asked. "Did he follow her out of the saloon?"

"No. Well, if he did, not at first, anyway. He went to the bar and ordered a whisky." Her tone was disapproving, as if he'd committed a grave sin. "I didn't pay him any mind after that."

"What did Miss Redhawk do?" Cordelia asked.

"She also went up to the bar, paid the bill, and then she went into the hotel."

I considered what Constance had said. It was clear Mr. Graves felt he'd been overlooked by Mr. Baxter, and he'd also not been keen on Mr. Baxter taking credit for his work, but why would Mr. Graves be angry with Miss Reynolds? Perhaps it had something to do with her accusations of Mr. Baxter stealing the Star Amulet, like he'd mentioned before? Or maybe he thought she had killed Mr. Baxter?

"Thank you, Constance. Like I said, we should be cautious. If any of you notice anything suspicious, please let me—or the sheriff—know." I wanted them to come to me with any information, of course, but I set my pride aside. What mattered most was catching the killer, or killers, no matter who uncovered the truth.

Cordelia, Bijou and I stepped outside to find that Mr. Ellis had not yet returned with the coach, which was odd.

"Where do you suppose he is?" Cordelia asked.

I shrugged. "Perhaps his errand took longer than he expected. But, let's put the time to good use. I want to head back to where we found Miss Reynolds—maybe we can uncover some evidence that sheds light on what really happened."

We quickly made our way back to the area at the edge of the forest, and Cordelia and I went in opposite directions, scouring the ground for anything that might be telling. Bijou went her own way, sniffing everything in sight. I weaved in and out of the large pines, my eyes scanning the pine-needle carpeted floor. My gaze settled on something at the base of one of the trees. It was a cluster of three blue feathers. I looked up into the branches and noticed a nest directly above me.

The poor bird, probably a Mountain Blue Bird, must have fallen out of its nest and then had been devoured by other wildlife.

I went back to the stone I'd noticed before, near where the body had lain, still wondering if she had tripped over it, either forward or backward, but I saw nothing out of the ordinary. I went a little further into the forest, examining the pine-needle strewn floor. Bijou had made her way to a bush, profuse with green and red leaves—poison sumac.

"No, Bijou!" I scolded. She dutifully sat down and looked over at me with sad eyes. "I don't want you getting into that," I said more softly. She blinked at me, but stayed put, and then stretched her nose out toward the bush again, sniffing at something.

"What have you found, girl?"

And then I saw it. A tubular object that looked very out of place. I knelt down to get a better view, but it was partially hidden in the undergrowth. I picked up a nearby twig and carefully guided the object out from under the poison sumac.

Glad I had not removed my gloves in case I came into contact with the glossy leaves, I picked it up. It was a roughly hewn wooden tube about a foot long and about one-half inch in diameter.

"What have you found?" Cordelia came up behind me.

I stood up and showed it to her. "Bijou found it."

"That's interesting," she said. "It looks like a blowgun. I saw a picture of one in a book I've been reading about the indigenous peoples of South America. They use it to shoot lethal darts at prey—or enemies—with the intent to kill."

"Did Miss Reynolds appear to have any kind of puncture wound?" I asked.

"Not that I could tell." She shrugged. "But the doctor will need to see this—not to mention the sheriff."

I let out a sigh. Now I had two pieces of information to relay to Clayton, and I just knew I was going to catch it for this. But what choice did I have? It was becoming more and more apparent that Eleanor Reynolds had been murdered.

Chapter Twenty-Five

Bijou, Cordelia and I sat quietly in the coach on our way back to the hotel. My mind was whirling with thoughts regarding Eleanor's death, and the information I'd obtained about her being followed into the woods, and now, the blow-gun. I definitely needed to tell Clayton about it, but I was having trouble summoning up the courage. My interactions with him lately had been unpleasant—and hurtful.

I wondered if Clayton also suspected Miss Reynolds' death was murder. There was a time he would have shared his thoughts with me, but clearly, he was not inclined to do so now. But why the change? I reasoned that whatever his feelings were on the subject of our relationship, I might never know. Perhaps our friendship was over. For good. But I wanted to know why. It wasn't often I was rebuffed, and it made me uncomfortable.

The only thing I could do now was to keep pushing forward with my immediate plan, which was to help Cordelia find peace with the death of her friend Anna by sussing out who killed Mr. Baxter. After I spoke to Clayton.

When we neared the Arabella, I broke our silence. "I'm going to the sheriff's office."

"I think that is a wise decision. Would you like me to come with you?" Cordelia said, offering her support.

"No, I'll be fine. Perhaps you should tend to business at the hotel. I imagine today will be as busy as the rest so far."

She gave me her assent with a nod. The coach stopped and Mr. Ellis soon appeared at the door to let us out.

"Could you take me to Clayton's office?"

He gave me a nod of his head. "Yes, ma'am."

I bid Cordelia goodbye, and soon Bijou and I were on our way—which didn't take long as my destination was just down the street.

When I stepped down from the coach, I found Deputy Fleming standing outside the sheriff's office, casually leaning against a post.

"Mrs. Pryce," he said, all smiles. "It's so nice to see you."

"Hello, Deputy."

He came down the steps to greet me. Bijou eagerly danced on her hind legs hoping for his attention. He reached down and cupped her head in his hands. Her tail wagged furiously.

"Is Sheriff Marshall in?"

He shook his head. "Nope. He went to Addison."

I blinked, surprised he would leave during the festival with so many visitors in town, and also in the middle of a murder investigation. Unless it pertained to the murder investigation.

"Really? Did he say why?"

"He said he had business to attend to and left me in charge." The deputy hooked his thumbs into his gun belt and puffed out his chest.

Though puzzled by the sheriff's absence, I was glad to see that Clayton was finally showing some trust in the young deputy's abilities. When Fleming had first arrived in town—thanks to a favor Archibald Archer owed his uncle, the police commissioner of Denver—the sheriff had been resentful, doubting the deputy's qualifications. But it seemed that opinion had since shifted.

"Did he say when he'd return?"

"Said he'd be back by nightfall."

"Oh, I see."

"Is there anything I can do to help?" he asked eagerly.

"Well, I have some information that might be pertinent to Miss Reynold's death."

He tilted his head toward the door and held his hand out to help me up the steps. "Come on in."

We went inside and he took a seat at Clayton's desk, which I thought was amusing, as his own was right across the room. Bijou jumped up into his lap and curled up. I took the chair opposite him.

"An eyewitness saw Miss Reynolds go into the woods last night, and someone followed her."

His face settled into a serious expression. "An eyewitness? Who was it?"

"Well, I really can't reveal my sources." I hoped he wouldn't press me.

"Did this person say who followed her into the forest?"

"They couldn't make them out. It was dark. And, there was something I found at the scene." I pulled out the tubular object. "I think it's a blowgun."

"Indeed, it is." He took it from me and examined it more closely. "It's a weapon commonly used by tribes in South America."

166

"That's what I'd heard, too," I said. "Do you know if the Tavani use anything like this?"

He shook his head. "No, their weapons consist of mainly bows and arrows, spears, knives—even firearms."

"So, why was this particular weapon found near Miss Reynold's body?" I mused out loud.

"Could have been Noya'Keen," he said. "Did you find anything else?"

I shook my head. "No."

"I'll give this to the sheriff and let him know what you've told me."

"Thank you." I smiled, truly grateful I would not have to be subjected to Clayton's disapproving scowl. I wished I could have asked that the deputy not reveal where he'd received the object and the information, but that would put him in a difficult situation with the sheriff, and I didn't want to upset the balance they seemed to have achieved. I would face the consequences if need be.

"Do you know if the doctor has determined anything further about Miss Reynold's death?" I asked.

The deputy gave me a sideways glance. "Mrs. Pryce, the sheriff said I wasn't supposed to give you any information regarding the matter."

"So, she was murdered."

He regarded me with that familiar look of admiration in his eyes and inclining his head toward mine, he whispered conspiratorially, "You didn't hear this from me, but yes. The doc said there was fluid in both Mr. Baxter's and Miss Reynold's lungs—and he's still not sure what caused it, but he was able to confirm it was not from illness."

"Do you mean pulmonary edema?" I recalled an actor I had once performed with in London had succumbed to the condition. He'd had a bad heart, which caused fluid to form in his lungs.

"I think that's the term he used." The deputy frowned.

"So, in essence, they drowned," I stated.

"That's what it sounds like."

"Curious." My mind turned over the details. "They both died from the same cause, which points to a single killer. But how did they manage it?" I took the blowgun from the deputy, turning it over in my hands. "Could they have used a poisoned dart? Did the doctor find any puncture wounds on either victim?"

"No, he said nothing like that."

I let go a sigh. "Thank you for sharing this with me, deputy, but unfortunately, what you've just told me has left me more confused than ever."

"Maybe for now. But I know you'll figure it out, Mrs. Pryce. You always do."

I appreciated his vote of confidence. But, honestly, I wasn't so sure I could agree.

Chapter Twenty-Six

When I returned to the hotel, I popped in to the Bella for some refreshments and a little time to contemplate my next move.

Mr. Johns, the elder bellman, was standing near the beveled glass and wooden door, and opened it for me. I gave him a nod of thanks, and entered to find, to no surprise, the place crowded with merry festival-goers. Kitty's girls were busy bringing the patrons their food and drinks, or settling in to keep some of the men company in their card games. It seemed she had all of her little doves present and accounted for.

Kitty was standing near the corner of the bar, talking with Bernice Baxter. It was good to see Bernice outside of her room. I had seen little of her since her husband's death.

I went over to greet them. Upon seeing me, Kitty immediately frowned.

"You look like you've got the weight of the world on your shoulders. Want to talk about it?"

"So, Cordelia didn't tell you?"

"Haven't seen her," Kitty said.

"Me neither," Bernice chimed in. "What would she have told us?"

I leaned in closer to them and whispered. "Miss Reynold's was found dead out at the Aurora Mystique this morning."

Kitty's coal dark eyes grew wide. "No! Eleanor? What happened?"

"We're not entirely sure yet. But I've just learned that she and—" I shifted my focus to Bernice—"your husband both died under the same suspicious circumstances. It's unmistakably foul play."

Bernice's face paled, and she raised a trembling hand to her throat.

Kitty audibly exhaled and shook her head. "I can't believe it. And right on the heels of Mr. Baxter. This is very unsettling."

"I found something at the scene. I believe it's a weapon. Kitty, have you ever heard of the native peoples here using a blowgun?"

A look of confusion swept over her face. "A blow gun? Never seen one in my life."

"They are primarily used by tribes in South America," Mrs. Baxter said, her voice trembling.

"Could it have been part of Mr. Baxter's collection?" I asked.

Her gaze shifted rapidly to Kitty, and then back to me. "No. We've never encountered one. But didn't the doctor say that Warren succumbed to an affliction of the lungs?"

"Yes. But he still doesn't know what caused it." I scanned the room. "Has there been any talk of Mr. Baxter's passing?" I asked Kitty.

"I've heard his name come up a few times. But, no one has said anything of note. Just surprise that he's gone."

"All right. Please let me know if you hear anything of interest." I turned my gaze to Bernice. "I'm doing everything I can to help find who killed your husband. But, in the meantime, do be careful."

She nodded. "I will."

"Arabella is a skilled detective," Kitty said, her voice laced with reassurance and a touch of pride. "You can trust that she'll get to the bottom of this."

Bernice offered me a tight-lipped smile, her expression barely concealing her fear.

"Are you staying for lunch, or just passing through?" Kitty asked me.

"I'd like a little something to eat. Would you join me, Bernice?"

Still shaken, she said, "Thank you, no. I've just eaten. I think I'll go back to the General. I'm very tired."

I walked her out to the hotel lobby, where Mr. Johns was standing sentinel.

"Mr. Johns, please see Mrs. Baxter safely back to the General, would you?"

He tipped his bell cap. "At your service, ma'am."

After I watched them leave, I went back into the saloon.

"Poor woman," Kitty said.

"Yes," I agreed. "She must feel so adrift."

"Well, if I know you, you'll find her husband's killer—and that will make it a little easier for her to move on with her life."

"I'll do my best," I said, pleased with her faith in me.

Kitty then motioned for Sally Dean to come over to us.

"Hello, Mrs. Pryce," Sally greeted me. Though she had left her days as a sporting girl behind, she still worked at the

171

saloon, now in a more modest role. Her attire had shifted as well—more reserved, like Kitty's—but unlike the older matron, Sally opted for colors other than the black Kitty always wore.

"What are you having?" Kitty asked me.

"Just some bread and cheese, please. And some Earl Grey."

"Coming right up," Sally said, and went to the kitchen.

"Kitty, would you be so kind as to have Clarence fetch Cordelia to join me?"

I went to my booth at the back of the saloon and not long after Bijou and I had settled in, Sally reappeared with the bread, cheese and tea.

"Thank you, dear."

She gave me an appreciative smile and then moved on to another table, whose occupant had raised a finger to get her attention.

After several minutes, Bijou suddenly jumped down from her perch on the other bench seat and scampered up to Cordelia, who had just entered the saloon. She spoke a few words to Kitty and then made her way over to me.

"I've ordered some refreshment for us," I said as she slid onto the seat. Bijou jumped up next to me and rested her head in my lap.

"Good. I'm famished."

"Did you see Bernice? She just left here with Mr. Johns."

She shook her head. "No, I didn't. Was she all right?"

"As well as can be expected. How are things going in the lobby with the hospitality stations?"

"It all seems fine. I didn't have a chance to check with Mr. Pettyjohn about it, though," she said, shaking her head. "I was dealing with a challenging guest."

"Oh, dear. What's the matter?"

"The woman had a complaint about the pillows in her room. She was really quite demanding and took up a great deal of my time, but we got it sorted."

"What did you do?"

"I took the pillows to Maggie, and she replaced them with some others from one of the rooms she was cleaning."

"Did that satisfy the guest?"

Cordelia frowned. "I doubt anything would satisfy that guest. She actually made me stay in her room while she 'tested' the new pillows. I stood there for nearly twenty minutes as she tossed and turned on the bed, then finally muttered something about them being 'slightly better.' She seemed a bit more appeased after that, so I left."

"Well, there's always one guest who won't be happy, no matter how much you cater to them."

"Yes, I suppose."

"Cordelia, I have some news," I whispered. I then told her what I'd learned from the deputy.

"But the doctor doesn't know what caused the condition?"

I shook my head.

Suddenly, Kitty arrived at the table with two saloon girls in tow. One, a smiling, sturdy young woman with straw-colored hair and dark eyes, carried a tray piled high with our tea, bread, and cheese. The other, much more slender, moved with a hardened air, her demeanor far less friendly.

The blond woman set our food and drink on the table. "Is there anything else I can get for you, Mrs. Pryce?"

"I don't believe so, thank you."

With a brief glance at Kitty, she then retreated, but the other girl stayed.

"This is Maybelle," Kitty said. "She has just come to me

with some information that might be pertinent to your investigation. You are going to want to hear this."

Chapter Twenty-Seven

"What do you have to tell us?" I asked the young woman.

Maybelle glanced at Kitty, a look of uncertainty in her eyes.

"It's a little sensitive in nature," Kitty said.

"I see. Shall we go somewhere more private?" I asked, looking longingly at the tea and bread that had just been put on the table. "We can go to my office."

"I'll bring your refreshments along," Kitty offered. She signaled to the blonde girl to return with the tray. Once everything was carefully arranged on it again, Kitty handed it to Maybelle and we all made our way to the annex.

Once we were in my office, Maybelle set the tray on the table between the two armchairs. Bijou trotted over to her small bed beneath the desk and curled up for a quick nap while I poured myself a cup of fragrant Earl Grey. The tea's aroma filled the room, drawing my attention to the girl, whose hardened demeanor had softened now that we were away from the saloon. I wondered if the tough exterior was merely a protective façade. After all, some of Kitty's girls had come from difficult circumstances.

"It's somethin' I heard the night that art dealer died," Maybelle said. "At Kitty's place."

"Go on," I encouraged her.

Cordelia took a seat, poured her own tea, and began nibbling on a small piece of bread.

"We was all in the parlor, entertainin'. Well, not all of us —some of the girls was upstairs with customers. Anyway, the art dealer was there with Mr. Archer and Mr. Chase."

This confirmed what Bernice had said about the three men meeting to discuss business. The sheriff had mentioned it as well. I didn't know Mr. Chase, or his proclivities, nor could I claim to know Mr. Archer well enough to be privy to his habits, but I'd never known him to frequent the brothel. It wasn't really my affair, but learning that Mr. Baxter—a married man—had been there left me uneasy for Bernice's sake. A quick glance at Cordelia showed she felt the same; her flushed cheeks weren't from the tea.

"Anyway, the talk got a bit heated." Maybelle continued.

"How so?" I asked. "What did you overhear?"

She looked over at Kitty, who gave her a permissive nod.

"Well, at first, they was all carryin' on, havin' a grand ol' time. Laughin', drinkin', and flirtin' with the girls. Mr. Archer wanted me to sit on his lap—so I did." Her expression hardened. "Funny how they think we're just things, like dolls, ain't got ears to hear or eyes to see."

I reached out and took her hand in sympathy.

"Anyway, they started goin' on about Miss Reynolds and Michael Two Trees, and how they were interferin' in their business."

"How?" I asked.

She shrugged. "Mr. Archer wanted me to get him

another drink, so I left before hearin' more 'bout that. But when I came back, the talk had gotten a lot less friendly. The art dealer, Mr. Baxter, said somethin' 'bout Mr. Archer and Mr. Chase havin' secrets—he told Mr. Archer somethin' 'bout his mines and the inspectors, and to Mr. Chase, some-thin' 'bout how he got his money illegally for the project—whatever that is."

"Was that all?" I asked.

"Yes. Well—no, he said somethin' to Mr. Chase like 'let's not forget who's really backin' your project.'"

"So, it seemed he was threatening both men?"

She shrugged. "That's how they took it. Mr. Archer stormed out, and I thought Mr. Chase and Mr. Baxter was gonna come to blows. Kitty was over at the saloon, and she left me in charge at the annex, so I told 'em to leave."

"And did they?" Cordelia asked.

"Yeah. They didn't give me any trouble."

"Well, that's good," I said.

She let out a deep breath and nodded in agreement.

"Is that all, Maybelle?"

"Yes, ma'am. I told Kitty, and she said I should tell you."

"I'm glad you did. Thank you, Maybelle."

"You go on back to the saloon," Kitty told her. Maybelle gave her a tight smile and left the office.

"Well." Cordelia brushed her hands together to rid them of breadcrumbs. "It seems that Mr. Baxter was holding something over both men's heads, which means—"

"They both have a motive for killing him," I finished for her.

"And they weren't too happy with Miss Reynolds, either," Kitty added.

"Right," I agreed. "Kitty, what do you know about Mr.

Archer and the mines? What do you think Mr. Baxter meant about 'the inspectors?'"

She blew out a breath between puffed up cheeks. "Archibald has had trouble with the inspectors before for unsafe mining practices."

"Yes," I said. "Dr. Tate was called to the mines just a while ago for some kind of emergency. And then there was the issue at the La Linda mines."

That particular matter had arisen earlier during my stay in La Plata Springs, following the murder of Ralph Stewart. Mr. Archer had uncovered valuable ore in the mountains overlooking the small town of La Linda. However, due to safety concerns, he had been compelled to shut down the mines.

"Do you think there is a safety issue at the mines, here in La Plata Springs?" I asked.

"I'd be surprised if there was. Archibald felt terrible about the accident at La Linda. I don't think he'd be stupid enough to skirt on safety issues here."

"Hmm," I murmured. "What do you know about Mr. Chase and these alleged illegal funds? And for what?"

She shook her head. "Nothing exactly. I know Mr. Chase and Archibald have discussed developing the land between Addison and La Plata Springs, but I'm not sure if that's the project Baxter meant."

"Right," I said, hoping the 'project' in question was not one that had anything to do with Mr. Chase's proposed sister hotels.

Chapter Twenty-Eight

When we had finished eating, Cordelia complained of a headache and went up to our rooms. I went into the hotel lobby to check on Mr. Pettyjohn. He had been so busy with the guests and all the visitors, I thought I might spell him for a few minutes so that he could get a bite to eat. He rarely ate in the Bella, but would take his repast in the kitchen at the small table under the window—well out of Lottie's way.

He had his back turned to me and was placing something in the pigeonholes behind the registration desk.

"Mr. Pettyjohn," I greeted him. "Would you like to take a break for dinner? I'd be happy to fill in for you for a little while."

He turned around and looked aghast. "You? Behind the reception desk?"

I blinked at him, a little affronted. Did he think I was incapable of the job? "Yes. Why not?"

He set the papers he'd been placing into the pigeonholes down on the counter with a loud *thunk*. "Madam, that would not be seemly. You are the proprietress, not a clerk. No, it would not do!"

I held back a chuckle. "I really don't mind, Mr. Pettyjohn."

"Absolutely not!" he said with conviction.

"Well, perhaps we could find someone else? I've hardly seen you from behind the desk for days."

"Don't worry about me, madam. I would not like to leave my post until later, when the crowds have thinned. Kitty will take up the coffee samovars soon. I will eat then."

"Very well. If there is nothing I can do to help for the moment, I believe I'll go for a walk." I was feeling rather full from dinner, and I also wanted some time to organize my thoughts about everything I'd learned about the deaths of Mr. Baxter, and now Miss Reynolds. The manner in which they died had been so similar.

"Come, Bijou." I didn't have her leash and thought about going upstairs to retrieve it, but I worried about bothering Cordelia. Her headaches had become much more infrequent since our arrival in La Plata Springs, but I figured this partic- ular headache was because of her having been so busy with the guests, the festival, and that she'd felt responsible for reuniting her deceased friend's spirit with the now dead Mr. Baxter.

"You will have to stick close as the town is very crowd- ed," I said to the dog. She merely smiled up at me in agreement.

As I had suspected, the street buzzed with activity, even as the shopkeepers began slowly packing up their wares and retreating into their shops for the night. Yet, the visitors lingered, savoring the evening's calm, and the atmosphere remained relaxed, a gentle hum of activity winding down without rushing.

I crossed the street and headed south, toward the train station and the view of the setting sun. Bijou trotted obediently at my side. I stopped to say something to Tilly Weston, the young woman who often helped Mr. Emerson at Archer's Mercantile, when Bijou shot ahead of me.

"Bijou!" I called after her, but she ignored me, her ears flying in the wind. She ran into the street just as a carriage was turning the corner. Fearing she would be crushed under its wheels, I rushed after her, flinging my arms in the air and shouting to get the driver's attention. Seeing the dog, the horse skidded to a stop and reared into the air. Bijou scuttled out from under its hooves and continued to make her way across the street.

The carriage driver managed to settle the horse and then turned to me with fire in his eyes. "Watch your damn dog!" he yelled. "It could cause an ugly accident!"

"I'm so sorry!" I said. "Are you all right?"

The man grumbled something, clucked to his horse and moved on. My heart hammering in my chest, I let out a breath. Where had Bijou gone?

After a passing wagon went by, I spotted her over at the train depot. She was sitting near a couple embracing. The man's back was to her, and neither one of them seemed to notice the little dog watching their display of affection. My chest seized when I recognized the set of the man's shoulders and his familiar leather vest. It was Clayton Marshall, holding a tall, slim, blond woman—for a notable period of time.

Finally, they broke apart. The woman wiped a tear from her cheek and then turned and went through the station doors as Clayton watched.

"I've heard she's from Colorado Springs." Constance

Chatterley's voice rang out beside me, nearly making me jump out of my skin.

"Constance, you scared me."

"Sorry, dear." She pointed her chin toward Clayton and the woman. "The sheriff's been spending a good deal of time there lately. No one seems to know who the mystery woman is, though. Looks like she might be going somewhere. Maybe back to Colorado Springs."

Was she a sweetheart? I wondered, my heart sinking at the thought.

I cleared my throat. "Well, I'm sure it's none of our business, Constance." Even though I wanted desperately to know who the woman was—and who she was to Clayton.

"Pretty little thing," she added, shoving the dagger harder into my chest.

My attention was diverted when I saw Simon Graves and Bernice Baxter leave the General and walk down main street, toward the Arabella.

"Those two have been inseparable since the death of that poor woman's husband," she said. "He must be a great comfort to her. They seem to be rather close. The other night I saw them at the Exhibit Hall. It was very late. I was taking some photos of the exhibits for the paper. It was the only time the place wasn't swarming with people. Anyway, those two were completely absorbed in something. They were sitting at a table with lots of papers and books around them. Had some of the artifacts out of their cases, too. The whole building could have fallen down around them, and I doubt they would have noticed."

"Mr. Graves is very devoted to his work," I said, still watching Clayton watch the woman walk away. Was he as sad as she seemed to be? Was it a permanent farewell, or just a temporary one? Would he be returning to Colorado Springs to be with her after the murders were solved?

A million questions ran through my mind as I was half-listening to Constance.

"When did you say you saw Mr. Graves and Mrs. Baxter working late in the exhibit hall?" I asked.

"The other night. The same day as Mr. Baxter's lecture."

"You're sure?"

"Absolutely sure."

So that would mean that Mr. Graves had an alibi for the night of Mr. Baxter's murder.

I turned my attention back to Clayton, who was still watching the woman. She boarded the train and turned back to wave at him. He lifted his hand in return and then spun around to leave.

Our gazes locked. Bijou, at his side, danced on her hind legs, patiently waiting for him to acknowledge her, but he stood frozen, his feet rooted to the spot as neither one of us looked away.

"Well, I'm off to the Mercantile," Constance said in her sing-song voice. "I've got to pick up some supplies before they close. Good day, Arabella."

Still frozen in Clayton's gaze, I didn't acknowledge her leaving. The range of emotions crashing through my head and my heart was suffocating—the most potent of them was a feeling of loss, but then it quickly shifted to anger. How could he have kissed me if he had feelings for someone else? Had I completely misjudged him? Feeling like an utter fool, I turned and began walking away—back to the hotel.

"Arabella!" he called out. I ignored him.

Soon, he fell in step with me. "I need to speak with you."

I wasn't sure I could look him in the face. "I'm rather in a hurry," I said, lamely.

"I need to warn you about something—someone."

I stopped in my tracks and finally turned to face him, but said nothing. He gazed down at me with those sea-blue eyes and my heart wrenched.

"I understand you are considering a business proposal from Theodore Chase," he said.

I raised my chin in defiance of my shattered feelings. "I am. What of it?"

"You need to be careful with him."

Even though I quite agreed, I gave him a sardonic smile. "It's really none of your concern."

"You know, he's a suspect in Baxter's murder."

I gave a brief snort. "I've been a suspect for murder before, and was I guilty?"

"Chase had motive to kill Baxter, and was seen in an altercation with him, and, need I remind you, he was out at the theater where you found Eleanor Reynolds—I also have it on good authority he threatened the woman."

"Threatened her? How do you mean?"

He opened his mouth to say something, but then stopped himself. "Nice try. I don't want you interfering with the investigation. Honestly, I'm not sure why I'm telling you this—it's just that I don't trust the man. And if he's a killer, you're in danger."

"Well, I believe there are others you should pay attention to," I said, not willing to give him the satisfaction of showing that I would heed his advice. "Given the evidence, you might want to consider Miss Redhawk, for instance. I've heard she was seen leaving Mr. Baxter's room late on the night he was found dead."

"Where did you hear this?"

I crossed my arms over my chest and didn't answer the question, still stinging from the scene I just saw at the train station, and feeling incensed that he had the nerve to insert himself into my business dealings.

"And given the evidence found in Mr. Baxter's suite—" I ventured, and then bit my lip. I shouldn't have mentioned it. How would I explain what I'd seen on the back of the door?

"What evidence?" His voice carried an edge. "How would you know what kind of evidence was found in his suite? It's been off limits to everyone except me and Deputy Fleming. He didn't say anything to you, did he?"

Oh dear. The last thing I wanted to do was to get the deputy into trouble.

"No, I have not spoken with Deputy Fleming about the evidence in Mr. Baxter's suite. I have my—I have my sources. And you're welcome, by the way," I said, trying to divert his attention from my blunder.

"You're welcome?" He scoffed. "For what?"

"For finding the blow gun. You obviously didn't search the area very well."

His eyes narrowed, and he rolled his jaw in annoyance.

"That symbol found carved into Mr. Baxter's door is very telling, don't you think?" I asked, deciding to forge ahead. "It was obviously someone who was warning Mr. Baxter to return the Sun Stone. Perhaps someone who was passionate about the cause of the Noya'Keen? Like Miss Reynolds, for example—although, I don't believe she killed Mr. Baxter," I added, having just learned from the deputy that she and Mr. Baxter had succumbed to the same condition, it was unlikely she was his killer.

"Did Bernice Baxter tell you about the symbol?"

Still, I didn't answer him but said instead, "Why would you suspect Theodore Chase of defacing the door of Mr.

Baxter's suite? He has no stake in the survival of the tribe. But surely the Noya' Keen man I saw in Miss Reynolds' company does."

Clayton's eyes registered surprise. "What man?"

"The man who was with her at the lecture. I saw them together on another occasion as well."

"Who is this man? Do you know his name?"

"No, but he—"

He held up a hand, his mouth settled into a firm line. "I'll find him myself. We're not doing this. I thought we agreed you wouldn't investigate."

I knew I shouldn't have rambled on, but hurt feelings had swept over me, and I was desperately trying to ignore them by being confrontational. It wasn't my best quality, but it happened when I was not in control of my emotions. The words spilled out, as if I was thinking out loud—my thoughts were not entirely cohesive. If Miss Reynolds hadn't carved the symbol into the door, someone else, like her companion, could have done so, either in solidarity with her or perhaps even to frame her. The idea of Mr. Chase doing it seemed less plausible—though, regrettably, I couldn't rule him out.

"I agreed to no such thing," I shot back. "You forbade me from investigating, which is entirely different."

He exhaled sharply, frustration clear in his tone. "I'm doing this for your own good, Arabella. I don't want you involved in this—or any other—case. And you need to stay away from Theodore Chase."

A wave of heat surged through me. "How dare you tell me what I need or don't need to do! I am not a child, Clayton—I am a grown woman, and I expect you to respect that."

His expression shifted, emotions flickering across his

face. Then, suddenly, he reached out and touched my arm. "Arabella, I'm—"

I jerked away, pride and heartbreak colliding within me. I couldn't stand to hear more of his concerns or whatever it was that had twisted our friendship into this unbearable strain. "Good day, Mr. Marshall."

Chapter Twenty-Nine

Later that afternoon, I sent a note to Mr. Chase at the General, expressing my eagerness for our dinner but requesting we meet at the Bella instead of traveling to Addison. I explained that with the hotel at full occupancy, I needed to remain on hand in case any issues arose, and I wasn't comfortable leaving the responsibility solely to Cordelia or Mr. Pettyjohn.

My actual reasons, however, were three-fold: first, I wanted to stay in La Plata Springs in case any new information surfaced about Mr. Baxter's murder or Miss Reynolds' death; second, after the look in Mr. Chase's eyes during our earlier encounter, I was uneasy about being outside familiar territory for our cozy dinner—just in case I needed a swift escape, and third; it pained me to admit, but Clayton's warnings about him had stuck in my mind.

Now, as the clock above the Bella's fireplace mantel chimed eight o'clock, I sat in my usual booth at the Bella, sipping a sherry, and awaiting his imminent arrival.

The saloon was quieter than it had been earlier in the

week, and the calmness was a welcome reprieve. Business had been bustling with the festival, and while I appreciated the steady flow of patrons, the crowds had begun to wear on me. Tonight's peace was a small blessing. Most of the townsfolk, I reckoned, were attending the barn dance hosted by Mr. Crawford of the La Plata Springs Post Office and Telegraph Exchange, at his farm a mile out of town.

A weighty presence filled the room, diverting my attention. Mr. Chase had come into the saloon through the door that connected it to the hotel lobby. He scanned the room and then his gaze settled on me and our eyes locked. I braced myself for his approach.

"Mrs. Pryce," he said smoothly, his voice warm, like honey laced with something sharper.

"Mr. Chase. Thank you for indulging me. I hope you understand."

He gave me that familiar, confident smile, the one that he seemed to wear like a perfectly tailored coat. "Most definitely. It shows your dedication and sense of duty to your hotel. How could I mind? It just further proves you are the right woman for me."

I nearly dropped my sherry glass. "I beg your pardon?"

"Forgive me. I suppose I should have said the right business partner for me." He glanced at the empty booth seat across from me, silently asking permission.

With a slight nod, I gestured for him to sit. He didn't hesitate, lowering himself into the seat with an effortless grace that I knew came from years of knowing how to command a room, and, more importantly, how to charm the people in it.

One of Kitty's girls appeared at the table. She was small and fragile looking, but the dear thing had a severe expression on her face; one that could chop wood. I had seen her before, but usually never outside of the annex.

"What can I get you?" she asked, her voice flat.

"What does Lottie have on offer tonight?" I asked, trying to soften the crassness of her demeanor.

"Beef Wellington, or Ham, or Beans and Salt Pork. Potatoes. Carrots," she answered in staccato.

I deferred to Mr. Chase.

"I'll have a whisky to start," he said. "Then I'll try the ham. With potatoes and carrots."

I ordered the same and another sherry. Without another word, the girl left.

"I apologize," I said, embarrassed. "She's usually not working in the saloon."

"Kitty's girls have been busy with the festival in town, no doubt."

"Quite," I agreed, made further uncomfortable by the remembrance that he, too, had probably been at Kitty's place for more than just a meeting with Mr. Archer and Mr. Baxter.

Soon, the barmaid returned with our drinks. We engaged in idle chitchat, and it wasn't long before our dinner was served, and while we ate, Mr. Chase launched into a series of questions about my career on the stage, for which I was happy to oblige him with answers. He seemed duly engaged and impressed and peppered in various and sundry compliments. I knew I was being charmed, but I saw no harm in it if I was aware.

Once we pushed our plates away, I wanted to get down to business. Not necessarily the business of the hotels, but the business of murder, and what, if anything, he might reveal to me about his conversation with Clayton.

"Did your conversation with the sheriff go alright?" I

suspected that it most likely had not given Clayton's warning.

He wiped his mouth with his napkin and then leaned back in the booth, looking satisfied and engaged.

"Perfectly well. He just had some questions about my meeting with Warren and Archibald."

As did I. I also wanted to know what 'secrets' he and Mr. Archer were harboring, and how Miss Reynolds played into their plans.

"I see. I've heard Mr. Baxter desired to build a museum on the same land you and Mr. Archer are planning to develop. Land that Miss Reynolds and the Tavani believe belongs to them."

Suddenly, the shine of his polished bearing seemed to fade as I hinted at the altercation between the three men. And the problems Miss Reynolds had created for them.

He quickly resumed a relaxed smile. "Archibald holds the rights to the land, but, to keep the peace, we are working with the Tavani to establish an agreement. However, since the government could move the rest of the tribe to the reservation at any time, their efforts to retain the land may ultimately be in vain." He said the words with a kind of confident certainty that made a shiver run down my back.

I thought about Michael Two Trees, Miss Redhawk and the other Tavani, and how devastating it would be to be forcibly re-homed.

"The sheriff no doubt questioned you about Miss Reynolds as well, given she opposed your using the land for your development."

His eyes squinted slightly, and he tapped his fingers against the table. "And, here I thought we were going to have a nice dinner?" he said smoothly. "Why all the questions?"

"Mr. Chase—"

He placed his hand on his heart. "Come now, dear Arabella. Let's drop the formalities. Please call me Theodore."

I cleared my throat, a little taken aback by his forwardness. "Very well. Theodore. If I am to entertain the prospect of going into business with you, I need to understand what is at stake here."

He raised his hands slightly, palms outward, and nodded, signaling his compliance. "Understood."

I lifted my brows expectantly, waiting for him to answer my question.

"Look, Eleanor Reynolds is—was—a woman of remarkable foresight and determination. Her involvement in the NSFTL has—"

"I beg your pardon, the NSFTL?"

"The Native Sovereignty and Fair Treatment League. She was deeply involved with the Denver chapter—a small but tenacious group—particularly in their work on land disputes. While her efforts might seem purely philanthropic, one couldn't help but wonder if her motivations ran deeper."

Now, this was interesting. "More to her motivations?"

He frowned slightly. "It was hard to distinguish where her loyalties lay. I assume you know that the Tavani and the Noya'Keen were natural enemies?"

I blinked in surprise. "No, I didn't know that."

"I believe Miss Reynolds was using her influence in the NSFTL to gain prestige in Washington, D.C., to make way for the Noya'Keen to emmigrate to this area. She claimed the tribe in South America had severely dwindled and they were facing extinction. She was using her position as an advocate for the Tavani in the NSFTL to secure land here for the Noya'Keen."

"So she wanted to use Tavani lands to benefit the Noya'Keen?" I asked.

He gave a confident nod.

So, this was what Miss Redhawk had been alluding to when she accused Miss Reynolds of doing the same thing Mr. Baxter had done, with securing items—or in this case, land—that belonged to the Tavani. But it seemed she was not the only one who had concerns over the land.

"And her agenda would be a direct threat to your plans with Mr. Archer—and even to Mr. Baxter's plans for his museum," I added cautiously.

Tapping his fingers on the table again, he said, "We were confident her efforts would come to nothing. The U.S. Government has little interest in the Native American cause."

"I see." I found myself a little sad at the notion. "I wonder if Michael Two Trees and Sarah Redhawk knew of her agenda?" I thought out loud.

"Oh, I imagine they knew something. Or, at least Michael Two Trees did."

"What makes you say that?"

"They had a public dispute several months ago. He actually threatened her. Said, and I quote, 'she would pay for her traitorous deeds.'"

Chapter Thirty

I studied Theodore Chase's expression intently, surprised at the idea that a man as noble and sweet natured as Michael Two Trees would threaten someone.

"So, you suspect Michael Two Trees for the murder of Eleanor Reynolds?"

Mr. Chase gave a half-hearted shrug. "I don't think he should be overlooked. And I told the sheriff as much."

"And what did he say?"

"He thanked me, and then told me I was free to leave—his office, not town, which is a little inconvenient, as I have much to do in Addison. Quite frankly, I wouldn't put it past Two Trees." He continued tapping his fingers on the table. "Some believed he was responsible for the death of a youngster in Addison. A Noya'Keen youth."

"You're serious?" I asked, shocked by this revelation.

"Two Trees is—or was—a medicine man. The youth was suffering an injury—apparently, he had gotten into a fight with one of the Tavani boys. Two Trees witnessed the altercation and went to the young man's aid, but the youth died. Not from his injuries, but from poison. Something having to do with his lungs."

I blinked. "Oh, my goodness."

"Some of the Tavani thought he'd killed the kid on purpose."

"Because he was Noya'Keen?"

"Yes."

"But it was never proven?"

"No, never proven. But it gives one pause."

"Yes," I said, still ruminating on the idea. Something having to do with his lungs. Exactly what the doctor suspected with Mr. Baxter and Miss Reynolds. As a historian himself, and one of the Noya'Keens' enemies, Michael Two Trees most surely had knowledge of their beliefs, and even their weaponry. Could he have carved the warning into the door—killed Mr. Baxter, and then Eleanor Reynolds, with a poisoned dart from a blowgun? Perhaps. But it just didn't feel right.

Mr. Chase leaned forward, resting his elbows on the table and clasped his fingers together. "Arabella? Where did you go?" he asked with a smile, shaking me out of my thoughts.

"Oh, I'm sorry. It's just that—"

"My dear, I don't want to talk about all of this unfortunate business," he said smoothly. "I want to talk about us. I've been thinking about our conversation earlier. About the hotels."

Naturally, I thought. I had also, though I hated to admit it—it was undeniably tempting. The idea of expanding my influence, of taking William and Percival's vision and growing it into something even greater, had lingered in my mind since he first mentioned it. Yet, I couldn't shake the nagging feeling that there was more to his proposal.

"I haven't forgotten," I said, my tone measured.

His smile deepened, and he leaned in further, as if we were conspirators in some grand scheme. "I know you haven't. And I know how much the Arabella means to you. But I can't help but think… we could create something extraordinary together. You and me."

There it was, again. I wasn't naïve enough to think that his interest in me might be more than purely professional. But I sensed Mr. Chase was a man who knew how to blur those lines—who used them to get what he wanted. And I wasn't about to be taken in by his debonair ways and smooth talk, attractive as they were.

Still, there was a part of me that was intrigued. Maybe it was the ambition in me that responded to his words, or that he was offering something that no one else—even Archibald Archer—had. The idea of being part of something bigger, of creating a legacy beyond what had already been built here in La Plata Springs, was hard to ignore.

But I would not let him know that. Not yet.

"I'm still considering your offer. But as I told you before, I'm not sure I'm willing to share the Arabella."

His eyes shined with something that made my pulse quicken. "I wouldn't ask you to share anything that didn't benefit you in every way, Arabella." His voice dropped slightly, taking on a more intimate tone. "This isn't just about business. I think together we'd be a force to be reckoned with."

"Exactly *how* together?" I asked in a tone that begged for clarification, but I knew what he was angling for.

He gave me a devilish grin. "I think you get my meaning."

I felt a twinge of something at his words—something I quickly tamped down. I couldn't let him get too close. Deep down, I knew men like him didn't pursue women like me unless there was something to gain.

His mysterious smile, sharp and calculating, softened into what seemed like sincerity—though I had my doubts.

"It's about the future," he said, his voice low and persuasive. "I'm offering you half of my personal venture, Arabella. That's no small thing. Together, we'd be unstoppable. Your brilliance and business savvy, paired with my resources—we'd create something untouchable."

I bit back a snort. Clearly, he had it backward. What he really meant was that with his brilliance and business sense —and my resources, my reputation, and maybe even my fortune—we would create something remarkable. How convenient for him.

"And what would you gain from this partnership?" I arched a brow. "Aside from the obvious."

His eyes held mine, and for a moment, the playful charm fell away, replaced by something more earnest. "You," he said quietly. "I'd gain you."

The words hung between us, and I felt my breath catch in my throat. It wasn't the first time a man had tried to win me over, but Theodore Chase wasn't like most men. He was calculated, determined, and used to getting what he wanted.

I couldn't deny the pull of his words. Our stations in life were well suited, compatible socially and economically—but to enter a relationship founded in business seemed hollow. My relationship with William had stemmed from convenience, and thankfully we had grown quite fond of one another—but to say we were in love would have been an exaggeration.

"I appreciate the sentiment," I said, keeping my tone

light, "but I don't think it prudent to mix business with… other things."

He chuckled softly, leaning back in the booth once more, though his eyes never left mine. "I wouldn't expect anything less from you. But think about it, Arabella. The future I'm offering isn't just about business or ownership. It's about building something bigger, something lasting. Together."

There was a part of me that was curious—he made it sound so easy, so alluring—but another part of me, the part that had kept me standing through all of my worldly experience in the past thirty-six years, knew better. And, to Clayton's point, annoying as it was, the man was a suspect in a double murder.

"I'll consider it." I offered a small, measured smile.

He nodded and rose with his characteristic grace, placing his hands behind his back. "I've enjoyed our time together, but I must go. I'd love to see you again. Will you be at the horse races tomorrow? I understand it will be a thrilling event."

"Yes, I plan to attend. I'm sure it will be very exciting."

"Undoubtedly." He extended his hand, wordlessly inviting a handshake—perhaps to seal an agreement, or maybe to honor the start of a new friendship. I offered mine, and in an instant, he turned it over, bowed low, and brought it to his lips, his dark eyes never leaving mine. A shiver ran through me as the tender kiss lingered longer than expected.

Finally, he released my hand. As he turned and walked away, the soft click of his boots fading, I let out a breath I hadn't realized I'd been holding. As he passed through the door into the hotel, my gaze drifted to the bar where Clayton sat, beer in hand. His stare cut through me, filled with an intensity that left me breathless. He then swiveled on the stool to face the bar once again, and my heart sank. What must he be thinking?

"You're not actually considering it, are you?" A voice, as familiar as my own, came from across the table, distracting me from my turbulent feelings.

I shifted my gaze to see Percival, his translucent figure lounging in the seat Mr. Chase had just vacated. He gave me a sideways grin, one eyebrow raised in mock disbelief.

"How long have you been here?" I said, the habitual feeling of panic rising in me at the idea that Mr. Chase might have seen him—but it quickly faded. Percival had become much more discrete in his comings and goings when I was in the company of others, and he'd clarified that Clayton's skeptical nature made him impervious to spiritual phenomenon.

"Long enough." His tone was laced with warning—and perhaps a little annoyance. "You realize he's playing you, Arabella. The charm, the smiles—it's all part of his plan."

"I'll admit, the words roll off his tongue like honeyed whiskey—tempting and deceptively smooth." I kept my voice barely above a whisper, my lips hardly moving as I spoke, careful not to draw attention to the fact that I was conversing with someone unseen. "But that aside, Percival. He's offering an opportunity to build upon your legacy. And William's. I would think you'd be pleased."

He crossed his arms tightly over his chest, his lips pressed together as he regarded me, a shadow of discontent crossing his face. "I fear you'll get in over your head, Arabella. And, for all we know, he's a murderer."

I lowered my eyes, a faint smile tugging at my lips—my way of showing I understood his meaning. "I realize Mr. Baxter was making things difficult for him. But, so far, there is no evidence to show that Mr. Chase killed him. Seems to me Mr. Archer had more to lose—as he has a claim on the land that both Mr. Baxter and Eleanor Reynolds wanted for their own purposes."

Percival huffed. "That dandy is like a hound on a scent, refusing to be called off until he's reached his mark."

The corner of my mouth twitched upward as I recalled Mr. Chase's efforts with a hint of amusement. "He's certainly persistent."

"Persistent, yes," Percival said. "Trustworthy? That's another matter. I'd keep both hands on your purse strings if I were you. And maybe on your heart, too."

I sighed, leaning back in my chair. "Don't worry, Percival. I know what I'm doing."

His luminous eyes narrowed, a guarded intensity in his stare as he faded from view. His voice echoed harshly in my ear. "I certainly hope so, my dear. Because he's not just after your hotel. He's after you."

Chapter Thirty-One

The Tavani horse races were a much anticipated event of the festival. Townsfolk and members of the tribe were to show off their horsemanship skills by racing a two-mile circuit that both started and ended at the livery at the far end of town. Spectators were encouraged to meet at the halfway point near Silver Lake, which was a mile away, to cheer on the participants.

Eager to get out into the fresh air, I had opted to go via horseback. I hadn't realized just how much I missed my lessons with Clayton until Mr. Parkhurst brought Monty, the horse I had been riding for the past several months, out to me. As I usually did, I pulled several sugar cubes from the pocket of my riding skirt. The beautiful white horse loved the sweet treats and he knickered softly as I held out my hand.

His lips tickled my palm as he gently pulled the cubes into his mouth.

"Hello, boy," I murmured, relieved that the bond we'd formed hadn't faded despite my time away.

Cordelia, standing some feet away with Bijou in her arms, looked on. I turned to her. "Would you like to ride? I'm sure Mr. Parkhurst will find you a suitable mount."

She vehemently shook her head. "No, thank you. I'll leave the riding to you, Arabella."

"It's rather a long walk to Silver Lake."

"I'll be fine," she said.

"You could ride Peanut," Mr. Parkhurst offered. He was a towering figure of strength and muscle, a colored man whose sheer size and physicality commanded attention the moment he stepped into one's presence. Though he was large and strapping, his face held a surprising gentleness—his eyes were warm and kind, and his wide, straight smile revealed a row of perfect white teeth. His demeanor was one well aware of his power, but he had a humility and grace that belied his size.

"Oh, I—I don't know." Cordelia's eyes grew wide with anxiety.

"At least come take a look," Mr. Parkhurst said. "He's just inside the barn."

"It wouldn't hurt to look at him," I encouraged.

She slid a glare in my direction, but I ignored her vexation with me and gave her a bright smile.

She rolled her eyes. "Oh, all right."

We followed Mr. Parkhurst into the barn, Cordelia holding Bijou securely while I led Monty. As we stepped inside, we were greeted with a low nicker from a small, sweet-faced chestnut horse in the first stall. He had a beautiful head, with large, expressive eyes and a nip of white between his nostrils.

"This is Peanut," Mr. Parkhurst said with a warm smile. "Gentle as a lamb, this one. Come, give him a pat, Miss Danson. He loves attention."

Hesitantly, Cordelia looked over at me.

"Here," I said, "I'll take Bijou."

I picked up the dog and settled her into one of the two woven baskets, which hung like saddlebags from a sturdy leather strap draped over Monty's back—perfectly designed for carrying various necessities. Like small canine companions.

Cordelia followed Mr. Parkhurst into the stall, but stood several feet away from the horse.

"It's all right." Mr. Parkhurst held his hand out to her. "I'll be right here."

Shyly, Cordelia put her hand in his and let him bring her closer to the horse.

"If you scratch his withers, he'll be your friend for life," Mr. Parkhurst said, demonstrating with a practiced touch. Cordelia hesitated, then tentatively reached up to mimic him. Peanut, the horse, lowered his head with a gentle nuzzle against her arm. To my surprise and delight, Cordelia let out a soft giggle.

"Now see there? He likes you." Mr. Parkhurst smiled broadly, his face brightening as he watched her.

Cordelia glanced up, her eyes meeting Mr. Parkhurst's, and for a brief, unspoken moment, something seemed to pass between them. A soft pink bloomed on her cheeks, and the smile that followed was genuine and warm. It wasn't forced or polite—it was something more. Watching their quiet interaction, I suddenly felt like an intruder. *How intriguing!*

"What do you think, Cordelia?" I reluctantly broke their connection. As amused as I was at this brief exchange, we really needed to move on, as the races would start soon.

She looked back at Peanut, her expression thoughtful. "He seems very sweet."

"I've put all kinds of riders on him, from seasoned adults to little ones. Youngest was four years old," Mr. Parkhurst said, pride evident in his voice. "Peanut took care of that girl, and he'll take care of you, too. Just trust him."

Cordelia inhaled deeply, the tension visibly leaving her shoulders as she exhaled. "All right. I'll try it."

Once Mr. Parkhurst had the saddle and bridle secured, he helped her up onto Peanut's back with the care and skill of someone who'd done it a hundred times. I couldn't help but marvel at how Cordelia looked on the horse, her back straight and poised as if she were born to ride. She looked entirely at ease—almost regal.

"Ready?" I asked, watching her closely.

She gave a brief nod.

Mr. Parkhurst, standing beside her, rested a reassuring hand on her knee. "You'll be just fine," he said softly, and Cordelia offered him a grateful smile in return, her eyes shining with admiration.

I turned Monty, leading the way, and Cordelia and Peanut followed and were soon in step with us.

"He's very handsome," I said with a sly grin.

"Yes, he's a nice horse." She reached down to pat Peanut on the neck.

"I meant Mr. Parkhurst."

Her cheeks, again, turned pink as a ripe peach in summer, and she cleared her throat. "Oh—well, yes, I suppose he is. I hadn't really noticed."

"Didn't you?" I asked, unable to keep the teasing out of my voice.

She shot me an annoyed look, and I let out a laugh, which only seemed to irritate her more.

Chapter Thirty-Two

The ride to Silver Lake was tranquil, the air cool and still, with only the soft rustle of the wind through the long grasses and the steady clop of hooves breaking the serene quiet of the morning. Along the way, we passed a few pedestrians and were joined by other race spectators, some riding in carriages, and others on horseback. Up ahead, I recognized Michael Two Trees, riding a beautiful bay horse with white stockings.

I recalled what Theodore Chase had mentioned—the rumor that he'd killed a young man. It was still hard to believe he'd do such a thing, but it seemed wise to hear his side of the story. I'd need to approach the subject carefully.

"Do you feel up to trotting, Cordelia?" I asked, eager to catch up to him.

She gave me a slightly panicked frown. "You mean go faster?"

"If it's not your cup of tea, we can stop." I offered a reassuring smile.

Biting her lip, she dipped her head in a silent yes.

"Squeeze with your legs and move your energy forward," I said as I urged Monty into a trot. I wasn't sure if Cordelia had done what I suggested as she was a fraction behind me, but Peanut moved into a trot and stayed at Monty's flank. Cordelia jostled awkwardly in the saddle, her movements unsteady, but a wide smile spread across her face.

Soon, we caught up with the beautiful bay.

"Good morning, Mr. Two Trees." I brought Monty to a walk beside them. Bijou, in the basket behind me, let out a whine of excitement at seeing him.

"Mrs. Pryce. Miss Danson. Lovely day for a race, isn't it?"

"Exquisite," I said, taking in the landscape. The early morning light bathed the distant mountains in a crisp blue glow. The horizon was a watercolor blend of gradually diminishing lavender and peach, as the sun slowly climbed above the jagged peaks. A light mist hung over the valley, giving it an almost ethereal quality, while the crisp, cool air carried the faint scent of juniper and earth.

"It's a beautiful day, but there's an underlying sadness with the loss of two such prominent figures from the festival," Cordelia added.

A hint of melancholy passed over the regal gentleman's expression. "Indeed, there is."

"The doctor said he suspects Miss Reynolds died of suffocation, just like Mr. Baxter," I said. "An internal sort of suffocation. Pulmonary edema. They both drowned from fluid buildup in their lungs."

"That seems more than a coincidence." Mr. Two Trees' brow furrowed with concern.

"It does. But Dr. Tate is having trouble determining

exactly what caused this affliction. Perhaps his examination of Miss Reynold's body will yield more answers."

"We can only hope," he said.

"Mr. Two Trees, I understand you are a medicine man."

He dipped his head respectfully in acknowledgement.

"Have you encountered this kind of rapid filling of the lungs before?" I studied his face, but there seemed to be no apparent reaction other than genuine sadness.

"Regrettably, yes," he replied, his tone steady, though his gaze held a hint of sorrow. "Years ago, our people faced an outbreak of pneumonic plague. I did all I could, calling upon the powers of the ancients—but even they couldn't save everyone. It was especially difficult to see the young die."

This could very well explain what had killed the young man Mr. Chase mentioned.

"I understand there is a small tribe of Noya'Keen—with which Miss Reynolds was affiliated—in the area. Did they, too, suffer from the illness?"

He nodded. "Their numbers dwindled even more."

"Did you treat any of them?"

"Only one. A young man. But it was too late." He glanced over at me with a knowing look that made me wither inside. It was as if he could read my thoughts, see into my soul. He knew what I was asking.

"The Noya'Keen claimed I had brought the illness upon the boy—but it was only their grief talking."

I swallowed hard, caught off balance by his deeply refined intuition. He was a man of great wisdom, and it wouldn't be difficult to believe he had supernatural powers —but was he a killer? I found it hard to reconcile, but I couldn't be absolutely sure.

"I know you worked with Miss Reynolds planning the

festival, amicably, I assume, but were the two of you close?" I asked, changing the subject.

His lips turned up in a slight smile, and he shook his head. "No. While I had respect for Eleanor, we had many differing opinions—and a long history of ancestral hostilities that stood in the way of a genuine friendship."

Interesting. I was not sure where to go from here and a silence filled the air. We walked on, our horses moving at a leisurely gait.

"I never knew where she stood on issues important to the Tavani," he finally continued. "I didn't know where her loyalties lay. At times she seemed true to the cause of the Tavani—but she also advocated for the Noya'Keen. The two tribes have warred for many moons."

"Yes, I've heard," I said. "But weren't members of both tribes united when it came to the confiscating of precious artifacts?"

"Indeed, we were."

"Miss Reynolds seemed passionate about the Star Amulet—and she wanted it returned to the Tavani," Cordelia said.

"That, too, we agreed upon," he said. "But she was more concerned by the loss of the Sun Stone, which apparently contained the life essence of the Noya'Keen."

"What do you know of this Sun Stone?" I asked.

"It represents the Noya'Keens' reverence for the sun. It was used in solstice ceremonies to celebrate the changing seasons and to invoke blessings for prosperity and protection. Eleanor spoke of an ancient prophecy which foretold that if the stone was ever taken from its sacred place, its loss would lead to the tribe's extinction, like plants deprived of sunlight."

"And this stone is in Mr. Baxter's collection?"

"According to Eleanor, it was. But, he claimed he did not have it. It was very valuable because of its powers. Much like the Star Amulet. She was enraged at his denials, and desperate to get the stone back. The Noya'Keen are suffering from starvation. Their crops have perished from great rains and flooding."

Cordelia drew in a sharp breath, her eyes wide with astonishment. "So, she believed the prophecy was coming true?"

He nodded.

"You seem to know much about Noya'Keen culture," I said.

His lips turned up in a small smile. "We were brought up to know as much about our enemies as ourselves."

"That makes sense," I said. "Do you know the Noya'-Keen man who was with Miss Reynolds at the lecture?"

"I've met him. Briefly."

"What sort of fellow is he?"

"He is a Faithkeeper—a holy man."

I studied his face. At the mention of this man, his expression took on a definite rigidness, as if the very word carried weight beyond what he was willing to say. His silence was telling, and it only deepened the questions swirling in my mind.

Thinking back on what Mr. Chase had said about the dispute between Miss Reynolds and Michael Two Trees, I wondered if she paid the ultimate price for her dual loyalties. I reached into my pocket and felt the crisp edges of the paper where I'd drawn the Noya'Keen warning symbol.

"Do you know what this is?" I asked him.

Mr. Two Trees' jaw stiffened, and his eyes rounded slightly as they focused on the drawing. He blinked, a flicker of recognition and alarm passing over his face. For a moment, his normally composed demeanor seemed to falter.

"Ah, yes. The Eye of the Ancestors." His voice lowered an octave, edged with tension.

It occurred to me that if Eleanor Reynolds hadn't murdered Mr. Baxter, Michael Two Trees could have, and then framed her for his death, killing two birds with one stone, so to speak, in revenge for Mr. Baxter's taking of the star amulet, and to stop Miss Reynolds work with the NSFTL to obtain Tavani lands for their enemies, the Noya'Keen.

He brought his horse to a stop, and Cordelia and I followed suit.

"It is a symbol that has meaning for both the Noya'-Keen and the Tavani. Our tribes were one once, a very long time ago. We, too, were Noya'Keen. As the ancestors told it, the Great Chief had two sons—twins. When the Great Chief died, both brothers felt they were to be the next chief. They couldn't come to an agreement, so one of the brothers gathered an army of supporters, gave them a new name, Tavani, and the two tribes warred over the land in the south. The Noya'Keen outnumbered the Tavani, and drove them north—to this area. It is here we've been ever since. The two tribes no longer fight, but there are still some hard feelings among both peoples."

He looked at me in earnest. "Mrs. Pryce, I too, have also been recently subjected to the warning. I assume it's because of my strong advocacy for keeping Tavani land in Tavani hands—something I would do anything to protect."

"I see." So, he might have thought the warning came from Eleanor Reynolds, and he was giving her a taste of her own medicine? Or, perhaps it had come from the Faithkeeper?

"Although I do not share the same sympathies with the Noya'Keen as Eleanor Reynolds, both our tribal lands and sacred ancestral relics are being taken from us, disrespecting our protectors, our gods. When the holy balance is disrupted, dire consequences ensue."

Dire, indeed, I thought.

Chapter Thirty-Three

In the distance, two white tents marked our destination—the half-way point for the race. Michael Two Trees excused himself when he saw a small group of Tavani gathered near the tents. We watched as he galloped away.

"I find it hard to believe Mr. Two Trees would kill anyone. He has such a peaceful nature," Cordelia said.

"Yes, but he also said he would do anything to preserve his people's stake in the land here," I reminded her, looking behind me to check on Bijou. She appeared content, sitting in her little basket, swaying with Monty's every step and silently taking in the view of the landscape.

"That's true, but, in killing Eleanor—or Mr. Baxter—wouldn't that put the whole Tavani tribe at risk? They are in a precarious position with the U.S. Government as it is. Mr. Two Trees is a leader of sorts for the tribe. I doubt he would do anything to put them in jeopardy. Besides, he seems so kind. I can't imagine him doing something so evil," Cordelia added.

"I'm inclined to agree with you, but we can't overlook

the fact that each of us could have many motives for murder, Cordelia—loyalty, retribution, desperation, even a personal vendetta. These may have played a part in Mr. Baxter's death, and perhaps Miss Reynolds' as well."

"I suppose you are right."

"Mr. Baxter said he feared for his life—from someone close to him, a colleague, perhaps."

"So that would definitely include Michael Two Trees," Cordelia said.

"And, Simon Graves," I added. "He seemed very resentful of Mr. Baxter—and, if I'm honest—quite smitten with his wife. I wonder if the feeling is mutual?"

A look of astonishment crossed her face. "You don't think Bernice and Simon are—"

I shrugged. "Mr. Baxter struck me as a man who was less than sentimental. Perhaps Bernice sought affection elsewhere." I remembered how she'd cozied up to Mr. Chase. "And she stands to inherit Mr. Baxter's business. Mr. Graves said she intended to keep him on as an assistant," I added.

Cordelia looked a little aghast. "So, you think she or Simon may have killed Mr. Baxter? But, in his letter, Mr. Baxter expressed Bernice was in danger as well."

"He didn't know where the threats were coming from. But both of them claim they were working together late into the night on a paper Simon is writing—the same night Mr. Baxter was killed. Constance even corroborated their story, saying she saw them there. However, I didn't ask her what time she saw them; she just mentioned it was very late."

I also remembered, with a sinking feeling in my stomach, what she had said about Clayton and the woman— how he'd been spending time with her in Colorado Springs. But I couldn't dwell on that now.

"And it's not clear to me why either of them would kill Miss Reynolds."

"Didn't the doctor say that Mr. Baxter was murdered between eleven o'clock and one a.m.?" she asked.

"Yes. I'll have to find out just how long the two were in the exhibit hall."

Cordelia let out an exasperated sigh. "It seems we're not making much progress."

"These things take time, Cordelia. Don't give up hope. We'll do everything we can to get Mr. Baxter and Anna reunited." I understood her worry and frustration—and her feeling of responsibility.

"So, have we ruled out Michael Two Trees for the murders?"

I offered her a warm, sympathetic smile. "Not quite yet, I'm afraid."

Up ahead, near one of the tents, a Native man and woman carried a small table and set it near what looked like an easel. The woman then set a canvas upon it and adjusted it with a focused gaze as she surveyed the scene she was about to bring to life.

"There's Sarah Redhawk." I pointed in her direction.

"It looks like she is preparing to paint," Cordelia said. "This might be an excellent opportunity to talk with her about the murders."

"How fortuitous," I agreed. "She definitely seemed aligned with Michael Two Trees in his concerns with Mr. Baxter's artifacts collection, and his intentions to build the museum. And, since she is Tavani, I am assuming she also disagreed with Miss Reynolds over her trying to secure the land for the Noya'Keen."

"And don't forget, Bernice claimed she was one of Mr.

Baxter's mistresses," Cordelia said. "Though I can't help but wonder if Bernice might have imagined it. She's always been the jealous type—jealous of my friendship with Anna and even of Anna's courtship with Mr. Baxter."

"It's possible," I said. "If Mr. Baxter made a habit of being unfaithful, she might have misread the friendship between him and Miss Redhawk. But, if they had an affair —and it ended badly, that might establish further motive for Miss Redhawk."

"That's true. And, Arabella, we mustn't overlook Mr. Archer and Mr. Chase as suspects either."

"Yes, I know," I replied reluctantly. I didn't want to add to Cordelia's frustration by admitting that, indeed, we'd made little progress in finding the murderer—and truthfully, I was at a complete loss.

While Archibald Archer would probably stop at nothing to get what he wanted, including the Arabella, it pained me to entertain the idea of Mr. Chase's guilt. Although he was likely adept at manipulation, given his charismatic ways and suave demeanor, I hadn't quite figured out what to make of him entirely. I couldn't deny I was attracted to his drive and ambition—and his intelligence. I also couldn't discount that if what he had told me about his feelings about the Arabella were true, he could help me protect her from Mr. Archer's clutches.

At last, we reached the cluster of white canvas tents. A handful of townsfolk were busy assisting Mr. Crawford and Mr. Emerson as they set up tables laden with refreshments and arranged chairs for the spectators. Nearby, Miss Mayes, Constance, and Sally were adding the final touches to the colorful pennants strung between the tents, lending them a cheerful, festive air.

"Look, there's Constance," Cordelia said.

"Yes." I eyed Miss Redhawk, who was now carefully arranging her brushes and palette on the table with careful precision. Once again, she wore her resplendent buckskin dress, adorned with vibrant beads and shells. Long, colorful feathers dangled from her ears. "But first, I'd like to speak with Miss Redhawk."

"We could split up," she said. "I'll go speak with Constance."

I nodded in agreement, and Cordelia guided Peanut toward the group of women hanging decorations on the tents. I directed Monty over to Miss Redhawk.

"Hello there," I greeted her as I dismounted.

She gave me a welcoming smile. "Good morning."

"Beautiful day for the race."

"Excellent," she agreed. "Perfect for finishing this piece. This time of morning, the mountains are even more picturesque. They will make a great backdrop for my rendering of the event. The race is an important rite of passage for junior members of the tribe, especially for young men or women proving their readiness for adult responsibilities. Participation in the race signifies bravery, skill, and maturity. It is a marker that a young person is ready to take on leadership roles or join the tribe's council discussions."

"How intriguing. It sounds quite significant."

"It certainly is." Her smile brimmed with pride.

I stepped over to the unfinished work of art on the easel. The landscape denoted a vibrant sunset over a vast expanse of rugged mesas and rolling hills, where the late afternoon sun cast a vivid shade of crimson across the red rock formations, igniting the earth in a fiery glow.

"The vibrancy of the colors is most striking." I leaned

in, studying the painting more closely. "Such bold and potent hues, especially the red of the cliffs." They were painted in the exact watermelon hue of countless sunsets I had watched since our arrival in La Plata Springs.

"I love using the color. It adds such richness and depth to the subject," Miss Redhawk said. "The pigment comes from clay found in South America, used by some of its indigenous peoples for their pottery. It is said to contain magical properties for the renewal of life."

I recalled what Warren Baxter had written about the Tavani Star Amulet. That it, too, had powers of renewal.

"I thought your depiction of the Star Amulet exquisite. Did you use the same color in that painting?" I asked, since I had only seen the painting from a distance.

She gave me a tentative smile. "I did. And thank you. The Star Amulet is very special to me—and my family. Since it is in Warren Baxter's possession—well, in his collection—my people only have memories and recreations of it through my art, and the art of others in the tribe. I feel compelled to keep those memories alive."

"So, do you agree with Miss Reynolds that Mr. Baxter stole the amulet?"

She met my gaze, her eyes sharp with conviction. "It's the only thing we ever agreed on. Warren Baxter had no right to take artifacts that hold such deep spiritual significance for our peoples. Pottery, clothing, even ancient structures—those can be used to educate others about our history. But spiritual totems? They carry the life essence of generations. Stealing those is a crime far worse."

"The Star Amulet. And the Sun Stone," I said, my voice barely above a whisper.

Her expression hardened, as if the weight of her words bore down on her. "The Sun Stone belonged to the Noya'-

Keen, and Eleanor Reynolds was desperate to reclaim it. She was so consumed by their plight, she forgot her Tavani heritage. She betrayed her ancestors."

She paused, her voice steady but cold as flint. "And now she's paid the price for her betrayal."

Chapter Thirty-Four

Miss Redhawk's reaction to Miss Reynolds' death was startling. My expression must have given me away, as she quickly raised a hand in apology.

"I don't mean to sound so cruel. I'm sorry."

I gave a shrug of my shoulder. "You have strong feelings about her."

"Listen." Her tone grew gentler. "Eleanor and I were never friends, but that doesn't mean I wished her harm. No matter how much she disliked me, or that she never failed to make me feel guilty."

"Guilty about what?"

She shook her head, the long feathered earrings dusting her shoulders. "She didn't approve of my … association with Warren Baxter."

Ah, exactly what I want to discuss!

"You two were close?"

"We were quite close."

"I see. Does that mean you were romantically

involved?" I ventured cautiously, wondering if she would deny it.

"I'm not proud of it now. But, yes. Like I told you before, we were first acquainted in St. Louis, where he expressed particular admiration for the Tavani art and artifacts I had brought to the Exposition. One piece, especially, an heirloom passed through my family for generations, caught his eye. His interest in my culture seemed genuine, and he professed a deep appreciation for both the art and the people from whom it came. He spoke at length of his desire to educate others, particularly the white man, about the significance of our heritage and the need for its preservation and respect. For that week we were inseparable, and we later continued to meet at various symposiums across the country."

Her eyes strayed from mine, and her expression softened, as if recalling a bittersweet memory.

"It sounds as though you held Mr. Baxter in great affection."

"I did." Her voice hardened, carrying with it a tone of vehemence. "Until I saw him for who he truly was. A cheat and a thief."

"You found out he was married?"

"Yes, I learned about it from a colleague. And it turned out his integrity as a historian and artifacts curator was questionable, too. His pride in his academic success caused him to become just like other collectors who have taken sacred relics for profit, amusement, or personal gain. Not just at the expense of the Tavani, but other tribes as well."

"I see. So, you ended the relationship?" I inquired, noting the sudden steely glint in her eyes as they met mine once more.

"Of course. I would never align myself with a man who is so unscrupulous—or married," she replied coldly.

The depth of her disillusionment was palpable. "You must have been terribly angered at learning he deceived you."

"I was. But what he did to my family far exceeded my personal grievance."

"Your family?"

"In St. Louis, one of the Tavani artifacts I had loaned to the Exposition—a medicine pouch that belonged to my great-great-grandfather—went missing. It contained feathers from the now extinct Shokawia bird, the sacred spirit animal of our family. Both my father and I were heartbroken. Several weeks later, there were rumors that Warren had stolen it. Foolishly, I defended him. But soon, I feared those accusations were true."

"You weren't entirely certain?"

She shook her head. "Not entirely, but I recalled a moment at the Exposition when I had come upon him at the exhibit case where the medicine pouch was kept, and it appeared as though he had just shut the door. At the time, I noticed nothing was amiss, but the following morning, the medicine pouch was gone. Warren was the last person seen near it. I have little doubt now that it was him."

"Did you confront him?"

A derisive laugh escaped her lips. "He denied it, of course. But later, after I found out he was married—and after I broke it off with him—I learned the pouch had been acquired by someone in San Francisco, a man with whom Warren had business dealings."

I let the silence settle between us, observing her. Anger glinted in her eyes, and it was clear she had every reason to want revenge on Mr. Baxter for the missing heirloom. I recalled that Mr. Brooks said he'd seen her leaving Baxter's suite on the night of his death.

"Miss Redhawk, did you visit Warren Baxter the night he died?"

She inhaled slowly, lifting her chin, a mix of defiance and grief in her posture. "I did. I went to tell him that my father had passed away—of a broken heart. He never recovered from the loss of the medicine pouch. I wanted Warren to know the full weight of what he had done to my family. But I didn't get the chance. His wife answered the door and told me he wasn't there."

"Bernice was there?" I asked, remembering both she and Simon claimed to be at the exhibit hall that night. And Constance had seen them. Perhaps it had been earlier, when Mr. Baxter was with Mr. Chase and Mr. Archer at Kitty's place.

"Yes. And she wasn't thrilled to see me. I tried to explain my side of the story—that her husband had lied to me by omission, but she slammed the door in my face."

"What time was this?"

She looked heavenward, as if trying to remember. "It was after the lecture, so maybe nine o'clock?"

"So, you didn't see Mr. Baxter—perhaps later?" I pressed.

Her expression darkened again. "If you're wondering if I killed Warren Baxter, I didn't. Yes, he did immeasurable harm to my family and my people, but we are peaceful by nature. Violence isn't something I carry in my heart. Besides, I believe your efforts at finding the killer of Warren Baxter might be in vain."

"Why is that?"

"Because the person who murdered Warren Baxter is dead."

"You mean Eleanor Reynolds?"

"The Noya'Keen are a vengeful people. And Eleanor was no different. I know from experience."

"You do? How?"

"She told the Tavani that I was a traitor to the tribe, that I was involved in Warren's shady dealings—selling artifacts on the black market. It took me years to rebuild my relationship with my people. Michael Two Trees has stood by me as my advocate, and I am forever grateful to him. As for Eleanor, I've tried to forgive her. Now that she's gone, finding that forgiveness might finally be possible."

I couldn't help but feel a surge of sympathy for Miss Redhawk. Being accused of betraying one's own people— by someone close enough to have known better—was a deep wound to bear. But questions buzzed in my mind. If Eleanor Reynolds had truly been spreading such malicious accusations, what had driven her to it? And could Miss Redhawk's resentment, however buried, have left room for something darker? I wondered if her pain had been laid to rest as fully as she claimed.

Chapter Thirty-Five

I left Miss Redhawk to her painting. Cordelia and Peanut were heading my way, and we took the horses to a spot where they could graze while we waited for the racers to appear on the horizon.

Dismounting, I removed Monty's bridle, and then helped Cordelia with Peanut's bridle. We left their rope halters on, attached the lead ropes, and then let them graze peacefully.

"What did you find out from Constance?" I asked.

"She said she saw Bernice and Mr. Graves at around eleven-thirty. She didn't know how long they stayed at the exhibit hall because she left at around midnight."

I sighed. "Were there any others in the hall who might have seen them?"

"She said there were several people there—but she couldn't recall who exactly."

"Ah," I said, with some disappointment. "That's not helpful."

We entered the nearest tent to find Atticus Brooks sitting

in the front row, one leg crossed over the other knee, notebook in hand.

"Oh, dear." I did not want him to catch sight of us. I didn't feel like making polite conversation while having to deal with his condescension. "Let's go to the other tent."

"But there are plenty of seats here." Cordelia set Bijou on the ground.

"I think we should go to the other tent," I repeated, this time under my breath as I tilted my head toward Mr. Brooks. Cordelia instantly got my meaning and we turned to go when the sound of Bijou's low growl stopped me in my tracks. She was sitting at Mr. Brooks's feet, staring up at him. He regarded her with a look of disdain on his face.

"Bijou, come," I said.

"Mrs. Pryce!" Mr. Brooks rose to his feet as Bijou barked sharply, almost in protest. They say a dog knows the true measure of a man. I had my doubts about Bijou's judgment on most occasions, but in this instance, she was decidedly correct.

"Mr. Brooks." I gave him a slight nod.

"And, Miss Danson. Beautiful morning, is it not? Won't you two ladies join me?" He gestured toward the two empty chairs next to his.

"Oh, well—I—" I stammered, trying to drum up an excuse, any excuse, not to sit with him.

"Please, I insist," he said with an ingratiating smile.

I let go a sigh. "I have no desire to banter with you, Mr. Brooks—"

"Banter? Heavens no. I thought we put that behind us." He leaned toward me and whispered, "I have some information about the recent murders you might find enlightening."

I couldn't hold back my own sardonic smile. "Really?"

He raised his brows and again gestured toward the chair. I glanced over at Cordelia and rolled my eyes, to which she gave a shrug.

"Very well," I said.

We settled into the chairs, with me taking the one closest to him. "Forgive me, Mr. Brooks, but why would you want to impart any information about this to me and not the sheriff?"

"Well, I could go to the sheriff, and may still, but I know you are investigating the case and—"

"How do you know that?" I asked, feeling defensive and a little worried he might tell Clayton.

He gave a soft chuckle. "Well, my dear, you seem to think I don't know you at all, but let me assure you, I do. Your insatiable curiosity won't let you stay away from this investigation. You've had some success with these matters before, and I know just how much that success means to you."

Offended at his insinuation that the only reason I wanted to solve crime was for my own vanity, I opened my mouth to retort, when Cordelia laid a hand on my arm.

"Arabella is investigating on my behalf, Mr. Brooks," she said. "Mrs. Baxter is a friend of mine, and I want to help her, so I've asked for Arabella's assistance."

"And I'd like to help you both," he said with a cat-like grin.

This benevolent eagerness was beyond the pale. "I'm sorry, Mr. Brooks, please forgive me, but I doubt your sincerity. Why would you help us?"

It was his turn to draw in a deep breath, and then let it out slowly. He dipped his head and looked at me from under those caterpillar brows. "Because I may need a favor from you."

A smile spread across my face. Ah yes. Now we were getting to the crux of the matter. "I see. And what might this favor be? Perhaps you need information for the story you are so obviously writing about the murders. Using the influence of my name to bolster your article, are you?"

His eyes clouded with ire, and he cleared his throat. I'd obviously hit a nerve.

"My dear." His voice took on a placating tone. "If we could just work together—"

"What?" I said with a snort. "Oh, Mr. Brooks, I had no idea you were so well versed in comedy!"

"Very droll," he replied with an indulgent smile.

"In all seriousness, Mr. Brooks, let's stop beating about the bush. What is it exactly that you need from me?"

He looked at me blankly before screwing up his face as if the idea of asking me for a favor pained him, which I'm sure it did. Finally, it seemed he was about to make his mouth work.

"I need you as a reference. I'd like to be a feature writer for the *Sun Herald* in New York, and, well, I understand that you—through your late husband and Mr. Rankin of the *New York City Times*—have met the editor-in-chief, Mr. Towery, and I thought that with your influence—"

"Wait a minute," I interrupted him. "I thought you were a freelance correspondent writing articles about your experience in the west and selling them to numerous papers."

He lifted a shoulder. "Well—I am—I have been, but— it's not as easy as you might think."

"You mean it doesn't pay well."

"A job on staff would provide a much steadier income for me—and—"

"So, you mean to leave La Plata Springs, then?" I asked, my interest more than evident. From the moment I'd seen him on the train and learned he was bound for an indefinite stay here as well, I'd wanted nothing more than for him to leave.

He gave a slow nod. "If I get the position. New York would be my home base, but I'd be traveling, of course."

Which would mean we would soon be in New York together, I thought. *Would I never be rid of this man?*

"Why don't you ask for a reference from Mr. Rankin?" Cordelia asked.

He cleared his throat. "As you know, he's fired me. Twice."

"Yes," I replied, my tone sharp. "It seems you've made a habit of reporting fiction instead of facts." I still wasn't ready to trust him. For years, he had targeted my mother and me, always with baseless claims. At least two of his stories about me had been retracted by Mr. Rankin, and those retractions had done no favors for the paper's reputation.

"Come now, Mrs. Pryce. I did right by you. In the end."

I raised my chin. But, without first putting a tarnish on my reputation. "And if I do put in a good word for you, what do I receive in return?"

"I would feature you in many of my stories."

"Feature me favorably?" I wondered if he could truly overcome the difficulty he'd had with this in the past.

"Yes, of course. We could finally put our little tug of war to rest, my dear. You would have a friend for life."

I scoffed. "I'm not sure that's necessary, but why don't you tell me what you know, and I will give your request the utmost consideration?"

He shifted in his seat. More people had gathered in the tent, eagerly awaiting the arrival of the racers. Several others had gathered on the sidelines where the horses would come thundering through and the riders would throw their numbered batons in a barrel, make the turn, and head back to town.

"This might not be the best time." He gestured with a tilt of his head toward the crowd gathering in the tent. "I wouldn't want what I have to say to become common knowledge. Besides, I'm covering the race."

"Don't toy with me, Mr. Brooks," I said flatly. "We could step outside for a few moments. The racers are nowhere in sight just yet."

"I'll watch Bijou, and save your seats," Cordelia said sweetly.

"Very well." He stood up. "Shall we?"

I gave Cordelia a smug smile as we left the tent. We found a spot near a lone piñon tree where we had full view of the proceedings, and also the designated track where the riders would come through.

Mr. Brooks sank his hands into his pockets and rolled back and forth on the balls of his feet. I looked at him expectantly.

"What do you know of Mr. Graves, Baxter's assistant?" he asked.

"He seemed devoted to the man—even though Mr. Baxter had supposedly taken credit for some of his work—the finding of the Star Amulet, actually."

"Exactly. And there is something else you might find interesting." He pulled a small book from his breast pocket. "Simon Graves's journal."

I gasped. "Where did you get that? You weren't snooping in his belongings, were you?" Not that I would have done anything less had I had the chance.

"No," he said. "Archibald and I were having a drink at the Bella. Mr. Graves joined us. He had the journal in his hand, set it on the table, and well, after many drinks later, left without it. There was so much frivolity going on we hadn't noticed it, but when we did, I offered to take it back to the young man."

"But you kept it instead?" I arched a brow.

"For the time being."

"And, you've—no doubt—read it?"

He lifted a shoulder. "I may have skimmed it. But I landed on a very interesting entry." He flipped through it. "Ah, here it is."

St. Louis, Hotel Henri, 1884.
I couldn't help myself—I followed her to the hotel garden again. She never saw me, but I was close enough to see the beautiful feathers—the ones I gave her—adorned in her hair. The distance between us is maddening. I feel an undeniable pull toward her, as if fate has bound us together, yet Baxter stands in the way. He wants it all, every last piece. Doesn't he have enough? Isn't she enough? He's the only obstacle between me and what my heart truly craves.

I looked up from the page. "Who was he referring to?" I asked, thinking out loud. But I kept the next thought to myself. Could it be Miss Redhawk? This was around the time when Mr. Baxter and Miss Redhawk had been engaged in the affair.

Mr. Brooks took the journal from me and flipped to another page. "Read this."

I took it back from him. The entry date was more recent. At the end of last year.

I see through his façade—pretending to care, pretending to be the loving husband. He's only keeping the beautiful bird caged because he knows what we share, even if she hasn't realized it yet. Does he think I won't act? Does he believe I'll just stand by and watch him hurt her? He won't get away with it for much longer—his pining for Miss Redhawk —humiliating Bernice.

"He's in love with Bernice," I said, reading the entry again.

He leaned over and flipped to the last page. "His last entry. Dated two days before Mr. Baxter was found dead."

She deserves to be free of him. He doesn't love her—he's proven that with every secret rendezvous, every deception. He's not worthy of her. I've been patient for too long, waiting for her to see what I've known from the beginning. Now I have the ammunition I need to set things in motion.

A deep thundering sound of hoofbeats echoed in the distance. The first wave of horses was approaching the half-way point.

"I must go back to the tent," he said.

"May I hold on to this?"

He raised his brows as if the question was impertinent.

I sighed. "All right. I'll consider speaking with Mr. Rankin about giving you a favorable referral. His word will have more weight than mine with Mr. Towery." I still did not trust Mr. Brooks, even though this information he'd supplied was noteworthy indeed.

"Thank you, my dear," he said. "Yes, you may keep the journal."

As we headed back to the tent, I noticed the Noya'Keen Faithkeeper standing off to the side of the nearest tent. Given that this was a Tavani event, it surprised me to see him here. I veered toward him.

"This looks like an exciting race," I said as I came to

stand next to him. He wore the same coat as before, which I thought must be terribly warm for this time of year, but he seemed unbothered. A flat-brimmed beaver hat, decorated with a colorful band, shielded his eyes from the sun. With his hands clasped behind his back, he turned stiffly to regard me.

"It is that," he said quietly.

"I'm Arabella Pryce." I extended my hand. "I own the Arabella Hotel in La Plata Springs."

His gaze dropped to my hand, but he didn't take it. Instead, he gave a gracious bow. "I am Tayanakwa."

"Do you have someone in the race?" I asked, pretty certain he didn't, but thinking it a good starting point.

"I do not. This is a Tavani tradition. I am Noya'Keen."

"Oh, yes. Of course. I've seen you before. You were a friend of Eleanor Reynolds. I'm sorry for your loss."

He gave another bow, his features etched with sorrow. Then he focused on the horses, which were thundering toward the turning point. "We have lost a great voice for our people."

"Yes, I'd heard she was trying to secure land in this area for your tribe."

He nodded. "We are in great need. And she was building bridges between our people and the Tavani. I hope to continue her work. In these times, the indigenous tribes must find solidarity."

"Yes, I suppose you must." Then, fishing for a reaction, I added, "I understand Mr. Baxter made her work difficult—with him wanting to take some of the Tavani land for his museum. And then there were the artifacts that had special significance to the Tavani, and your people. She expressed her anger openly during his lecture."

His dark gaze slid to meet mine. "Justifiably so. The Star Amulet and the Sun Stone belong with their peoples."

"I wonder," I said carefully, "do you think Miss Reynolds was angry enough to..." I let the rest of the sentence hang in the air, studying his reaction. I didn't truly believe Eleanor Reynolds had killed Mr. Baxter, but I couldn't ignore the possibility this man might have.

Several horses dashed past us in a flurry of dust and speed, the ground quaking with their hoofbeats.

"She did not kill Mr. Baxter," he said, his voice raised above the din of the cheering crowd.

No. But who did?

The horses made the turn and sped away. The crowd's enthusiasm quieted as they waited for the next wave of riders.

Finally, a smile broke through his weathered features. "Violence solves nothing, Arabella Pryce. And, to address your unspoken question whether I killed Mr. Baxter, after the lecture, I left promptly for the livery to fetch my horse. I was due at a Noya'Keen wedding ceremony. You may verify this with the liveryman, Mr. Parkhurst, and the young couple I wed."

I pulled my chin back in surprise. Apparently, I hadn't been as subtle as I thought. "Right, not that I was—well, thanks for clearing that up."

"I wish you luck in finding the person who killed Mr. Baxter. And my friend, Eleanor."

I nodded. "Thank you, Mr.—er—I mean—"

"Tayanakwa," he finished for me.

"Oh, yes—yes. Good day." I hurried away, suddenly feeling very awkward. To say the man was intimidating was an understatement.

As I moved toward the tent, I noticed Mr. Chase

standing near the entrance, speaking with a woman. The
two were laughing, and as I got closer, I realized it was
Bernice. She gazed up at him with admiration, her expression that of a woman utterly smitten. I wondered again
what exactly their relationship was.

But it was Simon Graves, standing a short distance
away, who really caught my attention. His cold, unblinking
stare was locked on them, his expression hard as stone.

Chapter Thirty-Six

Later that afternoon, fatigued from the ride and the excitement of the race, Cordelia and I retired to our suite. Percival joined us and lounged on the settee, quietly blowing smoke rings into the air. Bijou slept soundly in her little bed under the window next to the fireplace. The room was quiet, each one of us caught up in our own thoughts.

As I sipped my tea, I read through Simon Graves' journal. There were no further entries about his apparent obsession with Bernice—just notes on various digs he'd worked on, historical artifacts he'd collected, and the projects he undertook with Mr. Baxter. Early entries revealed Simon's admiration for the man, but over time, his words grew tinged with resentment as Baxter's reputation soared, leaving Simon to fade further into the background.

"Well, I'd never really considered that the Noya'Keen man, Mr. Takana—Tawake—" Cordelia began.

"Tayanakwa," I said, quite pleased with myself for remembering the pronunciation.

"Yes. Him," she continued. "—could have killed Mr.

Baxter. But, even so, I suppose it's a good thing that his alibi checked out. It would be a shame if Miss Reynolds' work to instill peace between the two tribes had died with her."

"Yes," I agreed, absently.

When we returned the horses to Mr. Parkhurst, I had asked him about Tayanakwa's story. He confirmed it, saying Tayanakwa had indeed come by the livery after the lecture to fetch his horse. Mr. Parkhurst also mentioned that Clayton had already asked him about it. So, the sheriff had followed up on my lead regarding Eleanor's association with the Faithkeeper. *You're welcome, Clayton.*

Seeing as Tayanakwa hadn't been arrested, I could only assume the sheriff had also verified the holy man's claim with the young couple he'd married. It seemed he was in the clear.

"Have you found anything more illuminating in the journal?" Cordelia asked.

"Only that Simon Graves felt completely overshadowed by Mr. Baxter. If Mr. Baxter had taken credit for his work, and if Mr. Graves had grown excessively fond of Bernice, it would stand to reason that he might come to hate the man. But we have no evidence, or proof, that he killed him."

"I wonder if Bernice knows that Simon Graves is in love with her?" Cordelia said.

"If she does, she certainly doesn't seem to feel the same way about him. It appears she only has eyes for Mr. Chase —which strikes me as rather odd, considering what you've said about her feelings for Mr. Baxter—and the fact that he's recently been murdered. Didn't you say that she always admired him—even when he was with Anna?"

"Yes." Cordelia nodded. "So much so it made me uncomfortable."

"My dear Arabella, do I detect a hint of jealousy?" Percival's voice echoed from the settee.

"Jealousy?" I said. "What do you mean?"

"I mean, that Bernice Baxter seems enamored of Mr. Chase."

I scoffed. "Don't be silly. Why would I care who is enamored of Mr. Chase? Our relationship is purely professional."

"You aren't still considering going into business with the man?" he asked.

I let go a sigh. "I'm considering a great many things lately."

"Well, for once I agree with your sheriff—on the character of Mr. Chase."

"What are you talking about, Percival?" I asked, growing annoyed with him.

"Your Mr. Marshall has taken a keen interest in Mr. Chase—has been asking around about him—more so than about anyone else, it seems."

"He's not my Mr. Marshall, and how do you know this?"

"I see things. Hear things. As you know, I can move about quite stealthily, my dear."

"What have you seen and heard?"

"Mr. Marshall has been asking around about Mr. Chase's business dealings of the past. Something about his involvement in a Cattle Syndicate."

"A Cattle Syndicate—what is that?"

"It's an exclusive group of cattle barons who use certain tactics, often aggressive, to take over land and muscle out smaller ranchers. They've been known to pay off certain officials to secure their claims."

"Oh—" I could not ignore the fact that, like his project here, it involved disputes over land.

"Don't forget, Arabella, both Mr. Chase and Mr. Archer were seen by Maybelle disputing with Mr. Baxter," Cordelia said. "They both have motive."

Could it be I was letting my business ambitions cloud my judgement of the man? Or, more disturbingly, was it something else?

"Listen," I said. "The only concrete evidence we have so far that indicates Mr. Baxter was murdered is the Noya'-Keen symbol carved on Mr. Baxter's door. Although, after speaking with Michael Two Trees, it could have been Tavani. He said the symbol has meaning for both tribes," I reminded myself.

"Anyway, everything else is based on speculation. Would Mr. Archer or Mr. Chase have done something like that? Did they even know about the symbol, or its meaning?"

"They could have," Cordelia said. "They are both on familiar terms with people of the Noya'Keen and the Tavani tribes. If one of them did kill him, perhaps they wanted to cast suspicion on someone else—like Eleanor Reynolds? She was rather a thorn in their side with her plans for the land they wanted to use for expansion, and the Addison train depot."

"Agreed," said Percival. "If she truly stood in the way of their plans, either—or both—could have framed her for Baxter's murder and then killed her to silence her, effectively halting her efforts. A tidy solution, all wrapped up in a neat little bow."

"But the doctor said she died of the same condition as Mr. Baxter. If what you say is true, whoever killed her used the same method she used to kill Mr. Baxter. If the blowgun I found near where Eleanor Reynolds' body lay was the means of murder, it seems unlikely that Mr. Archer or Mr. Chase would have used a weapon like that. Why not strangle her? Or use something else readily accessible and harder to detect, like poison?"

"She has a point there," Cordelia said to Percival.

"It just doesn't feel right that either of those men committed the crimes," I said. "Besides, Mr. Chase and Mr. Archer, in particular, have friends in high places. Miss Reynolds might have annoyed them, but she probably didn't stand a chance of getting the government on her side. It has to have been someone else."

"We did get some interesting insights from Michael Two Trees and Sarah Redhawk today," Cordelia said.

"Right. They both harbored grievances against Warren Baxter and Eleanor Reynolds. Especially Sarah Redhawk."

I was about to close the journal when it slipped out of my hands and landed on the floor, its pages splayed. One of them looked like it had ripped itself from the spine.

"Oh, dear. Now look at what I've done," I muttered to myself. I went to pick it up when the torn paper fell to the floor. It looked different from the other pages in the journal. In fact, it was—it was a separate piece of paper—a note that read:

Mr. Graves, don't think for a moment that your 'anonymous critiques' have gone unnoticed. I know exactly who's behind the articles undermining Dr. Baxter, and I have no problem ensuring he finds out, too. Unless, of course, you're prepared to do something for me in return. Find the Sun Stone, Simon, and your secret stays safe. Fail, and I'll be happy to watch your carefully laid plans unravel. E.R.

"My goodness." I held the note out for Cordelia to read. Percival looked over her shoulder.

Her eyes quickly scanned the page, and then she raised them to meet mine. "E.R. Eleanor Reynolds. She was black-mailing Mr. Graves."

"That's what it sounds like." I tucked the paper back into the journal.

"So, that gives him further motive," Percival said. "For both murders."

"Exactly." Cordelia agreed. "Yet, he was seen with Bernice in the exhibit hall around the time of Baxter's murder. But where was he at the time of Eleanor's murder?"

I shook my head. "It's perplexing."

A quiet knock on the door interrupted our conversation. Bijou awakened from the noise and barked. Quickly, I went to the desk and shoved the journal into the top drawer.

"I'll get it," Cordelia offered. Percival made himself scarce.

"Bernice!" Cordelia said.

The woman looked positively ashen.

"Good heavens, Bernice, is something wrong?"

Her eyes wide with fear, she said in a strained voice, "I need to speak with you both."

"Please come in," I said, as Cordelia took her arm. "Would you like some tea?"

Still mute, Bernice nodded again, pressing her fist to her chest. My attention was drawn to the beautiful silver broach at her neck—the bird in flight. I notice she carried some folded-up papers in her other hand. Cordelia led her to the settee, and I poured her a cup of tea. Trembling, she took the cup and sipped.

"Thank you. I'm so upset."

"What's happened, Bernice?" Cordelia asked, sitting down next to her.

"I found these." She held the folded papers out to me.

I unfolded the one on top, and something fluttered to the floor. It was a beautiful bright blue feather. I picked it up and then read the letter out loud.

Warren,
Old wounds fester, and ghosts don't rest without their reckoning. The debts of the past are due, and blood calls for blood. You know the price of broken promises and shattered trust. Look to the crimson horizon when the sun dips low—where shadows stretch, there lies the truth you've long tried to bury.
Remember, Warren, everyone has something they hold dear. You took what was mine, and now you will lose something in return. Tell your lady-bird to guard herself well, for birds of prey seek vengeance.

"Where did you find this?" I asked her. Could this have been from Simon Graves? It seemed vaguely reminiscent of the journal entries. Or perhaps Eleanor Reynolds— although the script was decidedly different from the hand-writing on the note that had fallen from the journal.

"In Warren's valise," she said. "He had not completely unpacked it. I thought I would donate some of his clothing to anyone who might need it, now that—" her voice hitched, and then she cleared her throat. "—Now that I would have no need of them. I saw the corner of one of the letters sticking out from behind the backing of the valise—there was a hidden compartment—the letters were there. There were several—but only one with the feather."

"What did the other letters say?" Cordelia asked.

"Just variations on this theme," she said, shaking her head, her voice quavering.

I opened the other letter. It read:

The past never truly dies, and old sins have a way of finding their way home. The score between us remains unsettled, and the time for collecting has come. Promises once broken still echo through these empty nights, and the hour of retribution draws near.

You stole from me what could never be replaced. Now, Warren, it's your turn to feel the emptiness of loss. Keep her close, for soon, you may find the shadows have a way of swallowing what is precious.

Justice waits for no man. Least of all, you.

"I had no idea Warren had received these letters," Bernice said. "He didn't tell me about them—but that was just like him. He wouldn't want to worry me. But, now that I have seen them, I'm afraid I'll be the next to die."

Chapter Thirty-Seven

Her hand shook as she raised the teacup to her lips and sipped gingerly.

"Bernice. In your letter to me, your husband said the threats were coming from someone close to him. Do you have any idea who it could have been?"

She let go a breath and then composed herself. "When I first read these, I thought it might have been Eleanor Reynolds—she'd been after him, quite aggressively, regarding the Sun Stone, even though he'd told her it wasn't in the collection. And then there was also the Noya'Keen symbol on the door. But then I remembered the sheriff said someone had come forward providing an alibi for her."

"Really? When was this?"

"The other day. Apparently, she'd gone to visit some of the Noya'Keen on the outskirts of town after the lecture. There was a wedding. She stayed overnight."

I nodded. So, like Tayanakwa, she'd also gone to the wedding.

I recalled Mr. Graves's journal entries, and the way he often looked at Bernice. "Do you think it might have been Mr. Graves?"

She blinked, shock registering on her face. "Simon? Why would Simon kill Warren?"

I shrugged. "He told me that Mr. Baxter had taken credit for some of his work—finding the Tavani Star Amulet, for example."

She shook her head. "I know Simon felt slighted by Warren over the amulet, but he knew what he was getting into when he became Warren's assistant. Anything found by those working under Warren belonged to him—it was part of the deal. Simon's young and ambitious, but I don't believe he'd have killed Warren. He worshiped him. Besides, Simon had too much to gain from his association with Warren."

"But what if there was something more personal at stake? For instance, how does Simon feel about you?"

She laughed, her fear seeming to evaporate from the room. "Me? Well, Simon is a dear, and we work well together. What are you getting at, Arabella?"

"What is your relationship with him?"

Her eyes fluttered rapidly and her complexion paled. "We are colleagues, friends. Nothing more."

I bit my lip, considering what I should tell her. I thought about showing her the journal, but I didn't want it to get back to Simon that I had it in my possession. I had no proof that Simon killed Warren Baxter—or Eleanor Reynolds. Nevertheless, I worried about her safety.

"Bernice, it might be a good idea if you distance yourself from Simon for a little while. Just until we find your husband's killer."

She shook her head. "Simon would never harm me.

And, we have much to do. He's helping me with the arrangements for Warren's funeral. We're also starting to pack and catalogue the artifacts for an exposition in Chicago, right on the heels of this festival—"

"So, you aren't going ahead with the plans for the museum?" Cordelia asked.

She shook her head. "That was Warren's dream. I don't want to be tied down to a place. I want to travel with the collection. See the world. It's what Simon wants, too. I think Warren would give us his blessing. He would want us to continue to educate the world abroad about the native peoples of this area—and the areas he studied in South America."

She obviously didn't know that Simon had been discrediting her husband, and she seemed convinced that Simon wasn't a threat to her. In thinking about it, if he was in love with her, that might be true—especially now that Mr. Baxter was out of the way. But still, he was a suspect with a powerful motive. He also had plenty of opportunity. But the means? That's where I needed to focus my attention.

"Please, just be careful," I said.

Another knock on the door interrupted us. Cordelia went to answer it and ushered none other than Simon Graves into the room. A chill escaped down my spine. It was as if he knew we were just talking about him.

"Ah, there you are," he said to Bernice, running a hand over his forehead. There was a slightly frantic look in his eyes.

"Hello, Mr. Graves." I greeted him.

He gave me a jerky nod, and then refocused on Bernice. "When you didn't show up at the exhibit hall, I was worried."

"Oh, dear!" She rose from the settee. "I'm so sorry,

Simon. I completely forgot." Her eyes traveled to the clock on the mantel. "We were supposed to meet ten minutes ago," she said to me. "We have some things to go over regarding the funeral and our plans for the collection. Would you please excuse me?"

"Yes. Don't let us keep you." My gaze flitted over to Mr. Graves again. Dots of perspiration glistened on his forehead and upper lip. "Are you all right, Mr. Graves?"

"What?" he snapped. "Oh, yes, yes I'm fine."

Bernice drew closer to him, and he shoved his hands in his pockets. "Simon, what's bothering you?"

He took out one of his hands and rubbed the back of his neck. He was clearly agitated. "Nothing. It's nothing. I've just—I've just misplaced something, and I can't for the life of me remember what I did with it."

Cordelia inhaled sharply, and I darted a warning glance in her direction. He was, no doubt, referring to the journal.

"Would you like for me to help you look for this thing?" Bernice offered.

He flinched, and then vehemently shook his head. "No, no." He swatted a hand through the air. "I'm sure it'll turn up. It's nothing to worry about. We really should go, though."

"Please don't let us detain you further," I said.

"Shall we?" Bernice took Simon's arm and Cordelia showed them both to the door. Once she had closed it, she spun around, her eyes wide as pinwheels.

"He was talking about the journal!"

I nodded. "I know. Given the threatening nature of his entries, he's most understandably concerned about someone reading it. But, now, it's evidence."

Still holding the letters Bernice had given to me, I read the first one again.

Warren,
Old wounds fester, and ghosts don't rest without their reckoning. The
debts of the past are due, and blood calls for blood. You know the price
of broken promises and shattered trust. Look to the crimson horizon
when the sun dips low—where shadows stretch, there lies the truth
you've long tried to bury.
Remember, Warren, everyone has something they hold dear. You took
what was mine, and now you will lose something in return. Tell your
lady-bird to guard herself well, for birds of prey seek vengeance.

Two things stood out to me: *Look to the crimson horizon*
when the sun dips low, and, *tell your lady-bird to guard herself well,*
for birds of prey seek vengeance.

I recalled the bright crimson sunset Sarah Redhawk had
been painting at the horse race, and the reference to birds in
the letter also made me think of her. She always wore feathers, either in her hair, on her garments, or as jewelry.

"Miss Redhawk said that Mr. Baxter had stolen a medicine pouch from her family that contained the feathers of
the Shokawia bird—the spirit animal of her family," I said
to Cordelia. "I wonder if this feather belonged to such a
bird. Do you know anything about them?"

"I don't. I've never heard of it. Didn't Miss Redhawk
say it was extinct?"

"She did." I twirled the feather between my fingers.

"Perhaps I can find a book at the library that would tell
us something about it," she offered.

"Excellent idea. Why don't you do that. In the meantime, I have a rather unpleasant task to do."

"Oh? What is that?"

"The sheriff will need to see these letters. And Mr.
Graves' journal," I said with some regret, for I liked both
Mr. Graves and Miss Redhawk. And while I understood

their feelings of loss and anger, if either of them had acted upon those emotions, they would have to pay the price.

Chapter Thirty-Eight

Queenie, the sheriff's beloved mare, dozed in the sun at the hitching rail in front of the sheriff's office.

A feeling of sadness washed over me at seeing her. I missed our outings. She and Monty were great friends, and riding out with Clayton had been some of my happiest moments here in La Plata Springs.

But, I had no time for sentiment now. I knew Clayton would be perturbed that I was still involved in the case, but in my defense, it was Mr. Brooks who had supplied the journal—without my asking—and Bernice who'd come to me with the letters. That I had actively questioned Sarah Redhawk might be more problematic, but Clayton had already seemed determined to end our friendship, so what did it matter?

Mustering my courage, I took in a deep breath and entered the office, only to find no one there. I stepped back outside just in time to see Clayton coming out of the doctor's office. Our gazes locked.

"There you are." I offered a polite smile. "I have something you need to see."

"Is it about the murders?" Dr. Tate asked, stepping outside to join us.

"Yes," I replied.

"Please, come in," he gestured for me to follow him inside.

"I can fill you in on what Arabella has to say," Clayton said to him with a dismissive tone.

"And deprive me of Mrs. Pryce's excellent company?" Dr. Tate smiled at me. "I won't hear of it."

Clayton shot me a mild look of annoyance, but I brushed past him and entered the office.

Dr. Tate showed us to the benches in his reception area. Clayton closed the door and remained there, arms defiantly folded across his chest.

"I was just telling the sheriff here that I've made somewhat of a breakthrough on the cause of death," the doctor said.

"That's wonderful, Dr. Tate!" I then turned my gaze to Clayton. "Has it led you to who the killer might be?"

Clayton remained silent, and his moodiness was getting under my skin. I was accustomed to Percival's bouts of melancholy—it rather suited him, actually—but seeing it in the sheriff was entirely different. It didn't fit his personality, and I found it more than a little unpleasant.

"Not yet," the doctor answered for him, rubbing his chin thoughtfully. "This case has been most perplexing. In my initial examination of Mr. Baxter's body, I concluded he'd died from pulmonary edema, which was accurate, but I couldn't pinpoint what had caused the fluid to fill his lungs. After examining Miss Reynolds' body, I found she had died from the same condition. Yet the cause still eluded me.

Then, I discovered something in the outer areas of her lungs—the lining. In Mr. Baxter's case, I had focused on the central area and the fluid itself, but in Miss Reynolds' lung lining, I found a rare toxin—Aquamortin."

"Is it a poison?" I asked.

"It functions like one. It's a mineral compound that reacts with moisture in the lungs, triggering a rapid and severe inflammatory response in the pulmonary tissue. This disrupts the body's ability to regulate heart and lung function, causing the heart to beat erratically, which leads to rapid fluid buildup—ultimately resulting in asphyxiation, like drowning from the inside."

"Where would they have come into contact with this Aquamortin?" I asked the doctor.

Before he could answer, Clayton stepped in. "You said there was something you wanted to show me?" He obviously didn't want to encourage any further curiosity on my part.

Annoyed, I gritted my teeth. "Yes." I took the letters and the journal from my handbag. "Bernice brought these to me." I handed them to him. "She said she found them earlier today—in a hidden compartment in her husband's valise."

Silently, he read them. He then handed them to Dr. Tate.

"This must be the threat Mr. Baxter mentioned in his letter to me," I said. "And Bernice is clearly still in danger."

"Agreed," Clayton said.

"Do you have any idea who might have sent them?" the doctor asked.

"Maybe." I darted a look at Clayton, expecting him to shut me down, but he simply folded his arms across his chest again. This time, I took his silence as a sign for me to continue.

"On a separate occasion, Bernice told us that her husband and Sarah Redhawk had an affair. Miss Redhawk herself also confirmed this."

"So, she just offered this information? About her affair with Baxter?" Clayton asked, his annoyance making itself clear again.

"I—I may have asked her about it."

Clenching his jaw, he shook his head. He was frustrated with me, but he hadn't made a move to throw me out yet. Inwardly, I smiled with satisfaction. I was bringing important information, and he couldn't deny it.

"Go on," Dr. Tate encouraged.

"Miss Redhawk claims she broke off the affair when she suspected Mr. Baxter had stolen a particular artifact, one that was precious to her family—a medicine pouch containing the feathers of the now extinct Shokawia bird." I held up the blue feather. "This was found in one of the letters, indicating she could be the sender."

Clayton reached out and took it from me. "That does seem plausible," he said—with a little reluctance.

"But I have something else that needs to come into consideration." I held up the journal. "I believe Simon Graves is in love—perhaps obsessed—with Bernice Baxter. He also has expressed resentment about Mr. Baxter having taken credit for some of his work. And, based on what I've found, it seems he was secretly discrediting Mr. Baxter's work—and Eleanor Reynolds knew about it. You can see it here in his journal."

Clayton let out an exasperated sigh. "And, just exactly how did you get this journal?"

"Mr. Brooks gave it to me," I answered, looking him square in those impossibly blue eyes.

"Mr. Brooks? How did he——?"

"They were having drinks the other night at the Bella. Mr. Graves was in his cups and left it behind."

His left eyebrow arched, a clear sign of his skepticism. "And why would Atticus Brooks—your sworn enemy—hand this over to you?"

"It seems he's trying to get in my good graces. He needs a favor."

Clayton leafed through the journal and then stopped, obviously having found the incriminating entries. The doctor and I waited in silence while he read.

"If Graves is in love with Bernice, then why would he be a threat to her?" he asked.

"That's what I thought, too," I said. "So, even though he had a strong motive for killing Mr. Baxter, it didn't quite add up that Mr. Graves was his killer. But, then I found this. It was tucked inside the journal." I handed him the note.

He rubbed the stubble on his chin. "E.R. Eleanor Reynolds."

"Exactly!" I exclaimed, unable to hide my excitement.

He looked over at Dr. Tate. "If you are correct, and the two victims died from the same thing, most likely by the same hand, it doesn't add up that Graves is the killer, because Bernice Baxter provided an alibi for him. And someone who saw them working together around the time of Baxter's death corroborated it."

"Constance Chatterley didn't know how long Simon Graves and Bernice were at the exhibit hall that night. She left at around midnight," I said.

Clayton turned his icy blue gaze on me. "How'd you know it was——" he shook his head. "Never mind. I don't

253

want to know. Besides, there were others that saw them together as well during that time."

After a minute, he closed the journal, took the letters back from Dr. Tate, and then raised his eyes to meet mine. "This is good, Arabella," he said quietly. "Thanks for bringing it to me."

Having expected nothing but cool indifference, or even hostility from him, my mouth nearly dropped open with surprise.

"You're—you're welcome," I stammered, my heart lifting with his appreciation. Feeling a little more emboldened, I turned to the doctor.

"I believe you were about to tell me about how one would come into contact with Aquamortin?" I asked, quickly casting a glance at Clayton, who, this time, didn't discourage my inquiry. I suppressed a smile. He couldn't deny that I had a knack for detective work—even though he didn't seem to want to admit it for some reason.

"I believe it comes from a specific type of clay—Rudrassite clay. However, it's not native to this region. The red clay found here is Adobe, which owes its reddish-brown color to its high iron oxide content—and it's not inherently toxic."

"Where does this Rudrassite clay come from?"

"It's found in parts of South America," Clayton said. "It's used for pottery, but it's also dried and ground down into a powder—to be used in paint pigments."

Paint pigments? Alarm bells suddenly went off in my head.

"Oh, my goodness," I said, "I have something else to tell you."

Clayton let go a sigh. "Why doesn't that surprise me?"

Chapter Thirty-Nine

Clayton looked at me expectantly. He'd just thanked me for bringing him the journal and the letters, which I found encouraging, but once again, his mood had changed. I couldn't blame him. I was outright defying his authority by continuing my investigations—but the truth of the matter was, once I got started, it was very difficult for me to stop. I didn't know if it was a blessing or a curse.

"What is it you have to say, Mrs. Pryce?" Dr. Tate encouraged.

I glanced back at Clayton who gestured with a wave of his hand that I continue.

"I think I may know where this Aquamortin came from. Miss Redhawk uses a particularly vibrant red paint in her artwork. She said the pigment came from South America, and it contains special powers."

The doctor pushed his spectacles further up the bridge of his nose. "You don't say?"

"The powder on Miss Reynolds' face?" I asked. "Did it contain this Aquamortin?"

"Yes. There were also traces of it inside the blowgun you gave to Deputy Fleming."

"So, what you are saying is that Miss Reynolds inhaled the substance? Someone blew it into her face with the blowgun?" I asked.

"There was bruising on her arms and shoulders," he said. "And her left hip."

I played a version of the scenario in my mind, speaking it out loud. "So, someone—in this case, Sarah Redhawk—followed her into the woods—"

"But why was Miss Reynolds in the woods so late at night?" The doctor interjected.

"I've been thinking about that, ever since Arabella told the deputy she had a source that witnessed her going out there." Clayton turned his gaze toward me, the edge in his voice returning. "And, by the way, I'll need the name of that source. Who was it?"

My heart skipped a beat. How could I tell him about Percival? "They—they requested to stay anonymous," I stammered. "I gave my word to keep their confidence."

He narrowed his eyes at me, but thankfully, continued with his thought. "The Noya'Keen encampment is out that way. She might have been going there for the night."

"All right," I said, ignoring his ire and continuing with my previous thought. "So, Miss Reynolds makes her way to the encampment, hears something behind her, turns to see the person—Miss Redhawk—following her. She startles and then trips backward over the stone, falls and lands on her hip—"

"Which would have knocked the fight out of her," the doctor added. "Giving the perpetrator the opportunity to hold her down and blow the red powder into her face."

"But how was it administered to Warren Baxter?"

Clayton said. "There were no traces of this powdered clay on his face—or even his clothing."

And then suddenly I remembered what I'd found in Mr. Baxter's study.

"The pipe!" I shouted.

"What pipe?" Clayton looked at me like I'd lost my wits.

I bit my lip, suddenly realizing I'd have to divulge the fact that I took the pipe from Mr. Baxter's suite.

"Mr. Baxter's smoking pipe," I said, somewhat timidly. "There was a red residue around the bowl."

His eyes narrowed once again. "How do you know this?"

"I, well, I—saw it."

"After his death?"

I swallowed. "Yes."

"How? How did you see this residue?" His gaze bored into mine. "Arabella?"

I knew I had to tell him. "I—I may have the pipe in my possession."

The muscles of his jaw tensed. "Why?"

"I—I found it."

"You found it? Where?"

I considered making up a story about finding it in the Bella, or perhaps some other place where Mr. Baxter might have dropped it, but looking into those sea swept eyes, my heart stuttered. Lying to him would make everything we once shared a farce, and I found I couldn't do it. I squeezed my eyes shut. "In his study."

I waited for the tirade, but it didn't come. Cautiously, I opened my eyes.

"How did you get into the—?" His mouth dropped

open as if a realization dawned. "So, this is also how you knew about the symbol on the door?"

"Yes, well, I—"

He held up a hand. "I think it's better if I don't know."

I gave him a weak smile. "Perhaps."

The doctor cut in. "If the Rudrassite clay was mixed into Baxter's tobacco, or if the bowl of the pipe was laced with it and he smoked it, it most definitely would have killed him. I'd have to examine the pipe to be certain it's the same substance."

"It's in my suite," I said. "But there is also something else you should know."

"Is this something I *want* to know?" Clayton asked, a flicker of caution in his eyes.

"Yes, don't worry," I said with a smile. "Miss Redhawk confirmed she went to Mr. Baxter's suite after the lecture. Bernice answered the door and told her he wasn't there. What if Miss Redhawk returned after Bernice went to the exhibit hall with Mr. Graves, and somehow got into the suite and placed the powdered clay in the pipe? Her belief that he stole a precious family artifact—which resulted in her father's death—coupled with her feelings of betrayal and disillusionment in his character, establishes motive. The red paint in her possession is the means, and her presence near the crime scene—corroborated by Bernice and Mr. Brooks, provides opportunity—which also means ..."

"She could have been the one who carved the symbol into the door to cast suspicion upon Eleanor Reynolds," Clayton said.

"Yes!" I said. "Michael Two Trees told me that the symbol had meaning for both the Tavani and the Noya'-Keen—so Sarah Redhawk would be familiar with it. She and Eleanor Reynolds were definitely at odds over the Tavani land in question."

"Sounds like I need to bring her in," Clayton said. "I'll see if she's at the hotel—and I'll also need to collect Mr. Baxter's pipe from you."

He opened the door and held it for me as we walked out onto the porch.

"This is nice," I said, looking back at him with a smile, hoping he wasn't completely furious with me for my persistence in pursuing my investigations. But how could he be? I'd brought him vital information. And maybe I'd just broken through the block of ice he'd build up around himself with my findings. Or perhaps he'd gotten past whatever had been bothering him before?

"What's nice?"

I shrugged. "You, know. Us. Working together, again."

He pulled the brim of his hat further down over his eyes. "I'm just following a lead, Arabella."

"Which I provided," I reminded him.

"Yeah, all right. Which you provided. But it doesn't mean we're working together."

Chapter Forty

We walked to the hotel in an uncomfortable silence. Clayton was right beside me, yet he felt a million miles away. I considered asking him again why he was so distant, but something told me that pushing might shut him out entirely. Despite the silence, there was a glimmer of our old teamwork, and that gave me a flicker of hope—though for what, I wasn't sure. Who was the woman he'd held in his arms? And what did she mean to him?

We arrived at the hotel to find the coach parked out front. Mr. Ellis stood by one of the two gray horses hitched to it, adjusting the blinkers on its bridle.

"Ellis." Clayton quietly greeted him with a nod.

"Hello, sheriff, Mrs. Pryce."

"Is everything all right?" I asked him.

"Yes, ma'am. Just busy helping the outta town folks get to the train station."

I offered him a gracious smile. "Thank you, Mr. Ellis." With only two days left until the festival ended, people would soon begin drifting out of town and back to their daily lives.

We entered the lobby of the hotel to find it quieter than it had been earlier in the week. At the reception desk, Mr. Pettyjohn assisted several guests, who were waiting in line to check out. Clarence and Mr. Johns were toting several pieces of luggage to the front doors to load onto the hotel coach, or the guests' private carriages.

"Mr. Pettyjohn, have you seen Miss Redhawk?" the sheriff asked him.

He shook his head. "No, but I've been rather busy here at the desk."

As we climbed the stairs to my suite, the sounds of children's laughter and pounding footsteps echoed from above. Just as we reached the first landing, three children came hurtling down, squealing with delight. One of them collided with me, and before I could react, I was tumbling backward. Panic surged through me as I flailed for something—anything—to stop the fall, my stomach lurching as the stairs loomed behind me. Then, just as suddenly, I was caught, cocooned securely in Clayton's arms.

"Sorry, ma'am!" One of the children called out as they continued their boisterous play. A woman came rushing down the stairs, and seeing my precarious position, her eyes widened as she realized what had transpired.

"Oh, my goodness!" Her hand covered her mouth in mortification. "I am so sorry about my children. Are you all right?"

Clayton righted me onto my feet on the landing, his hands still encircling my arms.

"Yes, yes, I'm fine," I managed to say, my heart pounding with adrenaline.

"They are so naughty!" she said. "Again, I'm very sorry. Are you sure you're all right?"

"Yes, don't worry yourself about it," I said, catching my breath. "Children will be children."

She gave me a quick smile and then hurried after her charges.

I placed my hands on my chest, trying to steady myself. I realized Clayton had not let go of me. I turned around and our eyes met. My breath froze as he looked down at me with that familiar, heart-pounding, sea-swept gaze.

"Thank you," I said, my voice barely a whisper.

He didn't respond, but continued to look deep into my eyes—so deep I felt as if I'd never take another breath again.

Finally, his hands released me and his gaze dropped to the floor, leaving me feeling empty and bereft.

"I'll get Baxter's pipe and be on my way. I need to find Miss Redhawk."

"Right. Yes." I continued upstairs like an automaton, my thoughts and emotions wrestling with one another. I could no longer deny my feelings for Clayton. Feelings I'd never had for another man before. Not even my husband. This was not optimal. I was lost. Lost in my ache for him. And I'd never felt so hopeless.

We reached the fourth-floor landing and turned toward my suite, and I stopped short. The door was wide open.

"That's odd." I rushed to the parlor and looked inside. "Cordelia?"

She wasn't there, and neither was Bijou in her little bed. I moved through the parlor and peeked into Cordelia's room, but it was empty as well. Continuing through the bathing room and into my bedroom, I found no sign of either of them.

"She would never leave the door wide open," I said to Clayton as he followed me in.

He shrugged. "Perhaps she thought she'd closed it? She can be a little preoccupied."

"That's true." Cordelia was often in her own head, but she'd never done something like this before.

"Arabella?" A woman's voice called from the parlor. Moments later, Bijou darted into the room, prancing excitedly at my feet. I scooped her up, and Clayton and I headed back to the parlor. There, Cordelia was hanging her hat on the peg beside the one meant for Bijou's leash.

"Oh, there you are." Her gaze bounced between me and the sheriff. "Everything all right?"

"The door was wide open when we got here," I said. "Did you not close it?"

Her face looked stricken. "No—at least I think I closed it. Maybe I didn't. Bijou was in a hurry to go outside. I-I must have left it open. I'm so sorry, Arabella."

"It's all right." I assured her, my heart flooding with relief.

Clayton cleared his throat, obviously eager to be on his way now that we had the mystery of the opened door solved. I went to the table where I'd left the pipe, but it wasn't there.

"Cordelia, did you do something with Mr. Baxter's pipe?" I asked.

"No. I thought you had it."

"I left it right here."

"You're sure?" Clayton asked.

"Positive." I looked at the table again, and then looked all around it, thinking it might have been knocked onto the floor. Getting on my hands and knees, I looked under the table, and under the settee. "It's not here."

"Then we have to assume that someone came into your rooms and took it. Most likely someone who used it to kill Baxter," Clayton said.

Cordelia's brow pressed downward, causing her eyes to scrunch. "What are you talking about?"

I explained about the red clay. "It's often used in pottery, or ground down into a powder to be used as paint."

She gasped. "Sarah Redhawk?"

I nodded.

Clayton headed for the door. "I'd best go find her." He turned and gave me a pointed look. "Be careful, Arabella."

I nodded, and then he left, closing the door behind him. Once again, shutting me out.

Chapter Forty-One

Sleep eluded me. The encounter I'd had with Clayton played over and over in my mind. For the life of me, I couldn't reconcile his behavior. He obviously had no intentions of a romantic relationship with me, given that he'd thought our kiss something to apologize for—that sentiment still felt like a lance driven into my stomach—yet, when he had caught me on the stairs, and we shared that moment ...

But, there was also the matter of the woman. Who was she? If he had feelings for her, then he had some nerve warning me away from what he thought were my romantic intentions toward Theodore Chase.

Although, as much as I didn't want to admit it, his words of warning had taken hold of me. Clayton was, if nothing, cautious, highly aware of potential risks and uncertainties. Setting my hurt feelings aside, he was a responsible and dependable man, always prepared for worst-case scenarios. He was serious, calculating, and logical. He must have had his reasons for warning me away from Mr. Chase.

But was it a warning against physical danger—or the danger that breaks the spirit—or perhaps the heart?

My thoughts then drifted to Sarah Redhawk. Had Clayton found her and taken her in for questioning? Had he arrested her?

As much as I liked the woman, and understood her feelings of betrayal and loss, caused both by Warren Baxter and Eleanor Reynolds, I struggled to think her capable of that kind of vengeance. She'd said she had no violence in her heart, and that the Tavani were a peaceful people. But even Michael Two Trees, who seemed an utterly peace-loving person, said he would do anything to protect what he believed belonged to the Tavani, whether it be lands or artifacts.

And, the red clay she used as a pigment for her art, her admission of being near Warren Baxter's suite at the time of his death, the symbol carved into the door—which could have been Noya'Keen or Tavani—the feather in the letter, and the feathers found near the blowgun were all pieces of evidence pointing directly to Sarah Redhawk. It was undeniable.

I rolled onto my side yet again, trying to get comfortable. Bijou, nestled beside me, let out a small whine, clearly annoyed by the disruption of her sleep. I squeezed my eyes shut, willing away thoughts of Clayton or the murders. Sleep was essential if I had any hope of functioning tomorrow.

Moments later, Bijou leapt off the bed and padded to the door leading to the washroom, scratching at it insistently. I sighed, assuming she wanted to go through to Cordelia's room in search of a quieter spot to sleep. Reluctantly, I got out of bed and opened the door for her.

After what felt like hours, my mind and body finally

surrendered. My thoughts drifted, becoming disjointed and dreamlike, with one fleeting idea dissolving into another. Soon, wakefulness slipped through my fingers like sand, and I was teetering on the edge of sleep—when a *click* brought me back to consciousness.

My eyes fluttered open. Then it happened again. *Click.*

"Percival, is that you?" I said, my voice thick with grogginess. "I thought we agreed you would not come in when I'm sleeping."

There was no answer.

I strained to hear the noise again but after a few minutes of silence, I turned my attentions back to dreamland, which, this time, didn't seem as elusive. My body melted into the bed, and soon my thoughts were dancing into oblivion. A rhythmic sound pervaded my senses and reminded me of something familiar. Breathing.

I opened my eyes again. Yes, there was the unmistakable sound of breathing next to the bed.

"Percival, I thought I told you—" and suddenly, something heavy was covering my face. In the blackness, I thrust out my hands and felt a body, sturdy and solid, leaning over me; arms on either side of me, and hands pressing the heaviness into my face. I was suffocating.

Struggling to fight them off, the heaviness grew more intense. Darkness oozed in around me and my heart pounded frantically in my ears.

And then the sound of something shattering echoed in the room, and the heaviness suddenly left me. I flung the object off my face and sat up, just in time to see a figure retreating through the doorway that led into the hall.

"Arabella, my dear, are you all right?" It was Percival, who was now standing next to the bed.

My heart still racing, I gasped for breath. "I think so," I managed. "Did you see who that was?"

"No, they were wearing a heavy cloak."

My hands scrabbled over the nightstand, searching for the matches I'd left near the oil lamp. Finding them, I quickly lit the wick.

The room was empty, save for Percival's shimmering figure. The door leading to the hallway was open. My gaze drifted to Percival's mirror, which was positioned over the bureau, and then down to the floor, where the crystal vase lay shattered in pieces.

"You broke my vase—again," I said, exasperated. The last time he'd done this was when he tried to scare off Clayton shortly after I'd arrived in town. His attempt had been a complete failure—Clayton, unbothered by anything paranormal, had remained entirely unfazed. The only result of his efforts had been the destruction of a valuable crystal vase.

He shrugged. "How else was I going to scare the person away?"

"Of course, I'm sorry Percival. I'm still a bit rattled."

"Naturally," he said, forgiving me.

"How did they get in here?" I went to the opened door. "I know I locked it when I went to bed." Looking down, I saw a small file lying on the wood floor.

I scooped it up in my fingers. "Someone picked the lock. And they must have done the same in the parlor earlier today. Percival, did you see anyone here this afternoon?"

Leaning against the doorjamb, he lifted his palm and curled his fingers toward his face to examine his fingernails —something he did when expressing boredom, or annoyance. "I was in the attic most of the day. I don't mind telling you, I'll be glad when the festival is over and these infernal people will be gone. It's growing quite tiresome."

"Well, that's not very helpful, Percival. And it's good for business to have so many people in town."

"By people, you mean murderers? Someone just tried to kill you, Arabella, and if it wasn't for my—"

"Thank you, Percival. I'm forever in your debt."

He smiled at the acknowledgement and then peered closer at me. "What's that on your face?"

I left the doorway and hurried to the mirror. Smudges of red streaked my face. It felt gritty under my fingers. As I pulled my hand away, traces of the strange substance clung to my skin. It looked like the same substance that had been on Eleanore Reynolds' face. A sinking feeling hit my stomach. Had I breathed it in? Was it coating my lungs, slowly causing them to fill with fluid, pulling me toward drowning? How long had the doctor said it would take to take effect? An hour? Two?

Cordelia had come through the door leading to the washroom. Bijou, too, scampered in and jumped up on the bed, her button eyes trained on me.

"Arabella, what's going on? I heard a crash."

I looked up at her, holding my fingers up for her to see. My knees turned to water, and I felt as if I might faint. "I— I don't know."

My heart racing, I crumpled and immediately she was at my side. She helped me to the bed and then picked up the pillow. When she saw the red stain, a horrified look crossed her face.

"Someone broke in and tried to smother her with the pillow," Percival said.

"Oh, no! Arabella, did you breathe in the dust?"

My head feeling lighter by the minute, I let out a meek little whine. "I—I'm not sure. I don't remember."

Bijou climbed on my lap to comfort me.

"We need to get Dr. Tate here. And quickly," she said. "But I don't want to leave you alone."

Percival, his reflection with hers in the mirror, laid a hand on her shoulder. She shivered with cold at his icy touch.

"I'll be with her. You go."

She nodded. "I'll hurry."

I took a deep, unsteady breath, testing the clarity in my lungs. Everything felt normal—for now—I told myself, clinging to the thought. But how long would it be before the walls pressed in, leaving me helpless against the darkness?

Chapter Forty-Two

With every precious minute slipping away, I glanced at Percival, who had now taken a seat in the chair beside my bed. His expression was calm, serene, and I took strength in it. Bijou, snuggled in next to me, slept, breathing steadily, calmly.

"What's it like? To die?"

He set his elbows on the arms of the chair and tented his fingers in front of his face. "It's quiet."

"Quiet?"

"Yes. There is a stillness that takes hold of you before you drift off into the ethereal plane."

I imagined myself walking toward a bright light, toward a doorway. What lay behind it? Who would be there? Would I see William?

A trembling overtook me, and my heart was still pounding a staccato in my chest.

"I—I don't feel very still. Can you—can you sense if someone is dying?"

"No, I cannot," he said calmly. "But if you are dying, you have nothing to fear."

He was trying to make me feel better, but I didn't have the heart to tell him he was doing the exact opposite. The lightheadedness returned, and the trembling increased. I lay my head back onto the pillow in an effort to relax, but fear gripped me like a vise. A tear escaped down my cheek. I didn't want to die—not with so much left to accomplish and experience. I wasn't ready yet.

Suddenly, Cordelia burst into the room, the doctor right behind her. Percival vanished from view.

Dr. Tate quickly came to my bedside and pulled a stethoscope from his bag.

"All right, Mrs. Pryce, Miss Danson here has told me what's happened. I'd like to have a listen to your chest."

I wiped the tear away and nodded. Cordelia had climbed onto the bed next to me and took hold of my hand. Hers felt warm to the touch, while mine was as icy as Percival's.

The doctor pressed the cold metal disk onto my chest and listened intently. His thinning hair was mussed from sleep and stuck out at wiry angles. I watched his eyes, which were nestled in a sea of fine wrinkles, as they flitted back and forth with concentration.

He took hold of my arm and helped me to sit. He then set the disk on my back between my shoulder blades. "Three deep breaths, please."

I obeyed, my head spinning with each breath. It was as if I couldn't get enough oxygen into my lungs. Had the Aquamortin started to take effect?

He encouraged me to lie back down, pulled the earpieces from his ears and gave me a wide smile. "You've no cause for worry, Mrs. Pryce—at least where your lungs are concerned."

Cordelia squeezed my hand with both of hers, and I let out a sigh of relief. Sensing our joy, Bijou uncurled herself, and stood up, licking my face.

"You must have been holding your breath when the intruder held the pillow over your face." Dr. Tate took a small cloth from his medical bag. "Which is not uncommon when startled or surprised. But we need to get the powder off your face. Do you have a water pitcher in here?"

I pointed to the bureau. The doctor tip-toed over the broken vase and poured some water on the handkerchief. He then carefully cleaned my upper lip, my cheeks, and my chin.

"We'll have to tell Clay about this," he said, lifting the stained pillow to more closely examine it. He shook his head in disbelief. "You're lucky, Mrs. Pryce. It's a horrible way to die."

"Did the sheriff find Miss Redhawk?" Cordelia asked.

"I'm afraid not. He was out looking for her as late as a few hours ago."

Her eyes opened wide. "So, she could very well have been the intruder."

"It's possible, I suppose," I said. "But she's such a small woman. I'm not sure she would have the strength to pin me down like that."

The doctor removed his glasses, took a handkerchief from his pocket and proceeded to clean them. "She might have been experiencing hysteria, which could have produced a fit of strength."

I tried to recall what my hands had felt as they flailed through the air and clawed at the arms of the person who held the pillow over my face. Had they been the arms of a woman, small and delicate? Or had they been bulkier and firm like a man's?

"I wish I could remember what the person felt like."

The males in question were Simon Graves—in love with Bernice and threatened by Eleanor's plan to expose him, or —and I didn't want to think it—Theodore Chase, Archibald Archer, and Michael Two Trees, all who were threatened by Mr. Baxter's ambitions over the land, and threatened by Miss Reynolds' lobbying with the Native Sovereignty and Fair Treatment League. But the fact remained—it was Sarah Redhawk who possessed the means of the murders, the red clay.

Cordelia squeezed my hand. "Given the evidence we've uncovered so far—and the fact that she has suddenly disappeared, makes it clear enough to me. Sarah Redhawk is the murderer."

I gave her a firm nod. "Then we'll just have to find her."

By the time we were dressed, the first light of dawn was creeping over the mountains, casting a warm, golden glow that slowly chased away the lingering shadows of the dreaded night.

We entered the parlor to find Bijou, waiting at the front door.

"Oh, dear. She needs to go out," Cordelia said.

"We'll just take her with us." I unhooked the leash from the peg next to the door. "Come on, girl."

"Where should we look for Miss Redhawk?" Cordelia asked.

"I think we should start with the General. We need to

check on Bernice—to make sure nothing happened to her last night."

We made our way downstairs. The lobby was still and empty, except for Clarence, who was standing behind the reception desk.

"Morning ma'am," he said quietly.

"Good morning, Clarence. Where is Mr. Pettyjohn?"

"He'll be here in a few minutes. I told him I'd get things started today. He's plumb tuckered out with the festival."

"That's kind of you, Clarence. Mr. Pettyjohn didn't mention anyone suspicious wandering about? Wearing a cloak, perhaps?"

He shook his head. "No ma'am. He didn't say anything like that. Is everything okay?"

I nodded. "Yes. It's fine. Thank you, Clarence."

Once outside, we pulled our coats tighter around us, the chill of the morning intruding upon our warm bodies. We made our way to the General, and passing by the reception desk, gave the sleepy clerk a quick nod before heading to room one-twelve. When we got there, the door was wide open.

With a look of concern on her face, Cordelia swept past me and went into the suite. "Bernice?"

I followed her in. Bernice was standing amidst several opened trunks and other luggage.

"You're leaving?" Cordelia asked.

Bernice folded her hands at her waist. "I'm not comfortable here—given that my life is in danger, and Warren's murderer has not yet been found. Simon and I have decided to go back to South America to continue Warren's work there. Besides, even though we never talked about it, I'm sure it's where Warren would want to be buried."

"But we're pretty certain we've discovered who the murderer is," Cordelia said.

Bernice's face paled, and she reached for the arm of the chair a few feet away from her and gently lowered herself down into it.

"Who?" she asked quietly.

"Sarah Redhawk," Cordelia said.

I then explained all that led us to that conclusion.

Shaking her head, she let out a deep breath. "It's just as I suspected. Although, I did not know about her anger toward Miss Reynolds. But, like I said before, she was obsessed with Warren. She couldn't accept that they were through. That he loved me. Clearly, the woman is mad. I'm sorry you had to go through that, Arabella. I'm glad she's been apprehended."

"Well, we aren't sure she has been," Cordelia said.

"What do you mean?"

"She's missing," I said. "We were just checking to see if she had been here, and to make sure you were safe—which you are, thank goodness. I suppose we should go to the sheriff's office to see if he's found her yet. If he hasn't, we're joining the search."

"You could still be in danger, Bernice," Cordelia added. "It might be best if you stay put for now."

Bernice let out a shaky breath. "I see."

I glanced around, looking for Bijou. She had made her way to the other side of the room and was sniffing around a small end table. I worried she was looking for a place to relieve herself. Because of the coolness of the morning she had been reluctant to piddle since we'd left the Arabella. And, in our haste to check on Bernice, we hadn't given her ample time to adjust to the cold and attend to her business. By now, I was sure her little bladder was about to burst.

"Bijou, come here," I said.

"But you two are obviously in danger as well," Bernice said. "Do you think it's wise to go out looking for her?"

"We'll be careful," I assured her. "The more people we have out searching, the more likely it is we'll find her."

"You should stay here," Cordelia said to her. "In your suite. Until she's found."

Bernice looked around the room at all of her belongings. "Well, all right. Simon should be here any minute. He was going to help me pack. I'll let him know what you've told me."

"We should go," I said to Cordelia. Bijou had wandered to another part of the room. "Bijou, come!" I said, a little more forcefully. Finally, she obeyed and followed us out the door.

We hurried back through the lobby and out onto the street. A few shop-keepers had made their way outside and were setting up their tables and displays out in front of their businesses for the festivities of the day.

In the distance, I spotted a horse and rider making their way down the street toward the sheriff's office. As the horse veered to avoid a dog in the road, I realized there were actually two people riding tandem. I quickly recognized the horse as Queenie, the sheriff's mount, and the person seated behind him—a woman with long, dark hair.

"Well, what do you know?" I said. "It looks like Clayton has Sarah Redhawk."

Chapter Forty-Three

We picked up our pace until I felt a tugging at the leash. Bijou was trying to stop near a bush.

"Oh, you poor thing," I said, feeling bad for her. She'd been so patient. "Hold up, Cordelia."

Soon we were on our way again. The sheriff assisted Miss Redhawk, who was handcuffed, as she dismounted the horse. He then secured Queenie at the hitching rail and took Miss Redhawk into the jail. As we neared the hitching rail, he re-emerged to fill a hay bag for Queenie. I assumed he'd put Miss Redhawk in one of the cells.

"You found her," I said, somewhat out of breath by the time we got there.

"She was headed out of town." He was untying a large Indian print carpet bag from the saddle.

"When was this? How far had she gone?" I asked, trying to piece together the timing of when she had broken into my room.

"About an hour ago—why?"

"We think she tried to kill Arabella," Cordelia blurted.

He stopped what he was doing. "What!?"

I explained what had happened. "When she failed, she probably decided to leave town. We were getting too close for comfort."

"Well, we've got her now," he said, relief evident in his voice.

"What's going to happen?" I asked. "Are you charging her?"

"I have a few more questions, but most likely yes. I have to go." He tilted his head toward the door.

"Of course," I said. "I'm glad you found her."

He gave a quick nod. "I'm glad you're okay."

We lingered in awkward silence for a few moments, and I found myself half-hoping he'd invite us in. I was eager to hear what Miss Redhawk had to say for herself. If Clayton hadn't put up a wall between us, I might have been able to observe—if not take part—in his questioning. But he had, and that left me, literally, standing on the outside.

"Let's go, Arabella," Cordelia said.

Clayton tipped his hat to us and went into the office. Through the opened door I heard Miss Redhawk's voice claim in protest, "You have to believe me, I didn't kill anyone!"

He closed the door, shutting out any other conversation from within.

Cordelia turned to me with a smile. "Well, you've done it again, Arabella. You've helped solve two more murders in La Plata Springs."

"You were with me every step of the way," I said absently. I should have felt victorious, but I didn't.

"I didn't do much," she said.

I remembered she had said she was going to the library to research the Shokawia bird.

279

"What did you find out about the bird? Any idea what it looked like?"

She nodded. "Yes. It's a non-raptor. A song-bird with bright blue, yellow and red plumage."

"Hmm," I murmured. The feathers I'd seen adorned in Sarah Redhawk's hair and hanging from her earlobes certainly matched that description, but I wondered about the other feathers we had discovered.

"The feathers that were found near the blowgun were blue—but I wouldn't say they were bright blue. Nor was the feather that fell out of the letter."

"A bird's plumage is layered," she said. "Those feathers could have been from the layer between the down and the contour feathers."

"I suppose."

As we passed by Archer's Mercantile, Mr. Emerson stepped outside and greeted us with one of his rare smiles.

"You two are out early. Sally told me you were investigating the murders. How's it going?"

"It seems the culprit has been found," I said.

"Really? That's wonderful news. Who was it?"

Cordelia and I shared a glance—she obviously felt as uncomfortable as I did in revealing her identity. She was much beloved in town.

"Please keep it quiet for now, Mr. Emerson, but it was Sarah Redhawk."

His eyes widened in surprise. "Sarah? Are you sure?"

I nodded. "I'm afraid so. The evidence really stacked up against her."

He shook his head. "What a shame. She seemed so nice. Always friendly. At first, I kind of thought it might have been that Graves fellow."

"Oh really? Why is that?"

He gave a slight shrug. "Can't really say. It was just a feeling. He rubbed me the wrong way. But, when the sheriff asked me about him and the widow being at the exhibit hall on the night of Baxter's murder, it was clear it wasn't him, 'cause he didn't leave till I had to lock up at around one o'clock—"

Something struck me as odd about that statement. "He didn't leave till you locked up, but wasn't Bernice Baxter with him?"

He nodded. "She was, but she left about a half hour before he did."

"Really," I said. That would mean she left at around twelve-thirty. Thirty minutes after Constance had left the hall. "Did you tell the sheriff that? About her leaving?"

"I didn't remember until just now. I was dog tired that night."

"I'm sure you were," I said.

He gave a shrug of his shoulders. "Well, I guess it doesn't matter anymore."

I nodded in agreement. The evidence against Miss Redhawk was indisputable.

"Have a nice day, Mr. Emerson."

We waved goodbye and continued down the street. I was lost in my thoughts, replaying everything about the case in my head.

"You're awfully quiet," Cordelia said, with a hint of concern in her voice. "You aren't feeling short of breath or anything?"

"What? No, no." I waved a hand in the air. "I'm fine, Cordelia. Don't worry. The doctor said I wasn't in any danger."

"I know. I was just making sure. That was really frightening."

"It was." I took hold of her hand. "But, I'm not going anywhere."

Bijou dragged her feet, tugging on the leash. I looked back to see her hesitating at the shrubbery. "My goodness, girl, again?"

We waited while she relieved herself. Once she finished, she hopped back into action, but the leash was wound around her paw, giving her a comical limp.

"Oh, dear." I chuckled and bent down to untangle her leg when I noticed something odd. Her paws were stained with something red. I blinked, to make sure I was seeing it right. What had she gotten into? The color was eerily reminiscent of the red clay containing Aquamortin.

"What's the matter, Arabella?" Cordelia said. She knelt down, and I pointed to Bijou's paws. "Why are they red?"

And suddenly I remembered. She had been sniffing around a table in Bernice's suite.

"Oh, no! Bijou!" I cried, my heart going into spasms. I took hold of her face to quickly examine it. The ends of her ears were stained red, but there was nothing around her nose and mouth, which gave me a modicum of hope that she had inhaled none of the substance.

"Cordelia, get Bijou to the doctor's office, immediately."

"What? What's wrong, Arabella?"

"I think she got into some Rudrassite clay."

"But, where? What about you?"

I picked up my beloved little dog, gave her a quick hug, and then shoved her into Cordelia's arms. "I'll explain later —just get her to Dr. Tate, and then tell the sheriff to meet me at the General."

Holding back tears, I turned and ran down the street, hoping it wasn't the last time I'd see my dearest little friend in the entire world.

Chapter Forty-Four

When I reached the General, I had to zig-zag my way around two carriages that had parked out front. Several people were standing on the front steps, waiting for their luggage to be loaded onto the waiting conveyances.

The lobby was now full of activity, with people checking out of the hotel and others standing around, talking and enjoying themselves. I hustled through the crowd and made my way to room one-twelve. The door was now closed, so I knocked.

"Bernice? It's Arabella. I need to speak with you."

I listened, waiting to hear footsteps, but there was nothing. I knocked again. "Bernice?"

After the third try, I turned the knob to find, to my relief, it wasn't locked, so I let myself in. Bernice wasn't there, only two remaining partially packed trunks.

My eyes scanned the room and settled on the fireplace mantel. The small, chipped red clay pot lay on its side—and appeared even more broken than before. Half of it was missing.

Near the fireplace was the side table that had so capti-
vated Bijou. I went over to it and looked around it, tipping it
on two of its legs to look beneath it.

A silver object, partially hidden under the settee next to
it, caught my eye. I knelt down for a closer look. It was the
silver brooch Bernice often wore pinned at her throat—a
bird in flight, maybe a hawk or falcon, with its wings
elegantly folded back. I picked it up, and as I examined it
further, I noticed tiny hinges along the wings, revealing it to
be a locket. The wings served as a delicate clasp, sealing
whatever secrets might be hidden inside, which in this
instance was a red, powdery dust—which had partially
spilled onto the floor.

Then, things fell into place—details reaching all the way
back to the beginning. Cordelia's unease over what
happened to Anna, Bernice's fixation on Warren Baxter,
and then Anna's pregnancy. How Bernice had not only
arranged Anna's abortion, but had also withheld care afterward. Bernice had told Cordelia that she and Warren were
practically estranged, revealing her jealousy over his affairs,
especially with Sarah Redhawk. And since the day Warren
had died, Bernice had been subtly casting blame in Sarah's
direction.

Having worked so closely with her husband and
Simon Graves, Bernice would undoubtedly have been
familiar with the Tavani and Noya'Keen warning symbol
—the Eye of the Ancestors. She would also have been
aware of Baxter's disputes with Mr. Archer and Mr.
Chase, as well as any tensions between the two men themselves. Furthermore, she had admitted knowing about Mr.
Graves' resentment toward Baxter for undermining him,
and possibly even Miss Reynolds' blackmailing of him.
Bernice and Mr. Graves appeared to have a very close

relationship. Could it be that he was complicit in the murders with her?

Also, there were so many convenient suspects. Even the deceased Miss Reynolds, who had been at odds with all the parties involved.

I thought back to the letters she'd brought me, and snippets of them flashed before me.

Now, Warren, it's your turn to feel the emptiness of loss.

And,

You took what was mine, and now you will lose something in return. Tell your lady-bird to guard herself well, for birds of prey seek vengeance.

Sarah Redhawk identified with the sacred bird that meant so much to her family. The Shokawia bird. A non-raptor. Unlike the hawk or falcon, which was a bird of prey. This could be read as an outright threat to Sarah Redhawk.

I had to share this with Clayton. My earlier suspicion was true. He had the wrong person in custody!

Carefully, I pressed down on the wings, closing the locket. Pulling a handkerchief from my dress pocket, I wrapped the brooch inside and then rose to leave.

When I saw Bernice standing in the doorway.

"What are you doing, Arabella?" she asked coolly, her tone as sharp as the look in her eyes. Gone was the grieving, fearful widow—what stood before me now was someone unrecognizable. Her once-soft features had sharpened, her cheekbones stark and angular, her gaze like flint, cold and unyielding. Her dress, the sapphire one I'd seen her wearing before, seemed to heighten the effect, its rich hue casting a striking contrast against her hardened expression. A chill ran through me and I fought an instinctive urge to step back, as if I'd just come face to face with evil itself. She was between me and the door. I had to, somehow, get around her.

I drew on my acting training to keep a neutral mask, holding steady eye contact and controlling my breathing to hide any trace of fear.

"I was just coming in to tell you that the sheriff has apprehended and arrested Sarah Redhawk."

"Really?" she said with a slight upturning of her lips. "Well, I'm glad to hear it."

I stepped toward her and a little off to the side in an effort to get her to mimic me, leaving room for me to skirt around her. I nodded toward the remaining trunks. "I see you've decided to leave, anyway. Before she was found." A tear at the hem of her dress drew my gaze. An odd detail given how meticulously she usually presented herself.

She blinked at me and gave me an impatient wave of her hand.

"I cannot live my life in fear, Arabella. And now it seems I won't have to. Thanks to your good detective work."

I clenched the handkerchief tightly in my hands as her gaze dropped to my fingers, her eyes narrowing. Slowly, her eyes flicked back up to mine, sharp and unblinking. "What is that you're holding?"

I looked down, horrified to see a visible smear of the red powder on the handkerchief.

"Oh, it's nothing. I had the sniffles." I moved to slip it into my pocket, but she lunged forward, snatching it from my hand. She unfolded the fabric, and the silver bird caught the sunlight streaming through the window, glinting brightly.

Her gaze met mine again, those flint-like eyes making the blood in my veins freeze.

"It's over, Bernice," I said. "The sheriff will be here at any moment."

With her other hand, she slowly reached into her dress pocket and pulled out a small handgun. A Derringer, by the look of it. She pointed it directly at my face.

She laughed. "Nice try. You just told me he arrested Sarah Redhawk for the murder of my husband."

Another chilling realization struck. "You've been planning this all along. You knew Sarah Redhawk was here in La Plata Springs. It was you who wrote those threating letters to your husband—and the letters you claim to have found in his valise. You planned to kill your husband and frame her for his murder."

She raised a brow. "Brava, Arabella. You've found me out. The harlot deserved it. I thought Warren would never want to see her again after she accused him of stealing that silly medicine pouch—but he didn't want to give her up."

"Did he steal it?" I asked, my eyes trained on the barrel of the pistol and my heart in my throat.

She smirked. "It may have ended up in our collection. Briefly."

"You stole it, didn't you? Then you spread the rumors he took it. You wanted to turn them against each other."

Her lips thinned into a firm line. "She stole my husband's heart. Turnabout is fair play. So now, finally, the man-stealer will get her just desserts. And, as for you," she clicked her tongue and playfully shook her finger at me, "the brilliant Arabella Pryce—I knew you'd figure it out. So, you need to be eliminated."

"You tried to kill me. Just like you killed your husband and Eleanor Reynolds."

She let go an irritated breath. "Yes. But, I failed. It won't happen again."

Something in the doorway caught my eye, and I was about to let out a sigh of relief that Clayton had come, but my heart sank when I realized it was only Simon Graves.

"Bernice?" Simon moved toward her. "What are you doing? What's going on?"

"Close the door, Simon. Mrs. Pryce was trying to kill me. Luckily, I was able to get the gun away from her."

He did what she said, and then turned to look at me with what seemed to be confusion, but I couldn't be sure.

"It's not true, Mr. Graves. She's the one who killed Warren Baxter—and Eleanor Reynolds. Or do you already know that? Were you in on it with her?"

His mouth dropped open, and he looked from me to Bernice, and then back to me again. "No. No! I didn't kill anyone, and neither did Bernice," he said. "This is outrageous!"

Bernice glared at me with a satisfied smile on her face.

"She used Rudrassite clay from South America to kill her victims," I said. "Surely, you are familiar with it. You have two or three pots made from it in your collection, don't you?" My gaze traveled to the pot on the bureau. "Like that one."

"Yes, I'm familiar with it," he said, "but what does it have to do with murder?"

I blinked. "You really don't know?"

His eyes were wide with bewilderment. "No! What are you talking about?"

"Don't listen to her, Simon," she said.

"Rudrassite clay contains a chemical called Aquamortin," I continued. "If inhaled, it causes the lungs to fill with fluid. I'm guessing she broke that pot, ground the shard to a fine powder and laced Mr. Baxter's pipe with it. Later, she filled a blowgun with it and blew the contents into Miss Reynolds' face, killing her."

A look of mortification swept across his face before he turned slowly to Bernice. "A blowgun? The blowgun from my personal collection? The one you asked me for? You said it was being shipped to Chicago for the exposition. Is this true? Did you kill Warren and Eleanor?"

She sighed impatiently. "We need to go," she said to him. "Didn't you say the train is leaving in thirty minutes?"

"Bernice, did you do this terrible thing?" he asked, with genuine hurt in his voice.

"She couldn't stand it that her husband was still in love with Sarah Redhawk," I said. "Or, perhaps, she was angry that he was still in love with Anna."

Bernice's head swiveled slowly in my direction, and her eyes grew wide with rage. "Anna? How did you know about —?" Realization dawned on her face. "Oh—oh, of course. Cordelia told you. The girl never could keep her mouth shut. And she was under the spell of that witch, Anna, too. She never deserved Warren! He pined for her like a love-sick girl. It was disgusting."

"Who's Anna?" Simon said with an edge of desperation in his voice.

"Simon, I'm leaving," she said. "Are you coming with me, or are you going to stay here and pay for the crime of killing Mrs. Pryce?"

"What!?" he shouted. "Are you mad?"

It was then I knew the poor young man had been in love with a mirage—an idea of who he thought Bernice was, and I was seeing his whole world crumble before him.

She leveled the gun at him. "Are you coming or not?"

He held his hands up and backed away from her,

shaking his head, his face contorted in disappointment. "I—I can't believe it." He raked his hands through his hair. "You killed—"

"Shut up!" She jabbed the barrel of the gun toward his face. Then, on the turn of a dime, her features softened. "Don't you see? I did it for us, Simon," she said, her voice dripping with a slow, honeyed sweetness. "I did it for you. I know how much it pained you that Warren took credit for all of your hard work. He didn't deserve you. Now, we can work together—be together. I know it's what you want."

She moved closer to him, looking up into his face with confidence in her powers of seduction. "The collection is worth thousands. And I have a private buyer for the most valuable piece of all. The Tavani Star Amulet. We'll be rich... Together."

Simon's face twisted in a mix of confusion and disbelief, brows knitted tightly together as his mouth opened slightly, as if he wanted to say something but couldn't find the words. His eyes darted from side to side, searching for something—a rationale, perhaps—that wasn't there.

"You'd sell everything Warren—and I—spent years of dedicated pursuit to obtain?" he finally blurted out. "You know how much I was against Warren selling the Sun Stone. It was more than just a means of monetary gain—it was a link to the past. A connection to a culture I intend to keep studying—a culture I greatly respect."

The feigned tenderness dropped from her face. "You're far too sentimental, my dear. Why cling to objects that only gather dust? Isn't it the thrill of the hunt that truly captivates you? Just think of the treasures we have yet to find—"

"Stop!" He raised his hands in protest. "This is utter insanity!"

A sense of relief that he wasn't completely prey to her manipulations washed over me.

She stepped back, leveling the gun at his chest. With her body angled just enough away from me, I seized the moment, kicking her sharply in the hip and knocking her off balance. The gun fired, and Simon crumpled to the ground, clutching his chest. She quickly regained her footing, her eyes flashing as she swung the gun back in my direction.

"Now, look at what you made me do."

Simon writhed on the floor, groaning, his face wrenched in agony.

"This has to stop, Bernice," I said. "If you shoot me, too, and then leave town, it will be obvious to everyone that you killed your husband and Eleanor Reynolds. One of the suspects is in jail, and the other two, Mr. Archer and Mr. Chase, are meeting with the land commissioner." I lied to buy myself time. "You are the only one left who could have killed me. Well, you and Simon."

A familiar sensation washed over me, one I'd often felt on stage—a flow state where I sank so deeply into character that the scripted lines faded away, replaced effortlessly by my own words. It was a moment of pure inspiration, with new ideas blossoming effortlessly in my mind.

Struck with this sensation, I was emboldened to ignore the pistol aimed at me and moved closer to her. "But, listen—he's probably going to die." I pointed at Simon. "If you let me go, we can tell the sheriff that it was Simon who killed them. The sheriff already knows he was in love with you—was obsessed with you—and how your husband was standing in his way. He wrote about it in his journal."

Simon, still conscious—but barely, made a grunting noise from the floor. My heart ached for him, but I continued. "And Eleanor Reynolds was blackmailing him. Did you know that?"

Her eyes shifted to Simon, and then back to me. I could tell she hadn't been privy to this. I went on.

"Apparently, he was publishing critical reviews of your husband anonymously, but somehow, Eleanor found out and was threatening to expose him unless he returned the Sun Stone to her. Since it was already sold, it only makes sense he would want her silenced. The sheriff knows this, too."

She paced the room, but kept the pistol aimed at me. Why hadn't Clayton shown up yet?

"I'm impressed," she said. "You really are good at this detective stuff."

I shrugged. "It's a gift."

"And you can convince the sheriff of this? That Simon killed them both?" she asked, considering my proposal.

"He's like putty in my hands," I said with a confidence that was a complete farce.

Still aiming the gun at me, she sidestepped over to her handbag, which was sitting on an armchair. With one hand, she opened the clasp and tucked the handkerchief with the falcon locket inside.

"But before you go, I would like to know why you killed Miss Reynolds. I haven't been able to piece that one together quite yet."

She snapped the handbag shut again. "She knew I killed Warren."

I raised a brow. "How?" I glanced down at Simon, who had gone still, and his face had turned a sickly shade of white. Was he dead?

"Right after the lecture, I went back to the suite," she said. "I knew Warren would be out late."

"You went back there to carve the symbol in the door—and lace his pipe with the Rudrassite clay."

She nodded. "Somehow, Eleanor got into the suite—she must have followed me."

"Was this after, or before, you carved the Eye of the Ancestors symbol into the door?"

Her jaw tightened. "After. She didn't see the carving in the door, but she did see me using a pestle and mortar—"

"To grind down the broken piece from the clay pot into a fine dust," I added. "Did she know what you were doing?"

She shook her head. "She didn't figure it out until later. After the doctor said what had happened to Warren—that he was mysteriously asphyxiated. She, being Noya'Keen, knew all about the Rudrassite clay. Her ancestors had used it to kill their enemies. Anyway, she came to me and told me she knew what I had done—and that she wouldn't tell if I could get the Sun Stone back for her."

"So, you agreed to do it."

"Yes. But I knew it would be impossible. The man who bought it is somewhere in Europe. So, I had to take care of the problem of Eleanor Reynolds." Her lips curled into a chilling smile. "Just like I'll have to take care of the problem of Arabella Pryce."

She took a step closer, the barrel of the gun practically pressing against my nose. My heart spasmed, my breath catching in my chest.

"B-but, we talked about this—we had a plan," I stammered.

"I've decided I don't like your plan. After I kill you, I'll put the gun in Simon's hand. I like that plan better." Her finger tightened on the trigger, knuckles turning white as she applied pressure. I squeezed my eyes shut, bracing for the blast. But I heard a hollow click. The gun was empty. The

Derringer only held two bullets, and apparently, one of them had already been used.

From the floor, Simon let out an enraged growl, clawing at her skirt, throwing her off balance. Seizing the moment, I shoved her with all my strength, sending her sprawling face-first to the ground. I lunged forward, pinning her arms behind her back, but before I could secure her, she twisted around, hands flying to my throat. She wrestled me onto my back, leaning in hard, pressing down with all her weight, choking the air out of me.

The memory of that smothering pillow rushed over me, panic mingling with a surge of anger. I managed to grab a handful of her hair, yanking with all my strength, throwing her off balance just enough to break free. Gasping, I scrambled to my feet just as Clayton burst through the door.

"Stay right there, Mrs. Baxter!" he ordered, his pistol leveled at her.

I nearly sank to the ground with relief. "Thank God you're here," I said with a ragged breath. "It's about bloody time!"

Chapter Forty-Five

The crowd, having risen to their feet, thundered their applause as the actors came out onto the stage for the final bow.

"That was really wonderful," Cordelia said, her voice raised above the din.

"Andrew's debut was a rousing success!" I said back.

Bijou, at my feet, barked happily. Luckily, she had experienced no ill effects from the Rudrassite clay and Dr. Tate had given her a clean bill of health.

Finally, the applause died down—only until Andrew Archer stepped out onto the stage, and a cacophony of clapping and shouting filled the air once again. He basked in the glory, his face beaming with pride. After a few moments, he put his hands out, tamping at the air, gesturing for the crowd to settle down.

"Thank you very much," he said with a bow once they had quieted. "But I couldn't have done this without such a wonderful cast and crew. This has been a dream come true for me."

More shouts and applause filled the theater once again. After they had settled, he continued.

"Bridging Worlds was my attempt to reenact the complex and multifaceted relationship between the early settlers of La Plata Springs—of which my uncle Mr. Archibald Archer played a huge role with his founding of the mines—" he held his hand out to Mr. Archer, who seated in the front row with me, Mr. Chase, Cordelia, Michael Two Trees and Sarah Redhawk, stood up and took a bow while the audience applauded. "—and the Tavani, who had been here for centuries," he continued, and then acknowledged Michael Two Trees and Sarah Redhawk, who also stood to receive praise.

"It's a complex and multifaced relationship, but through it all, we have fostered cooperation, cultural exchanges, and respect for one another."

Many in the audience nodded their heads in agreement.

"But, there was one person in particular who was passionate about her heritage, both Tavani and Noya'Keen —" his gaze traveled to the back of the theater where Tayanakwa stood in his heavy wool coat and flat-brimmed hat, before he continued "—and passionate about equality for her people whom I must acknowledge, and that was Eleanor Reynolds. May she rest in peace."

There were several murmurs from the crowd.

"For those who knew her, you might agree that Eleanor rarely showed individual displays of affection, yet there was never any question about her dedication to her people— both tribes she belonged to. She dreamed of a haven for the Noya'Keen and unity between them and the Tavani, striving always for a peaceful coexistence between the tribes and those of us who came here to settle on their land. And it is for this reason that I would like to dedicate Bridging Worlds to the memory of our good friend, Eleanor Reynolds."

Again, the crowd erupted into applause.

"There are a few more people I would like to mention," Andrew said above the noise. Soon, the crowd quieted.

"I'd like to recognize everyone who worked tirelessly to make the Historic and Cultural Festival a success. The townsfolk, shopkeepers, hoteliers—" he paused, offering me a quick smile, "the artifact collectors, and lecturers who devoted themselves to educating us about the native peoples of this land, including Michael Two Trees and Mr. Simon Graves, who is currently recovering from an injury. I must also acknowledge the late Mr. Warren Baxter, who contributed much to our understanding of indigenous cultures, even if some of his methods have recently come into question. May he, too, rest in peace."

Another murmur rippled through the audience.

"And finally, I'd like to extend my deepest gratitude to my friend and mentor—a person who has helped me recognize my potential and encouraged me to pursue my dreams. And someone to whom we all owe a debt of gratitude for her remarkable detective skills: Mrs. Arabella Pryce!"

Another round of applause filled the theater as I sat there, stunned, mouth agape as faces beamed my way. People stood, their applause swelling to a roar that left me overwhelmed. I glanced over at Archibald Archer, who applauded politely, but remained in his seat. Mr. Chase, however, was on his feet, shouting, "Brava! Brava!"

Cordelia jabbed me with her elbow. "Stand up," she whispered loudly.

Slowly, I rose to my feet. Tears pricked at the back of my eyes as I turned and waved to the audience. My heart swelled with gratitude for these wonderful townspeople, who, I could scarcely believe it, had become my friends. True friends. Friends who appreciated me, not for my fame, or my money, or my acting talent, but who appreciated me for what I had done for their community. And I appreciated them for what they had done for me; accepted me for who I was, flaws and all.

Later that night, the Bella was full to capacity with folks celebrating the end of the festival. I sat alone in my booth, sipping champagne, delighting in the merriment. My bliss was soon interrupted when I noticed Atticus Brooks making his way over to me.

"Well, my dear, you never fail to disappoint," he said, sliding onto the seat across from me.

I gave him a tight smile. "Good evening, Mr. Brooks. What can I do for you?"

He shrugged. "I was just coming over to congratulate you on solving the murders of Mr. Baxter and Miss Reynolds."

I gave him a nod. "Thank you."

"I suppose you found the journal helpful?" He gave me a smarmy smile.

I chuckled. "Not really. Simon Graves was innocent of the crimes. It actually only clouded the waters, if I'm honest."

His smile faded. "That was not my intention."

I sighed. "I know. And I appreciate the gesture. You were trying to help—in your way." I still didn't trust him, but he had made an effort. "I'll mention your good faith effort to Mr. Rankin. But, I'm afraid that's all I can do at this point. Given our past... differences … I'm not sure I'm ready to endorse you completely."

A tightness surrounded his eyes, but he gave me a polite nod. "That will have to do, then. For now."

I blinked at him, but offered no more conversation.

"Well, I bid you goodnight," he said, understanding my subtle hint that I no longer required his company.

When he left, my gaze drifted to a table near the bar where Theodore Chase and Archibald Archer were sitting with a group of well-dressed men. Catching my eye, Mr. Chase picked up his whisky, excused himself, and came over to my booth.

"Arabella, you are radiant as ever," he said, the dimples in his cheeks deepening with a wide smile. "May I join you?"

I gestured my acceptance with a nod and he slid in across from me. "You really are something else, Mrs. Pryce."

I arched a brow. "Is that a compliment?"

His dark eyes sparkled with a charming hint of mischief that made my breath catch. "The highest compliment. You're smart, courageous, talented, generous, beautiful, and quite the detective. Well done on uncovering that it was Bernice Baxter behind the murders."

I regarded him thoughtfully for a moment. "Thank you. And, speaking of Mrs. Baxter, what exactly was the relationship between you two?"

He blinked. "I'm not sure I know what you mean."

I smiled. "You two seemed rather cozy at times."

He shook his head. "Nonsense. She was the wife of someone I was trying to do business with. I find it's best to be cordial to all parties involved. After her husband passed, I felt sorry for her—until you uncovered the truth. Now the woman will get exactly what she deserves. I must hand it to you, Arabella. I never would have guessed her capable of murder. It's you this town has to thank. And, it's yet just one more reason I want you to be my partner."

I laughed off the statement, still not sure how I felt about the whole proposition—or his continued boldness. I liked the fact that he was so direct, but it also made me a little uncomfortable.

"There's something else I want to know," I said, changing the subject.

"Anything," he said, opening his hands wide.

"What was the trouble between Mr. Baxter, Mr. Archer, and you? I understand there was quite a disagreement between you three at Kitty's place."

I took a sip of my champagne, waiting for his answer. I thought I should know, seeing as if I were to agree to Mr. Chase's plan of the sister hotels, I would be caught in the middle of this proposed development deal between Mr. Chase and Mr. Archer.

With his hand perched over the top of his whisky glass, he slowly spun it around. "Baxter told Archibald that if he didn't get the land for his museum, he would go to the authorities with information he'd learned about Archibald under reporting the amount of ore he was extracting because he didn't want to pay taxes on it."

"Oh, so it wasn't about the safety of the mines," I mused. "And is this true? Was he under reporting?"

Mr. Chase tapped his fingers on the table. "I don't know. All these mine owners are always going to get away with what they can. It's not the most ethical practice in the world, but it's not unusual."

"I see. And you? How did this affect you and your relationship with Mr. Archer?"

He gave me a lopsided grin. "How, exactly, did you know about this little disagreement?"

"I have my sources," I said, not willing to give them away. "You were saying?"

"Baxter came to me and convinced me that Archibald was going to back out of our deal to give him the land for his museum. He said he had some leverage with Archer and would use it if I gave him the capital to build the museum."

"The business with the mines?" I interjected.

He nodded. "That and the Tavani Star Amulet. Archibald wanted it for his display case at the hotel—to make it more of a tourist attraction."

"So Baxter had all the power," I said.

"Right."

I cocked my head. "You and Mr. Archer seem to be on friendly terms again."

"After Baxter's death, we got together and talked. It was then we realized he was playing us against each other. Archibald had no intentions of backing out of our deal, and he still plans to use his influence with the railroad to get the train depot in Addison as well."

"How do you know?" I asked, my skepticism rearing its head.

He tilted his head toward the table with Mr. Archer and his companions. "The gentleman on his right is from the land commission, and the one on his left is one of his old pals from the railroad."

"Ah," I said. "That's good."

"Yes, and I really should get back to them," He finished the rest of his whisky.

"Mr. Chase," I said, wanting to delay him. "I have something else I want to ask you about."

"I can spare another moment for you." He gave me that dazzling smile again.

"What is this I've heard about your involvement with a Cattle Syndicate—possible illegal involvement pertaining to the exploitation of ranchers?"

Stunned, the smile faded. "What exactly have you heard?"

"I asked you first," I said flatly.

He picked up the empty glass and twirled it in his fingers again. With a sigh that hinted of annoyance, he obliged me. "The syndicate was formed under legal contracts, approved by the territory's officials. Every step we took was recorded, with settlements, grazing rights, and taxes paid by the book. I wouldn't risk my reputation on a scheme that wasn't legitimate."

He held my gaze steady, barely blinking. A man who was lying might look away or flinch. I was inclined to believe him.

"I see. Thank you for clearing that up for me," I said with a gracious nod.

"Any time." He released the glass and held his hands out in an open gesture. "Anything for you."

"Oh, and one more thing," I said. "As you know, Mr. Archer has always wanted the Arabella. What does he think about the prospect of you taking half-ownership of it with me?"

He let out a chuckle. "Archibald doesn't like it—but he doesn't have a vote. He knows our hotels will be good for the economy, and his name is still going to be all over this town, Addison as well. He'll get all the glory any man could want. Now, as much as I hate to leave your exceptional company, I have business to attend to."

He slipped out of the booth, and standing next to me,

bent down to take my hand. "I know you still need time to think about my proposal, Arabella. Just let me know when you are ready." His lips lightly brushed the top of my hand and he bade me goodnight.

I watched him return to his companions, my mind drifting over everything that had unfolded over the past week—and especially this evening, where I'd felt a genuine warmth in contributing something meaningful to this town and being so appreciated by everyone. The opportunity Mr. Chase presented would allow me to put down real roots here in a place I was, despite myself, beginning to love. I felt a sense of hope I hadn't felt since William died.

In just a few short months, I'd gain my full inheritance —a milestone that now felt like so much more than a financial windfall. I smiled to myself, a deep, satisfied smile, proud of how far I'd come. I'd learned to navigate a life that once felt foreign, breathed new life into the hotel, forged friendships I hadn't known I needed, and uncovered a knack for helping others through my unexpected talent for investigation.

This town had changed me, perhaps as much as I'd changed it. And as I looked out over the landscape of my new life, I felt the thrill of belonging and purpose settle in my bones. For the first time since I arrived, I knew I was exactly where I was meant to be.

Chapter Forty-Six

"How are you feeling?" I asked Mr. Graves as his eyes fluttered open.

At Dr. Tate's suggestion, we had set him up in a room at the Arabella to recover from his gunshot wound. The doctor had also stated that someone needed to be at his bedside for the next forty-eight hours, and now, it was my turn, having relieved Cordelia an hour ago.

"I feel like I've been shot," he replied groggily, but with a slight upturn of his lips.

"The doctor says you were very lucky. Based on your injury, you shouldn't have lived."

"Must be the power of the Tavani Star Amulet," he said with a sarcastic smirk.

I cocked my head, surprised at his statement. "You don't share Mr. Baxter's belief that it has magical powers?"

"Oh, I believe it does—when it is in the hands of the people with whom it belongs. It needs to be here in this area. Where it came from."

"From what I understand, Mr. Baxter had promised it to

Mr. Archer—in exchange for some land to build his museum."

He scoffed, and then winced, laying a hand on his wound. "That doesn't surprise me—that he promised the amulet to him, but Baxter was never going to let it go."

"Because he was ill, and he believed it would cure him?"

Mr. Graves nodded.

"Are you still going to keep it in the collection?" I asked.

"I'm going to give it to Michael Two Trees. He's the leader of the Tavani in this area, so it only makes sense that it should be with him. For the good of the tribe."

Relieved, I nodded. "That's a very noble thing to do."

"We can learn so much about the past through artifacts." He smiled. "And it's important to share those artifacts with the wider world, so that we can understand and appreciate cultures that differ from our own. But when it comes to artifacts that have deep spiritual significance to a tribe—they need to remain with them, through the generations. Like the Star Amulet."

"And the Sun Stone?" I added.

"Yes. And the Sun Stone. I want to see it returned to the Noya'Keen where it belongs. Once I've recovered, I'll do everything I can to track it down." A determined light flickered in his eyes. "Both Michael Two Trees and Tayanakwa have offered their support—not just of me, but of each other. I believe they're trying to mend the age-old rift between their peoples."

I nodded, the weight of his words settling over me. "Solidarity."

He gave a nod.

"But isn't the Sun Stone in the hands of a private owner in Europe who paid a handsome sum for it? Would you be able to afford to buy it back? Do you think they would let it go?"

He shrugged. "I don't know. But, it's important to me to try." His face blanched, and it was clear the effort of speaking had worn him out.

"You need your rest. Why don't you go back to sleep?"

He muttered under his breath, "I was such a fool. How could I have been so blind to who she really was? I was ready to turn on my friend and mentor for her. I'm so ashamed."

I took hold of his hand. "Love makes us think and do rash things sometimes. Don't be too hard on yourself."

His eyes drifted shut, unable to stay open any longer, and within moments, his breathing deepened. He'd fallen asleep.

The door creaked open, and Sally Dean came in for her shift.

"How's he doing?" she asked.

I rose from my seat and gave her a smile. "He's going to be all right. In time."

I went back to my suite to find Cordelia pacing in the parlor, a look of grave concern on her face. Bijou, sitting in her little bed, turned her head from side to side, watching her walk back and forth in front of the fireplace.

"Cordelia, what's wrong?"

She rubbed a hand across her forehead. "Have you seen Percival? I can't find him anywhere."

"No, I haven't seen him. Not for a while." It was rather unusual that he wasn't present in the suite when one or both of us were here. "Perhaps he's gone down to his spot by the river. He'd said he was tired of the crowds here at the hotel."

She set her hands on her hips. "But the festival is over, and most of the guests have checked out."

"True. What do you need him for?"

"I want to know about Anna. And Mr. Baxter. Are they together now?"

"Oh, of course. That would be good to know."

She shook her head. "I wish I had done something when Anna was in such trouble. I shouldn't have listened to Bernice. I should have insisted on getting care for Anna. I had my suspicions about Bernice's character—why didn't I listen to my intuition?" She bit at a fingernail.

"Bernice left much damage in her wake," I mused, thinking about what Simon had just told me. "There's a special place in hell for people like her."

The room suddenly chilled and the spicy fragrance of pipe smoke filled the air.

"My goodness, Arabella. Such uncharitable thoughts. That's not like you." Percival's translucent form appeared on the settee. Bijou, still in her bed, let out a yip.

"I know—but Bernice Baxter ruined so many lives. It's hard for me to reconcile."

"Me, too," Cordelia said. "Speaking of which—Percival, have you seen Anna or Mr. Baxter?"

He dipped his head in a gracious nod. "I have. They are not yet together, divided by separate planes—but they have had glimpses of one another. It will take time, but rest assured, they will be united."

"And their baby?" she asked.

"The child is already in the afterlife. Infants' innocence gives them a direct line to final tranquility. But once Anna and Warren find their way to each other, they will also find their way to their child."

Cordelia flopped down onto the armchair and let out a heavy sigh. Tears sprang to her eyes, and she covered her mouth with a trembling hand. Bijou sprang from her bed and jumped up onto her lap, ready to comfort.

"Oh, my dear!" I knelt down in front of her, setting my hands on her knees. "It's going to be all right. We've succeeded in leading them toward one another. They will find peace."

"Yes, I know. I'm just so relieved. I feel like I've been holding my breath ever since Bernice and Mr. Baxter came to town."

"It's been a whirlwind of a week," I agreed, rising to my feet.

Percival blew a series of smoke rings into the air. "But all is well in the end. And, despite everything that's happened, I think the festival was a success."

"Everyone seemed to have a wonderful time," Cordelia said.. "At least everyone at the hotel."

Percival tamped the ash out of his pipe and it sparkled in the air and then vanished. "I'm curious. Have you accepted Mr. Chase's proposal?"

"Proposal?" Cordelia said, a look of shock crossing her features.

"Not that kind of proposal. You know, the proposal of the sister hotels," I reminded her.

"Oh, yes, that." She frowned.

"You don't think it is a good idea?"

She tilted her head, considering. "I'm not sure. I like things the way they are. Besides, aren't you worried about people discovering your secret—your clairvoyance—and the rumors of the hotel being haunted? You've said you always lived in fear of it."

"It is an old fear—and one that is deeply ingrained. But I'm coming to agree with Percival—and Mr. Chase, the spirit world fascinates people. I don't plan on promoting my abilities, or that a ghost—"

Percival's brows shot up with annoyance.

"I mean, or that a *spirit* resides here, but if people are curious enough to book a room here to find out, it will only help with business. It could be beneficial."

"I promise not to be too frightening," Percival said with a smile. "But I'll give the occasional thrill to the curious."

We all laughed at the sentiment.

Suddenly, there was a quiet knock at the door.

"I'll get it," I said.

Percival heaved a sigh. "And we were having such fun!" He then popped out of sight.

I opened the door to find Clayton standing there, and my heart gave such a jolt it nearly knocked me off my feet.

Chapter Forty-Seven

"Clayton? How may I help you?"

How may I help you? What a ridiculous thing to say!

"Can I have a word?" He glanced in and gave Cordelia a nod in greeting. "Alone?"

"Oh—yes, of course—come in."

"I was just leaving," Cordelia rose from the chair. "I'll fetch some soup for Mr. Graves." She brushed past us and I closed the door.

"Please, take a seat." I gestured toward the settee.

I took the armchair perpendicular to it.

Sitting down, he swept his hat off his head and ran a hand through his thick, sandy hair. "I haven't had a chance to see if you are all right. You know—after the incident with Bernice Baxter."

"I'm fine. And grateful for Mr. Graves. He was very brave."

"As are you," he said with a faint smile. "You really are something special."

My heart fluttered with his praise, and hope bloomed in my chest that we might be friends again.

"You solved this one on your own," he continued. "Despite my asking you not to be involved." He stared at me, and there was something in his gaze that held a trace of sorrow—or perhaps pain.

"I'm sorry if I stepped on your toes. It's just that, well, I was doing it for Cordelia and—"

He held up a hand to silence me. "You are only doing what comes naturally to you. You have a gift for getting to the truth, and it was wrong of me to try to stop you. It's just that—" His gaze fell to the hat in his hands, his fingers gripping the brim as if searching for the right words. "I can't do this anymore."

I blinked, confused at his statement. "Do what anymore?"

He gazed up at me again. "This. Us."

My heart sank. "Oh. I see."

The image of the woman at the train station, wrapped in his arms, had lingered in my mind, unsettling and persistent. I hesitated before finally asking, "Is she someone special?"

His brow furrowed. "What?"

"The woman I saw in your arms at the train station. Who is she?"

He let out an amused chuckle. "She's my sister-in-law. My late wife's sister."

I nodded. "And... she's important to you?" I ventured cautiously, unsure if I truly wanted to hear the answer.

"Yes. But not in the way you're thinking she is—but because she is a friend. She's had a difficult time since—since Elizabeth died. I've been spending some time with her

—trying to help her. But I'm afraid I've just made things worse."

"How so?"

He shook his head. "Because I can't seem to move past it. The guilt."

"What do you mean?"

He hesitated, threading the brim of his hat between his fingers. "It's because of me she's dead," he finally said.

I blinked in surprise, momentarily at a loss for words.

"I used to work in Colorado Springs," he continued. "That's where we were living before we—I—came here. There were a series of murders at one of the brothels in town. Elizabeth, occasionally, liked to help me with certain cases—like you do. She came up with the idea that if she got a job at the brothel—as a maid, not a—"

"Yes, I understand," I said, reassuring him. "She went undercover."

"Right. I was against it at first, but she insisted. She was like you in that way—strong willed, persistent, stubborn—"

I held up a hand. "I get the idea."

"Anyway. She was found out, and it resulted in—" he stopped short, holding his hand over his mouth, as if he couldn't let the words out.

"Her death," I finished for him.

"The killer got away. After her burial, I went after him. I looked for him for a long time, only to discover he died in a shootout in Kansas." He went silent, his eyes still trained on his hat. "Why did I wait? Why didn't I track him down immediately? I was so lost in my grief, I was paralyzed. But I should have gone after him sooner. It should have been me that killed him."

Choked with emotion, I cleared my throat. "I'm so sorry

that happened to your wife. Elizabeth." Saying her name felt odd, but comforting at the same time.

"I haven't been able to forgive myself for it." He finally raised his eyes to meet mine. They were so full of hurt and despair it nearly broke my heart.

"Arabella, I never thought I would ever have feelings for another woman. Until you came to La Plata Springs."

"You mean until you fished me out of the river?" I said, laughing softly to lighten the mood, remembering how when he first gazed at me with those fathomless blue eyes, I could barely speak.

He laughed, too. "Yeah. Then." His mood sobered again. "I can't let myself fall for you, Arabella. I have too many unresolved feelings about Elizabeth. And I can't have you work with me. I can't be responsible for something happening to you."

"But Clayton, I can take care of my—"

He shook his head. "I'm thinking of moving to New Mexico territory. There is not enough law enforcement there, and I could be useful."

I could barely comprehend the thought. "But you are useful here. La Plata Springs needs you. I need—"

I stopped, shocked at what was about to come out of my mouth, and so was he, by the look on his face. We stared at one another, both of us unable to speak. Like so many times before, looking into those beautiful blue eyes, I could barely breathe. His gaze slid from mine and refocused on his hat. He cleared his throat.

"Deputy Fleming is green, but he's getting the knack of detective work. He actually figured out the murderer was Bernice Baxter, probably about the same time you did."

"Oh? How so?"

"When we were searching for Miss Redhawk, we split

up. He returned to the theater—back to where you discovered Eleanor Reynolds' body. There, he found a piece of fabric caught on a bush. He immediately recognized it as the same color and texture as one of Mrs. Baxter's garments."

Remembering the torn hem of Bernice's dress, I sucked in a breath. "Was it a deep blue? Sapphire?"

He nodded. "That kind of attention to detail is crucial to an investigation. He's a lot more savvy than I'd thought before. He's smart. A quick learner. He'll make mistakes—Lord knows I have—but he's determined to keep La Plata Springs safe. And he has the support of Archibald Archer. He'll be fine."

I had to agree, but my heart grew heavier by the minute. A weighty silence settled between us. While I was glad Clayton was finally recognizing Deputy Fleming's potential, the realization carried a bittersweet edge—it meant he had no hesitation about leaving.

He finally spoke, his voice cutting through the quiet. "So, have you accepted Chase's marriage proposal?"

Still reeling from my errant emotions, I stared at him blankly, and then the question finally sunk in.

"What?" I choked out. "Marriage proposal?"

"I heard you two at the Bella. I was sitting in the next booth."

"No! He wasn't proposing marriage. He was talking about the business proposal. The sister hotels."

A look of relief swept over his features. "Oh. Of course." A faint blush colored his cheeks. "So—have you accepted?"

I shook my head. "Not yet. I'm still thinking about it."

He nodded. "Be careful, Arabella. The man's reputation is—dubious."

"I know about the Cattle Syndicate," I said. "He explained it all to me. I'm very familiar with being a person of note who is subject to unfavorable rumors about them, Clayton. And, the one thing I've always wanted is for people to see beneath the façade. Beneath the rumors. So, I'm going to do the same for him."

His jaw tightened. "I'm not sure that's wise. The man is cunning. Don't be charmed by his swagger, Arabella. I don't want you to get hurt."

I scoffed. He'd just told me he had feelings for me, feelings that he couldn't handle—and that because of those feelings, he was leaving town. Like a coward. And, yet, he was still trying to tell me what to do?

I stiffened my spine. "Maybe it's not me you're worried about getting hurt. Maybe it's yourself."

His gaze met mine, steady and cool, as if he were grappling with unspoken words. But instead of responding, he abruptly rose to his feet and set his hat back on his head.

"I should go."

"I think that's best," I said, anger bubbling up inside. Yet, beneath it, I wished he would stay, wished he would wrap me in his arms, pull me close and kiss me as if he never wanted to let go.

He made for the door and I followed him. When he opened it, Clarence was standing there, about to knock.

"A telegram for you, Mrs. Pryce," he said.

Without another word, or even a look back, Clayton left.

To keep myself from crying, I snatched the telegram out of Clarence's hands, tore it open, and read it. The world shifted beneath my feet and I faltered. Clarence took hold of both of my elbows to steady me.

My hands trembled so violently I could barely make out

the words on the telegram as I reread it. The paper crinkled under my grip, a fragile thing against the storm rising in my chest. Tears brimmed over, and I could no longer hold back my resolve. Tears for Clayton. Tears for what I'd just read:

Dear Mrs. Pryce,
A man showed up at the theater claiming to be your father. He said his
name was Mr. Wendell Milton...

"This isn't right," I whispered, looking up at Clarence. "That's not his name."

The boy blinked in confusion, his head tilting as if to piece together my meaning. But my thoughts were racing too fast to explain, tumbling over fragments of memories. But then something dawned on me. Wendell was my father's middle name—Alistaire Wendell Janes. Milton had been my grandmother's maiden name.

Why would my father use an altered name? Unless ... unless this person wasn't my father at all. Could it be a coincidence?

I turned back to the telegram, devouring the words.

He said it was of the utmost urgency that he speak with you, and that
he was in grave danger. I asked him to come into my office for some tea
—he really was in such a state—but he refused. When I told him you
were in Colorado, he asked that I write down your whereabouts. I
excused myself to get some paper, but when I returned, he was gone.
It's been five days, and he hasn't returned. I thought you should know.

A knot of dread coiled in my stomach. Five days. Five days to disappear—or worse.

"Ma'am, do you need to sit down?" Clarence asked

316

cautiously, likely fearing I'd collapse into a heap right there on the carpet.

"No," I said, shaking my head fiercely. "No, Clarence, sitting is the last thing I need to do."

I held up the telegram, its edges quivering between my fingers. "This is about my father," I said, my voice raw but resolute. "And it seems he's in terrible trouble. What I need to do now—" I folded the telegram with renewed determination. "—is whatever it takes to help him."

This man claiming to be my father had reopened the wound of his leaving, but despite the uncertainty, my love for him ran too deep to ignore his plea—I would step into the unknown—no matter the cost.

vinci-books.com/ThePryceOfFame

Her past just demanded a ransom.

When a ransom note reveals her estranged father is in danger, actress-turned-hotelier Arabella Pryce leaves 1887 Colorado for Gilded Age New York. Accused in a literary forgery scandal, she must untangle secrets and betrayal before time—and the truth—destroy everything.

Turn the page for a free preview…

The Pryce of Fame: Chapter One

LA PLATA SPRINGS, COLORADO

June 2, 1887

The beveled glass doors into the hotel lobby swung open, ushering in a rush of cool, pine-scented air and a man with a tapestried carpetbag in hand.

I quickly closed the financial ledger, straightened my shoulders, and summoned a well-practiced smile to offer the guest. He paused for a moment, taking in the surroundings: the polished brass fixtures, the plush Queen Anne furnishings, and the faint scent of bright yellow chocolate flowers drifting from a vase on the desk.

"Good day, sir." I greeted him with a honeyed voice to disguise the mild panic in my chest created by what I'd seen, or rather had not seen, in the ledger.

"Welcome to The Arabella Hotel. Might I offer you a room—or perhaps you'd like to enjoy some refreshment in the saloon?"

He frowned. "Just need a room for the night. Nothing fancy."

"Of course." I reached behind me, plucking a key from the pigeonhole. After jotting the room number in the registration book, I slid it, along with the pen, across the counter to the man.

His smile conveyed the weariness I'd so often seen in travelers. He wrote his name next to the room number.

"Here at the Arabella, we pride ourselves on offering every guest the utmost comfort." I took the book back. "I trust you'll have a pleasant stay. Take some time to enjoy the wonderful food and drink we offer at the Bella Saloon, just through that door." I pointed to the singular wood and beveled glass door on the opposite side of the room. "That will be two dollars, payable now or upon departure."

As if on cue, Clarence, the freckled-faced young bellhop, emerged from the hallway behind the reception desk. At seeing our guest, his eyes widened in a mixture of apology and embarrassment, his hand hovering over his mouth as he chewed furiously, probably having just visited the kitchen for breakfast.

I handed him the key with a faintly amused smile. "Clarence, please show this gentleman to room two-twenty."

Still chewing, he swallowed so hard his eyes watered. "Yes, ma'am."

The man slapped two silver dollars on the counter, tipped his hat curtly before following Clarence upstairs. As soon as the man was out of sight, I let my shoulders sag.

I opened the registration book and once again let my gaze fall on the sparse entries scattered across the page. Business had been unusually slow since the Historical and Cultural Festival wrapped up a few weeks ago—a curious slump, considering this was typically the height of tourist season. With the hotel nearly empty, the profits I'd been counting on seemed to vanish.

Was the General facing the same struggle? Or could this downturn be linked to the General itself—Mr. Archibald Archer's newly refurbished hotel, drawing away the clientele I'd once relied upon?

I closed the book with a sharp snap, forcing myself to breathe. I couldn't afford to show my doubts, not even to myself. Besides, I had other equally serious problems to contend with.

I pulled the letter from my dress pocket. It was from Mr. Blackthorn, my theater manager, and it had arrived two weeks ago.

My eyes scanned the page:

. . . A man showed up at the theater claiming to be your father. He said his name was Mr. Wendell Milton . . .

. . . He stated it was of the utmost urgency that he speak with you and claimed he was in grave danger. I asked him to come into my office for some tea—he really was in such a state—but he refused. When I told him you were in Colorado, he asked me to write down exactly where. I excused myself to get paper, but when I returned, he was gone. It's been five days, and he hasn't returned. I thought you should know . . .

Suddenly, a coolness settled in the air, carrying the rich, mellow scent of toasted tobacco—warm and slightly leathery, laced with hints of vanilla and cinnamon.

Percival materialized on the corner of the reception desk, his translucent frame haloed by pipe smoke. Dressed in his burgundy velvet dressing gown, he exhaled a smoke ring, his Byronically moody eyes fixed on me with faint amusement.

"Oh, my." He pursed his lips in a playful pout. "I recognize that look."

"What look?" I shot back, slightly perturbed at his comment.

"The worried one. What's got you so troubled?"

Shaking my head, I sighed and shoved the paper back into my pocket. "What hasn't got me troubled?" I answered rhetorically. "Suddenly, everything seems to be going wrong."

His gaze traveled through the lobby and then back to the desk, as if he was looking for something, or someone.

"And why are you behind the reception desk and not Pettyjohn? I thought he deemed it unseemly for the hotel proprietor to be laboring as a clerk?"

I shrugged. "He does. But he is in bed with a cold. Cordelia and I are sharing the job in shifts. She's taken Bijou for a walk to get the mail and to run a few errands for me."

"Ah, well then, tell me, my dear, what's got you in such a downhearted frame of mind?" His gaze traveled to my pocket. "The business with your father?"

I bit my lip, not really wanting to discuss the matter. My father left twenty-six years ago, trading my mother and me for a wealthy benefactress who promised to make him a celebrated poet. I'd spent years burying the pain, only for his sudden reappearance to rip it all open again. And now, he was in danger—or so he claimed—and gone once more.

Percival blew another smoke ring into the air. "Do you plan to go to New York?"

"To what end?" I said, exasperated. "He's vanished. He doesn't know where I am because he left before Mr. Blackthorn could tell him, and I have no idea where he might be. For all I know, he could have gone back to Europe."

323

A flicker of thoughtfulness crossed his features. "It's quite mysterious."

I hesitated to bring up another complication—the fact that my leaving Colorado, and the hotel, would most certainly jeopardize my inheritance. My late husband's will had stipulated that I remain in La Plata Springs for a full year. While that year had passed, I'd had to borrow against the estate to restore the hotel to its former glory. Unable to repay those debts financially, I'd agreed to extend my stay as repayment—a decision that had turned out to be practical, given that the refurbishment was still unfinished. Three more months stood between me and securing my inheritance—a substantial sum I could ill afford to lose.

"Besides," I continued. "I'm not sure my father deserves my help."

Cordelia came around the corner by way of the kitchen, her tone sharp as she interjected, "He's caused you so much pain and suffering—abandoning you like that, and at such a tender age."

"You're back," I said. "Where's Bijou?"

"Lottie prepared a special breakfast for her this morning."

Percival harrumphed. "That dog eats better than any human."

"Lottie has a sweet spot in her heart for Bijou." Cordelia's smile conveyed the fact that she did, too.

I sighed. "She does, but I'm not sure it's good for Bijou to eat such rich food. She's become rather plump."

"I'll tell Lottie to scale back on the 'special' meals." Cordelia offered a reassuring glance before steering the conversation back. "You were discussing your father. Did you receive more news?"

"No. It's just the news I have received of him is weighing heavily on me."

"I know you're concerned about him, but if he truly wanted to contact you, why didn't he wait for Mr. Blackthorn to write down your address?"

I could tell she was trying to make me see reason, but her words cut deep. I had always clung to the dream of my father returning to me—even for just a moment—but he had not tried to do so in all these years, and that wound was harder to bear than I cared to admit.

"Besides," she continued, "newspapers across the country have featured your life in Colorado. He must know you're in La Plata Springs."

I nodded, but the pang of worry persisted. He mentioned he was in trouble. "What if something has happened to him? Yes, his leaving hurt me deeply, and it changed my life forever. I've often wondered what would have happened if he had stayed. Perhaps my mother wouldn't have driven me so hard to succeed on the stage. We might have been a normal family. Yet, despite what he did, I still do not wish him any harm or ill will. Though his actions angered and saddened me, I have never stopped loving him."

Percival laid his transparent hand on my shoulder to comfort me, and I took solace in the coolness that cascaded down my arm.

"I'm sorry." Cordelia's expression softened. "I know you do. And this is very distressing for you. What can we do to help?"

I shrugged my shoulders. "I'm not sure there's anything we can do. My only option is to await further news—if there is any."

The Pryce of Fame: Chapter Two

Cordelia took over at the reception desk, giving me a chance to retreat to my office in the hotel's annex. The annex consisted of several charming one-, two-, and three-room dwellings arranged in a U-shape around a grassy courtyard. It served as a small community within the hotel, housing some of the permanent residents and traveling miners and their families. While it functioned as a world of its own, the care and maintenance of the annex ultimately fell to me as the hotel's proprietor.

Craving a cup of Earl Grey, I lit a cozy fire in the wood-burning stove and placed the kettle on one of its burners. I then settled into one of the two armchairs placed in front of it. As I waited for the familiar rumble of boiling water, I unfolded the business contract Mr. Theodore Chase had recently offered me and read. The words seemed to blur together, their meaning slipping through my grasp. The dense legal jargon was overwhelming, and the more I tried to decipher it, the more my head spun.

A sharp clearing of someone's throat jolted me from my muddled thoughts.

Kitty Carlisle, the madam of the two-story bordello—the largest building in the annex—and the manager of the Bella Saloon, stood in the doorway.

"You look like someone just handed you a map with no compass." Her voice was firm, with a slight cutting edge to it, and her piercing dark eyes carried a glint of hardness. A pointed look from her could send the toughest cowboy running with his tail between his legs.

Kitty was a force to be reckoned with, but beneath her formidable exterior lay a surprising kindness that occasionally revealed itself.

I tilted my head toward the contract. "It rather feels like that."

"Anything I can do to help?"

"I'm afraid not. I need to handle this myself."

Kitty shrugged. "Suit yourself."

I had kept the stipulation in my late husband William's will—and Mr. Chase's proposal—a secret from everyone except Cordelia, who knew everything, and Percival, who was only aware of the business offer. Sheriff Clayton Marshall also knew about the business proposal and had taken it upon himself to warn me against any involvement with Mr. Chase. But he had no right to do so, especially now that the nature of our relationship had changed.

"I was wondering if you had a minute to discuss the Bella?" Kitty continued.

"Of course." I gestured to the chair opposite mine. "Please have a seat. I was just about to have some tea. May I offer you a cup?"

"Yes, thank you."

The tea kettle shook, signaling the water was ready.

After a few moments, we both had a steaming cup of the bergamot-infused beverage.

As she sipped her tea, I noticed a weariness in Kitty's eyes. The woman worked hard managing the bordello and the saloon—and though she seemed strong as a bear, she wasn't a young woman, and I wondered if it had all become too much for her.

She lowered her teacup and then met my gaze. "I'll just give it to you straight, Arabella. The Bella's numbers are down. Seems we're in a bit of a dry spell. And it doesn't help that we still owe the supplier for the spirits we had to purchase for the Cultural Festival."

I bit my lip, the weight of the news sinking in. This was the last thing I wanted to hear—it felt like I'd never get ahead of the mounting bills. Still, the one glimmer of hope in all of this was my impending inheritance—but that wouldn't come for a few months. I forced a smile. "I'm sure things will turn around soon."

She took a deep breath and let it out. "The supplier is getting impatient. I'm afraid he's going to come after us—legally, of course. And there's another thing."

A cloud of dread enveloped me. "What other thing?"

"I heard Archibald is adding a saloon to his hotel—and bringing in entertainment, no less. I'm afraid he's planning to give the Arabella a run for her money."

A sharp pang of anxiety coiled in my chest. "I see."

So, this was his retaliation. Denied the chance at owner-ship of the Arabella (because I refused to sell to him as per further instruction in my late husband's will), Archibald Archer was determined to outshine me instead.

The Arabella had always been the crown jewel of La Plata Springs—a gleaming tribute to William and Percival's shared vision of greatness—and it fell to me to see that vision realized. And truth be told, I had no intention of letting anyone outshine me.

Suddenly, the situation with my father loomed larger than ever. If I had to leave La Plata Springs before the stipulated time—the Arabella would founder, and it would be my fault. A knot twisted in my stomach, and closing my eyes, I pressed my fingers to my forehead. Mr. Chase's proposal was looking more and more attractive by the minute.

"There might be a solution," I said. "But it's not optimal. And I'm not sure I'm ready to commit to it—yet."

"Oh?" Kitty's brows lifted, her curiosity unmistakable.

"Theodore Chase has come to me with an intriguing business proposal. He's suggested a partnership to transform the Arabella into one of two sister hotels under joint ownership. According to the contract, Mr. Chase would gain a 49% stake in the Arabella, while I would gain an equivalent 49% share in the hotel he's building in Addison. He's also suggested we expand beyond the two towns."

She let out a slow whistle. "Are you sure that's a good idea? There's something shifty about that dandy. He doesn't play by the rules."

I sighed impatiently. "I suppose you are referring to his involvement in the Cattle Syndicate scandal?"

She gave a curt nod.

The Cattle Syndicate consisted of a group of cattle barons who reportedly used aggressive tactics, including paying off certain officials to take over lands previously claimed.

I lifted my chin, injecting confidence into my words. "Mr. Chase swore that the entire operation had been 'by the book,' and the lands were obtained legally. He assured me he would never risk his reputation on anything untoward."

That was one thing we had in common, among others — a fierce commitment to maintaining a sterling reputation.

"I still think there's something shifty about him."

"I appreciate your concerns, Kitty, but I know firsthand that achieving a certain amount of acclaim and success often breeds contempt in others, and attempting to malign one's reputation is the favored mode of attack."

I'll admit that when he'd first mentioned the idea, I'd been hesitant, but for other reasons. The Arabella was one of William's most cherished possessions (and he'd had many), and I wasn't sure how he would have felt about such a proposition. Initially, I'd planned to sell the hotel and leave La Plata Springs once I fulfilled my obligation to stay for a year. Yet, over time, the thought of handing over the Arabella to someone else had lost its appeal. I'd grown unexpectedly attached to the old dame, and it had become increasingly important to me to honor William's legacy—as well as Percival's, who had designed the hotel with such care and vision.

"Besides, I don't think I can handle this burden alone anymore," I said. "I am also responsible for my theater in New York."

The Pryce Theater was my very own possession, and I cherished her like a favored child. Performing on the grand stage had always been my purpose, my reason for living— and the thought of leaving all of that behind was beyond painful.

"My business manager at the theater has implied that my absence is affecting the bottom line," I continued. "I can't be in two places at once. What Mr. Chase is offering would be very beneficial to me, and the Arabella. She would be taken care of while I attend to matters concerning my career. And it would definitely help with the present financial burden." I lifted my teacup to my lips.

Tilting her head, she narrowed her eyes. "If you don't mind my boldness, Arabella, but why would you need the financial help? Aren't you filthy rich?"

I nearly choked on my tea. After I quickly composed myself, I looked at her in earnest.

"It's complicated."

She nodded slowly, her eyes still squinting at me in question.

I waved a dismissive hand through the air. "Money aside, both businesses need my attention—and my presence. Having a partner would allow me to take care of both the Arabella and my theater."

She gave a click of her tongue, her disapproval wafting over me like a dark cloud.

"Sounds like you might be ready to commit, after all."

My back went up at her chiding tone. I thought she might have been more supportive. I raised my chin in defiance.

"Perhaps I am, then."

She rose from the chair. "Far be it from me to tell you what to do, Arabella. If you think this plan is for the best... "

"I do." The words came easily—too easily.

But did I believe them?

The Pryce of Fame: Chapter Three

Still flustered from my conversation with Kitty, I folded the contract, tucked it into the desk drawer, and left my office for the Bella. A hearty breakfast was exactly what I needed to steady my nerves—both for the weight of my looming decision and the uncertainty surrounding my father's whereabouts and well-being.

I passed by the reception desk to find Cordelia reading a book, showing once again the lack of activity at the hotel.

"I'm going to the Bella. Need anything?" I asked her.

"No, thank you. I had breakfast in the kitchen earlier." She glanced up briefly before burying her nose in the book once again.

I stepped into the saloon and headed straight for the back corner booth—the one always set aside for me and my special guests. Kitty was at the bar, going over what I assumed were the accounts, while Sally Dean, the head barmaid, took an order from a customer. Several people occupied tables, which was a welcome sight, but usually the place was full to capacity at this hour.

Lottie, the cook, had earned quite a reputation for her "miner's breakfast," a plate piled high with her famous bread steaks. The dish featured thick slices of bread soaked in milk, dipped in eggs, rolled in bread-crumbs, and fried to golden perfection. Parsley often adorned the top for a savory touch, but those with a sweet tooth could drizzle on maple syrup for an indulgent twist. It had become an overnight sensation, drawing locals to the Bella in droves. Unfortunately, its popularity wasn't quite enough to make a dent in the accumulating debts.

Sally approached the table with a quick, purposeful stride. Petite, with large dark eyes that seemed to hold both innocence and wariness, she had the angelic face of a child—though it was often shadowed by a hardened expression shaped by the hardships of her past. Sally had been in Kitty's employ for years, starting as a sporting girl, but now, engaged to Everett Emerson, the manager of Archer's Dry Goods, she had transitioned to the more respectable role of head barmaid at the Bella.

"Good morning, Mrs. Pryce," she said with a broad smile. Her bearing this day had a buoyancy that indicated an exceedingly good mood.

"Good morning, Sally! Don't you look like the cat who got into the cream—and so early, too. What's the secret behind your glow today?" I found her effervescence infec-tious, lifting the weight of my earlier troubles.

Her eyes shone with delight. "Everett and I have set a date for our wedding!"

"Oh, that's wonderful, darling. Congratulations!"

"Thank you—and Mrs. Pryce, I'd like to ask you a favor."

"Of course, anything."

"We'd like to get married here. At the Arabella. It's so beautiful, and I think it would be perfect."

"Well—well, certainly. When is the big day?"

"October second."

"I don't think that would be a problem. Yes, by all means! I'll let Mr. Pettyjohn know."

"Thanks ever so much!" She beamed, and then her expression turned surprisingly serious. "I have one more favor to ask. Would you—I mean, if you can't I understand, but I was wondering if you—well, what I'd like is ... "

"My goodness, Sally!" I gasped, laughter bubbling in my voice. "What's the matter?"

Her gaze dropped to the floor, her lashes fluttering before she lifted her eyes back to mine, apprehension etched across her face. "I'd like to know if you would consider being one of my bridal attendants?"

I pressed a hand to my chest, touched at the notion. Sally and I had not exactly started out on the right foot, as we both had feelings for Clayton Marshall. But all of that was behind us now.

I reached out and took her hand. "Oh, Sally, it would be an honor."

She exhaled a relieved sigh, a smile breaking across her face. "That's wonderful. Thank you, Mrs. Pryce."

I chuckled. "I think it's time you started calling me Arabella."

She hesitated for a moment, then blinked shyly. "All right. Thank you, Arabella."

"You're welcome. Now, if you wouldn't mind, I would love some Earl Grey, toast with marmalade, and a hard-boiled egg."

"Coming right up." Her cheeks glowed pink with excitement.

As she left, I leaned back onto the backrest of the booth, basking in the joy and contentment of the moment. I closed my eyes, willing away the other pressing matters that had had me so flummoxed just minutes before my conversation with Sally.

A sudden commotion jolted me from my moment of contentment. I opened my eyes to find Constance Chatterley, sole reporter and owner of the town's newspaper, The La Plata Herald, bustling toward my booth with determined purpose.

"Oh, my dear, Arabella! I have just heard the news. This is just terrible! What a disgrace! How are you holding up, dear?" She awkwardly maneuvered her considerable frame into the booth across from me, her hat—a riot of color adorned with satin ribbons, silk bows, and a cluster of faux fruit attended by a bright, feathered bird—sat slightly askew on her head, as usual. Her equally flamboyant dress, embellished with a cascade of ruffles and pleats, was so voluminous it spilled unceremoniously outside the booth, as though threatening to topple her over.

I blinked, shaking my head in confusion. "What are you talking about, Constance?"

From seemingly out of nowhere, she produced a thick newspaper and slapped it onto the table. It was the *New York Gazette*, one of the smaller publications that came out of the city, and the headline read: "A New York Literary Scandal?"

I looked up at her. "I don't understand."

Her mouth dropped open, and she gasped. "Oh, my heavens! You don't know. Oh, my dear! Read it!"

My gaze fell to the paper, and I read:

In the complex underworld of New York's literary world, a fresh scandal has surfaced—one that could tarnish some of its most esteemed figures. Anonymous sources claim that a network of manuscript smugglers has been operating in the city, trafficking stolen or forged works of notable poets and authors. Rumors say this enigmatic ring spans continents, and its connections stretch from London and Paris to New York and beyond.

The literary elite here in New York have quietly murmured one name in particular: Wendell Milton. Though he has been in the city for nearly five years, people know little about Milton himself, and reports say he has frequented salons where literary works exchange hands, often under less-than-reputable circumstances.

Known for his eccentricities and claims of greatness, Milton's connection to a celebrated name in theater circles has added fuel to the speculative fire. There is speculation that he is somehow connected to New York's own stage diva, Arabella Pryce.

I blinked in disbelief, a shudder of dread stealing the breath from my lungs. My hand instinctively moved to my stomach to steady the anxiety that swirled there. The threat of failure, damnation, and shame loomed over me like a gathering storm, its weight pressing down so heavily I could scarcely breathe.

My father was allegedly involved in criminal behavior—and, even worse, he had drawn me into his web of lawlessness, threatening to unravel everything I had worked so hard to protect.

Gathering my strength, I read on:

Could this be mere coincidence, or does the scandal reach farther than the backrooms of New York's literary clubs?

For now, the accused remain elusive, and the truth lies buried in secrecy. But as investigations continue, one cannot help but wonder how far the stain of scandal will spread—and whether it might tarnish not only the scribes of literature but also the luminaries of the stage.

The Gazette will report further developments as they unfold.

My gaze traveled to the byline, and my heart sank to the pit of my stomach. The article had been written by none other than Atticus Brooks.

Grab your copy…
vinci-books.com/ThePryceOfFame

About the Author

Kari Bovée is an award-winning author of historical mysteries, weaving suspense and unforgettable characters into captivating tales. Her enthusiasm for storytelling began in early childhood, as illustrated by a note sent to her parents from her third-grade teacher praising her talent for writing. This passion flourished during her pursuit of a Bachelor of Arts in English Literature at the University of San Diego. There, she customized her studies to include independent projects in short story writing, playwriting, novel writing, and even a debut as a theater director.

Her acclaimed Annie Oakley Mystery Series, Grace Michelle Mysteries, and The Pryce of Murder Series have earned recognition in national and international writing competitions. Her awards include the Chanticleer International Goethe Grand Prize for *Peccadillo at the Palace* (2020) and the New Mexico/Arizona Hillerman Award for *Girl with a Gun* (2019).

Before turning to fiction, Kari worked as a technical writer, educator, and consultant, but storytelling has always been her true passion. She and her husband, Kevin, spend their time between their horse property in the beautiful Land of Enchantment, New Mexico, their home on the sunny shores of Hawaii, and their travels to inspiring destinations.